THE FALL OF MIDAS

The Fall of Midas

Juliet Astley,

Lofts, Norah (Robinson)

Coward, McCann & Geoghegan
New York

First American Edition 1975

Copyright © 1975 by Juliet Astley

SBN: 698-10680-6

Library of Congress Catalog Card Number: 75-10462

PRINTED IN THE UNITED STATES OF AMERICA

Part I

The man in the gig halted his horse at the prearranged place and took out his watch. Six o'clock. Absolutely on time, as was his habit. He hoped the girl would not be late, a hope that ran counter to experience. In all his days he had known only one woman to whom six o'clock meant exactly six o'clock and not ten, fifteen minutes past.

This girl was not quite punctual; he had time to look about him. It was flat country, the road before and behind him running as straight as a ruler, interrupted only by the hump of a bridge under which the River Rad, swollen by the spring rains, gurgled. On either side of the flat road there were cornfields—looking well, he noted. They were separated from the road not by hedges but by ditches, on this May evening beginning to froth with meadowsweet.

To his left—and that was the direction to which he looked most often, separated from the road by a cornfield— loomed the bulk of Monkswood, thickening out into its summer finery. By the edge of the field of well-doing barley which lay between the wood from the road at this point, there was a little footpath. And presently the girl appeared upon it, sauntering along.

He knew that perched in the high gig on the flat road, he was not only visible but conspicuous. From the moment she emerged from the wood she must have seen him, waiting there. But she did not hurry.

He thought: Insolent!

He thought: But of course, she knows that she has me by the short hairs.

He thought: Even her walk betrays her, that pace which could not strictly be called loitering and yet was an invitation to be overtaken.

As, moving at her own leisurely pace, she approached, he looked at her with avid curiosity. Not at all what he had expected. Seen at close range, with only the bit of grass verge and the ditch between them, he was astonished to see her so young, modest, and demure-looking.

She had black hair, neatly smoothed back and gathered into a chignon that looked a trifle too heavy for her very slender neck. She wore a cotton dress, extremely simple, white sprigged with green, with a close white collar at the neck, little white cuffs at the wrist. As she came nearer, hesitating on the far side of the ditch, he who knew what hussies looked like, though he had never made personal contact with one, thought: Methodist!

Failing to find one of the planks which sometimes spanned such ditches, she gathered her skirt and jumped with an agility that was in marked contrast with the languid air with which she had approached. She came to the side of the gig and leant against the footboard, looking up at him with an expression both mocking and sullen. The man looked down at her and thought: Charlie must have been bewitched! Beautiful, he'd said; so sweet and lovely. By God, she wasn't even pretty! She didn't look healthy; too thin, almost hollow-cheeked, and sickly pale. Eyes very black, very bright and big—too big for her face really; but perhaps with a friendly instead of a hostile look, not unattractive.

She spoke first.

"You know that I'm doing this for Bill's sake. Nothing else would have made me."

Curious voice, too, tired, almost hoarse. Possibly just right for murmuring endearments.

"I know the terms," he said.

"And he did tell you a hundred?"

"I have it here."

He opened the small version of a Gladstone bag which sat at his feet and produced a canvas one, the kind of bag which banks provided. Its neck was drawn close by a cord. The girl reached into her pocket and brought out five letters, four in stout white envelopes with a small neat crest on each flap, one pale-blue and flimsy.

"I left it open so you can read it."

"You wrote what I asked?"

"More or less. I added a bit to make it sound human. I daresay you'll find this hard to believe, but I was fond of Charlie—and he was fond of me. But you had me cornered. So there you are. . . ."

The man in the gig had been born one skin short; to compensate he'd grown in many areas of mind and body a carapace, resistant as a turtle's. But his eyes, his ears, his instincts were sharply, almost painfully acute.

So were the girl's. She knew that there was a possibility—no more, but nevertheless a possibility that the canvas bag might contain less than she had bargained for. A hundred pounds was a lot of money; if she handed over the letters half a minute too soon, what was to prevent him from whipping up his horse, leaving her with half what she'd asked for or even nothing. She'd been reared in a hard school, too.

"Come on," she said, "let's see the colour of your money." Something of the hostility, sullen and cold, left her eyes as he tipped out onto the flat part of the gig's footboard a hundred shining examples of the most sought-after currency in the world: the gold sovereign. There were a hundred of them, and he treated them as though they were pebbles. Possibly to him they were. When she had counted fifty and saw just as many remained, she made a swift scoop.

"That'll do," she said. "Here you are." She handed him the five letters.

A bargain made and kept.

In a sky the colour of hyacinth the sun tilted down, throwing fantastic shadows ahead of the man, his gig, his horse and upon the girl, once she had crossed the open cornfield, the deeper, darker shadow of the wood.

She reached her destination first. A pretty cottage with a deep thatch; lonely—a gamekeeper's cottage. The kind of place which anybody, exiled from it, might feel sentimental about. Roses, one yellow, one crimson, not yet in flower, but budding, sprawled over its whitewashed front and rustic porch; the path between door and gate was bordered by lavender and rosemary bushes, all neatly trimmed; behind them were beds of old-fashioned, homely flowers, sweet William, marigolds, Canterbury bells.

Once upon a time life within the cottage had been as pleasant as the exterior of the place seemed to promise. William Thorley lived there, with his wife, Ellen, as good a wife as any man ever had, and his son, a sturdy, healthy child, christened William but always called Bill. They were comfortably off, for as a gamekeeper William earned rather more than twice as much as a farm labourer and Ellen was a splendid manager. He was content with his one son, but Ellen wanted a daughter, someone to whom she could pass on all the little skills which she herself had acquired and was proud of, and when Bill was six, it looked as though Ellen would have her wish fulfilled. But something went wrong. The baby—and it *was* the girl she had dreamed of—was born dead, and Ellen died so soon afterwards that the one coffin held, the one grave engulfed them both.

He had never even visualised the possibility of marrying again. Why should he? Bill needed no woman's care, and he himself could cook and clean, not quite as Ellen had done—who could?—but well enough. He'd always been a fairly religious man, a Methodist, and now, bereaved, he sought consolation in the belief which, in varying forms, had from time immemorial made bereavement bearable. The loved one was not lost forever, simply gone ahead, waiting. In another world, where no sorrow was and all tears would be dried, he and Ellen would meet again.

When Ellen had been dead for eighteen months—it was October, and misty, though with a moon, he came upon just the situation that he was paid to guard against. Poachers, of the travelling kind. Local poachers didn't bother him much; they knew him, always on the prowl, and knew, too, that they would do better on the other side of the river. Travellers, who fell into three categories—gypsies, didikis, and tinkers—were less well informed. They took a chance, wherever in the daytime they noticed a likely place, to come back after dark and exercise their peculiar art. They could creep up to a roosting pheasant so stealthily that it made no cry, no flutter. Picked off like gooseberries.

But not here, and not tonight, William Thorley thought, raising his gun and taking aim at three figures, enlarged as well as blurred by the mist.

It was common practice to give that kind of poacher a peppering of shot, aimed low, not intended to injure *much*, just a warning. And even if injured, what redress had they, the gypsies, didikis, and tinkers? Go to the police and say: "Somebody shot me in Monkswood." One answer to that: "What were you doing in Monkswood?"

Two of the mist-enlarged figures ran away. The third attempted to follow, fell down, got up again, stumbled, almost fell again but, clutching at the bole of a small tree, remained upright, waiting.

He approached cautiously. It *could* be a trick; all the travelling people carried knives. Cornered, they could be dangerous, which somewhat excused the gamekeepers' habit of shooting first. Self-defence. Coming close, William Thorley saw with astonishment that this was a girl. Totally out of pattern. All the travelling people used their women, as they used their horses, their donkeys, their dogs, mercilessly, but he'd never known or heard of a travelling woman, of whatever grade, being a poacher. But there she was.

He said, "Can you walk?"

"I can try." She took a stumbling step, lurched, and fell not backwards towards the tree which had supported her, but forward, into his arms. She said, almost apologetically, "You got me through the knee."

He lifted her, carried her home, probed about, swabbed her hurt with a crude, but never yet superseded, disinfectant, and bandaged it. He then made tea and, since she said she was hungry, fetched a cold meat pasty and cut her a good wedge. He felt some admiration for the fortitude she had shown under his ministrations and, watching her devour the food, thought that washed and tidied up a bit, she'd be pretty. Presently he carried her upstairs and put her to bed in the tiny spare room. He apologised, rather awkwardly, for having injured her, and she said, "We all gotta live, I suppose. It'll be better in the morning."

In the morning it was worse. She made valiant efforts to stand, to stumble about, clutching at the bedrail, the little dressing table, the windowsill. Under the grime her face was grey with pain, and sweat broke on her forehead and round her mouth.

"You'll only aggravate it," he said. "Get back in the bed. I'll bring you some breakfast."

Showing emotion for the first time, she said, "But I gotta get after them. They've got my baby."

She looked young to be a mother.

"How old?"

"About a year."

"Well, for a day or two, your husband. . . ."

"I ain't got one. He's dead. Them I'm with now wouldn't look after her. She ain't big enough to be useful." A whole

way of life was summed up in that last sentence. William
thought for a moment.

"I'll fetch her for you. Where shall I find them?"

"Oh, they'll be on the road by now, after what happened
last night. They got a good horse, too."

"Which way were they going?"

"Making for Stonebridge Pot Fair."

"I'll hire a horse. Don't you worry."

They weren't real gypsies, just the one van with a canvas
cover. Three villainous-looking men. He was not actually
afraid; his job was not one for the nervous, and he had faith
in God. Still, it would be prudent not to reveal his identity.
Mounted on a good horse, wearing good whipcord breeches
and gaiters, he looked like a fairly prosperous farmer. He
played that part. He told them that a young woman, very
lame, had managed to reach his house in the early hours
and was worried about her baby. So he'd come to fetch it.

They had no desire to be cumbered with a useless female
child; but this fellow wanted it, and *anything* that *anybody*
wanted had a price.

"What's it worth to you, mister?"

"Nothing. The young woman is fretting for her child.
The baby is crying for its mother. All I want is to get them
together."

"So you can. Cost you a guinea."

He had no time to haggle. The girl was waiting; the baby
was wailing; the hired horse was costing money by the
hour; his work was being neglected. He handed over the
coin and received in exchange a malodorous, ragged bun-
dle.

He never tried to excuse himself to the Almighty—always
watchful—that it had been pity or any other respectable
motive that made him marry Rosanna. It was sheer lust.
Washed and tidied up, she was, as he had imagined, very

pretty; tempting bait for a man who had been happily married and then lived celibate for many months.

Some pity—she'd plainly had a hard life—and some sense of responsibility—he'd lamed her for the rest of her days—were involved, but mainly, God who knew the inmost secrets of every man's heart knew these were minor considerations compared with the desire to get her into his bed. And for a man of his kind that meant marriage.

So he married her.

He was well and truly punished.

Until the ring was on her finger, she'd seemed anxious to please, limping about, cooking in her outlandish way—she could make quite a tasty dish from nettles—keeping the place reasonably clean. Then bit by bit she revealed her real self: a slattern and a sloven and a drunkard. He did his best to control her; he kept her without money; she retaliated by taking Ellen's things and either selling or pawning them. Ellen, until she married, had been in good service and had received, when she married, presents, things not often found in cottages: a marble clock; silver forks and spoons; a bedspread of real eiderdown, light as a feather but warm; and two matching vases of some sort of ware called majolica.

He had recovered them all, put them in the little parlour, and locked the door. But Rosanna was not to be outdone. She let his ferrets loose; she hid his gun, his gaiters, once his very breeches. He could never bring himself to hit her as most men would have done. (And that she knew, because she could see auras. She always had done and, when she was about seven, had been surprised to learn that everybody didn't see people as she did. Most people saw other people just as faces and figures. She saw more. A kind of cloud about the head. Blue was good; red was bad. And even when William was very angry, his never turned red— just a murky dead lilac colour. So, not afraid of him, but willing to exploit him to the utmost, she made a compromise. If he allowed her a quart of gin a week, she'd leave

Ellen's things and his things alone. She'd cook, too, in her own way, but she didn't want to hear any more about how Ellen did this and Ellen did that, and what was the use of scrubbing the kitchen table, which would just get dirty again?

He kept the parlour immaculate and the garden tidy— memorials to Ellen—while the rest of the cottage declined into squalor. He washed his own shirts and Bill's and the clothes of the little girl who was christened, rather belatedly, Anna, not because it was part of her mother's name but because it had been that borne by his own mother.

Except when Rosanna's uncertain temper was affected by gin, she was not unkind to the children; for Anna in the early days she appeared to have some feeling, but it did not extend to keeping the child clean or providing regular food. Her shopping, as well as her cooking, was haphazard. Extravagant, too, since she never made anything, as Ellen had done.

Bill had taken to the baby wholeheartedly; here was the little sister whom he had heard talk of and who had not arrived. Anna returned his devotion, followed him about on uncertain and then on steady feet, cried when he went to the village school, cried when he and his father set off for chapel on Sunday mornings. "We could take her *there*, Dad." "We will, when she's bigger. She couldn't walk the distance now." "I could never give her a piggyback part of the way." So Anna from a very early age became a regular attendant at the little chapel at Wyck-on-Rad. She remained rather puny, pale and thin, but she was hardy and mentally very forward, picking up the Lord's Prayer, the Sermon on the Mount, the Ten Commandments, and various texts with astonishing ease.

William had had high hopes of Anna. . . .

On this spring evening Anna walked round to the back of the cottage and entered the cluttered, smelly kitchen. The bulk of the money she had tucked away in her bodice; one sovereign she carried in her hand. Ever since just before Easter when she had obtained, she said, some evening work, she had contributed a pound a week towards household expenses. She had told two stories about the nature of her work; one would have sufficed, but lies came naturally to her, and so did the instinct to shape the story to the listener's taste. Rosanna was given to understand that Anna spent her evenings behind the bar at the Brewers' Arms; William believed that she was helping with the bedroom work and the serving of supper at Mrs. Evans' most respectable boardinghouse.

It was Friday, the day when Rosanna received her money and went shopping and had her brown stone bottle replenished. It was becoming more and more difficult to make the quart last out the week, and she was always making resolutions to go gently on Friday, Saturday, and Sunday, so as not to be entirely deprived on Thursday or even Wednesday. Such resolutions were never kept. Her will, as well as her mind and her memory, seemed to be failing—in her dead sober, miserable moments, she realised that. She was uncertain of her age—didikis did not note such things—but she felt old, heavy, fat, ugly, and lame. Sometimes she saw herself as a wild bird, trapped. William Thorley had shot at and wounded her, made her unfit for the didiki life. Then he had made the cage, baiting it with regular food, a roof overhead, security, and she'd taken the bait. When she was young, she had helped to make birdcages of pliable osiers, and she'd seen many a wild bird—only the pretty ones— trapped and caged, fed poppyseeds so that at markets and fairs they did not beat wild wings against the bars, but looked, as the buyers said, "sweet and pretty," well worth a shilling and another for the cage.

Rosanna said, "You're early." Not that she took much notice of what she called clock time, one of the things that ruled William's life. He had a fat silver watch with a yellow face, and he was always looking at it, measuring out his time. When she said to Anna, "You're early," Rosanna meant no more than Anna was for once home for supper.

"I'm sacked," Anna said. She put the shining coin down on the filthy cluttered table. "Make the most of it. It'll be the last. I'm off back to London.. First thing in the morning."

Rosanna said, "You ungrateful little bastard! Came crawling back here, coughing your guts out. Who took you in? Looked after you? Got you on your legs again? Now, as soon as you're useful, off to London again, easy as kiss your hand." To this accusation Anna made no reply. Rosanna said, furiously, "So you got the sack. Ain't there plenty other jobs? Both sorts." The last was a vicious stab of the kind which Rosanna had so often administered to William while the struggle for mastery had gone on.

Unperturbed, Anna walked through the kitchen and up the narrow twisting stairs. Being called a bastard did not affect her at all. She was, and she'd known it for a long time, ever since Dad had rebuked Mum for using such a word and Mum had said, wishing to hurt Dad, rather than Anna, could he think of a better word for a child born in a ditch— the result of a fairground encounter? As for the jibe about both sorts of job, that was equally unhurtful. What girl in her right senses would stay in service, plodding up and down long flights of stairs, being at anybody's beck and call, lugging coal hods, cans of water, bedroom slops, and heavy trays, when she could take to the gay life, which was all right as long as your looks and your health lasted. With her, health had failed first, and she had come home, sick, beaten, penniless. Now she was cured, and she was going back, astonishingly enriched; she had a pound or two left of the money Charlie Orford had given; she had ninety-nine pounds of the sum she had exacted from Charlie's father. Of these she put away ten, to help Bill out of *his* muddle— the muddle had been the root cause of the whole miserable, though profitable, transaction. God knew that poor old Bill,

with that little bloodsucker, Effie, round his neck, could do
with a bit of help. She was sorry for Bill.

Sorry, too, in a different way, for Charlie. But hurt was
bound to come to him sooner or later; he was so *soft*. So far
as the world and its ways were concerned, Charlie Orford
wasn't born yet. But he was sweet, and she'd never forget
him: her first real *lover* , you might say, if you discounted
Bill and a fumbling, inconclusive experiment amongst the
bluebells, years and years ago. Poor Bill, afterwards he'd
been so ashamed; he'd actually cried.

Transferring her money to a shabby old reticule, she
thought of the future and, so far as her idle, easygoing nature permitted, made plans. She'd replenish her wardrobe,
find a room in a better neighbourhood, live in style for a bit
and be choosy. Her cough was almost gone now; she was
getting back some flesh on her bones; there was still hope
that she might attain the aim of every prostitute, except the
old and defeated—a permanent rich gentleman friend.

Mr. Orford drove briskly away. At the turning to the left,
over another bridge under which the river dawdled, a turning which would have taken him home, he hesitated, decided to drive on to Bressford, look in at the stores, put Bill
Thorley out of his misery—and peruse the letters in undis-
turbed privacy.

Bressford was a small, but prosperous, market town
which in the last fifty years had expanded: to the west with
suburban houses, loosely known as the Avenues, and to the
east with the railway station and all its satellites, including
other new houses of a different kind, loosely known as the
Terraces. Its real core had remained untouched: two ancient churches and some streets and squares of calm-faced
Georgian houses, behind which lurked the slums. In the
lowest of these—lowest in every sense, since it was prone to
flooding in a wet season—known as the Pike, Mr. Orford
had been born and had spent his youth. He passed the entry

to it without a glance or a reminiscent thought and drove on to what was known as New Town, which focussed about the railway station. Here everything except the stores was downright ugly. The railway station, built high, dominated an area given over entirely to utilitarianism: coal dumps, with little shedlike offices; timberyards; cattle pens, in which beasts awaited transport to distant slaughterhouses. Even the public house, calling itself the Station Hotel, was a grim, uninviting place.

It had no need to be attractive. Custom was on its doorstep.

Mr. Orford tethered his horse to one of the lengths of railing provided for that purpose and walked towards the store—his first independent venture; in the business world his firstborn. Preoccupied as he was at this moment, he looked at it with affection and approval. It had been such a shabby, despondent little place when he bought it; now it was not only resplendent, obviously prosperous, but pretty. It was painted cream—an obvious extravagance in an area where even the lace curtains in the windows of the houses in the Terraces and the flowers in the hopeful front gardens were all too soon sullied by the smoke from the station, but what, after all, did a coat of paint cost? The station store at Bressford was washed down twice a year, and painted once. It had wide shining plate-glass windows, behind which a tempting array of goods—including this week's bargain—were displayed. And from its walls four iron bars projected, supporting hanging baskets of flowers and ferns, high enough to be out of reach of greedy fingers, low enough to catch and gladden the eye of all those, who like Mr. Orford in the past, craved some relief from drabness.

Mr. Orford's spectacular success had taken off from the springboard of his own needs. He knew what people wanted, even if they did not actually know themselves.

He walked into the shop and saw that, as usual, the cooked meat counter was busy. It was his own innovation;

born and bred in the Pike, he knew that there were two hundred houses without ovens, without any place to store food. And in the new houses, in the Terraces, occupied as they were by the aristocracy of the working class, men on the railway, men in the post office, clerks in the timber and coalyards, a whole ham, a whole joint of salt beef or roast beef was practically unknown. He had set himself, from knowledge and nudging ambition, to supply a need, not perhaps immediately recognised by the needy, but insidious, and the seed once sown, became a lusty growth.

The cooked meat counter was topped with marble, easy to keep clean and impressive. Behind it, wielding a sharp and cunning knife, was Bill Thorley, exercising his peculiar knack of carving so delicately that a quarter pound of ham or beef looked a lot, enough for a family supper. He was so sure of himself, so precise; he slapped the slices down on a piece of paper and passed them on to the boy at the scales. Hardly ever enough discrepancy to be worth noticing; perhaps once in ten times a sliver to be taken back or added.

Bill Thorley was aware of Mr. Orford's entry, towering over the evening crowd; he looked up, his face a mask of anxious enquiry. Mr. Orford gave him a nod, reassuring, not particularly friendly. Well, of course, there was a lot to be forgiven, even yet.

Mr. Orford walked to the back of the store, towards the place that served both as stockroom and office, and did not hear, or so Bill Thorley hoped, an angry protest. "You gone deaf or something? I said beef!"

The storeroom was quiet, the desk in the corner tidy. Mr. Orford lowered himself into the chair behind the desk and took from his pocket the five letters which had cost him twenty pounds apiece. He looked at the blue one first. With contempt and again with the wonder as to what could possibly have got into Charlie. Imagine a man at St. John's College, Cambridge, welcoming a letter addressed in such a

way, in such writing, half capitals, half small letters, used
without any consistency.

His own education had been of the scantiest—two much
interrupted sessions at the rightly, if cruelly, named Ragged
School—but he had learned to read and write after a fashion, and a good copybook cost only a penny; *Dr. Walker's
Grammar for Beginners* was more expensive, threepence.
Mr. Orford now wrote a beautiful copperplate hand, and
his grammar was slightly on the pedantic side. He'd been in
full employment—seven in the morning to any unspecified
hour at night—from the time he was ten.

The girl had written what he had, from a distance, dictated:

> dere Charlie im afriad this letter will be a bit of a shok to
> you Im going back to london to be marryd you see dere chal-
> ie with you the wayting and everyboddy upset this frend of
> mine is Reddy now and nice and ritch Imight never get such
> a chance enny more i hope you see wye and dont take it two
> hard forget me with luv Anna.
>
> p S I shant never forget you or the happy times we had i
> shant nevver luv my friend like I luv you.

Mr. Orford recognised in the postscript the bit which the
girl had said she had added—to make it sound human—and
his mental verdict on it was "satisfactory." He was not a
man without feeling, but he was not sentimental. What pa-
thos there was in this ill-written, misspelt, and unpunctuat-
ed screed missed him entirely. The girl had given value for
money, and God, look what Charlie had been saved from!

Now, what had Charlie written to her?

Skip the "darlings," the "my dearests," "my lovely
ones"; look for the sentences in which the silly boy had
committed himself. As he had, in no uncertain fashion and,
to a man whose sexual impulses had always been weak, in a
way almost obscene. Quite apart from the promise to marry
her the moment he was of age and independent, Charlie

had written a lot of sheer filth, gloating over memories of ecstatic times in woodland glades.

As had so often happened before, Mr. Orford had bought rather more than he bargained for, but he had bought well, as always. Had he not known that Charlie was incapable of getting drunk, having such a weak stomach that he threw up before he was even mildly inebriated, Mr. Orford might have thought that Charlie was raving drunk when he wrote such things. Not that ecstatic reminiscence was all. There was poetry too. A part of Mr. Orford stood off and wondered what an ignorant and obviously vulgar little hussy made of such statements as "Now I know what Byron meant when he wrote, 'She walks in beauty, like the night.'" Or of Charlie's own: "My heart is caught in the net of your midnight hair."

Nothing in Mr. Orford's upbringing or background would have indicated that he should be fastidious to the point of squeamishness, but when it came to licking the blue envelope which the girl had handled, he couldn't do it. Fortunately the standard of hygiene in this store was high, and there was a little washbasin, with a tap of cold water, a piece of red carbolic soap, and a towel. He dribbled a little cold water on the flap of the blue envelope and thumped it down, put on a stamp, and put it into his pocket. Charlie's letters—and really for them the girl *must* be largely to blame—he screwed together and carried out to the cooking shed, a structure which occupied most of the yard of the store.

The old woman in charge of the place had almost finished work. Tomorrow's offerings of cooked meat were ranged on a shelf, near a slatted unglazed window. They were shrouded in butter muslin to protect them from flies and the ubiquitous smoke from the passing trains. The old woman was scouring a pot at the sink. She had a short black pipe clenched between her teeth, and at the sight of Mr. Orford she snatched it away and dropped it into the pocket of her hessian apron.

Mr. Orford said, in the kindly, yet remote manner that made all his employees adore him and some of them confuse him with God, "One day, Mattie, you'll set yourself on fire. You should know by now that I don't mind your smoking when you're well away from the food."

The fire had died down to a red glow into which he pushed Charlie's letters, watched them smoulder, then blaze.

Then he went to look at the dog. This store was extremely vulnerable from the rear because of the railway embankment which stood higher than any fence could be. So inside the narrow backyard there was a dog, big, shaggy, of no known breed but of known bad temper. It was Bill Thorley's last job of the day to let him loose, his first in the morning to feed him and hook him back on his chain, coaxed by his meal.

With some displeasure Mr. Orford noticed that the dog's drinking bowl was empty. When he looked in at the cooking shed door, his voice and manner had changed. He said brusquely, "The dog has no water. See to it."

Then he went in, and just outside the stockroom door there was Bill Thorley.

"Excuse me, sir. I was anxious to know. Did everything go all right?"

"Exactly as arranged," Mr. Orford said.

And not by him. In his time he had arranged a thousand things, all to his own advantage, but this bit of business, like two or three others, had involved chance, coincidence, sheer luck. The kind of thing which often happened in books—Mr. Orford was a voracious reader—but seldom occurred in real life.

On the day when Charlie was returning to Cambridge, he had stood fidgety and blushing a bit before his father. He wanted to tell him something, he said. His discomfiture was not due to trepidation, for Mr. Orford was a most indulgent parent; Charlie blushed and fidgetted because he knew that he was about to deal a blow. On Maundy Thursday he had

met, had subsequently seen a good deal of, had fallen in
love with, and wanted to marry a girl named Anna Thorley,
whose father was a gamekeeper at Monkswood. Mr. Orford
did not connect the surname with that of his trusted manager for the simple reason that it was such a common name in
the district; almost everybody below a certain income level
was either a Thorley, a Pryke, or a Snell. Charlie said that
he knew that his father would not exactly welcome this
news, so he had waited until he was absolutely certain.
Now he was. And Anna was the most wonderful girl in the
world. Not only beautiful, but an angel. Imagine, she had
given up a good job in the millinery trade in London to
come home and help care for her father, the gamekeeper,
because he was ill. And when Charlie met her in the road,
she was actually crying because she had been into Bressford to collect his outdoor relief and had heard that it was to
be discontinued.

One of the copybook headings had been "Honesty Is the
Best Policy." Mr. Orford knew that it was true. Honesty
saved time, prevented complications and misunderstand-
ings. Now, with his son, he was honest; this news was not
welcome; he did not think that a gamekeeper's daughter,
however pretty and filially dutiful, would fit in. He said
that he understood—which he did, but in a purely academic way, having no firsthand experience—how the spring,
and pity, admiration even, and of course a pretty face had
led Charlie to a hasty and possibly erroneous conclusion.
He advised Charlie to think about it. "Marriage, my dear
boy, is a life sentence with no remission for good conduct."

He had not alienated Charlie. In fact, in the course of an
extremely successful career Mr. Orford had alienated singularly few people. Nor had he so far exploited anybody, using wealth and power as weapons.

Charlie went off to Cambridge happy because he had
made his stand. And his father had been neither angry nor
lacking in understanding.

* * *

Income tax, on incomes over 300 pounds a year, was fourpence in the pound, and quite apart from the ordinary day-to-day bookkeeping, there were returns to be made. It was in the process of making such returns that Mr. Orford, with some astonishment, saw a discrepancy. He trusted his managers—Bill Thorley was one of four—they were paid enough to ensure honesty. Three pounds a week when the average clerk if he was lucky earned a guinea, and the ordinary manual labourer anything between nine and twelve shillings. And there was in addition the yearly reckoning—a bonus of threepence in the pound on any increase of turnover.

Bill Thorley, called to account, confessed immediately and excused himself. He had only *borrowed.* He had felt an obligation to help his sick father, and then his ailing sister. . . .

"Anna?"

"That's her name, sir. She came home . . . from London . . . in a very poor way. . . . And my father was ill at the time. I didn't somehow feel I could let them starve, sir. And Effie—that's my wife—she's a bit hard. She wouldn't have liked . . . I mean she wouldn't have agreed. So I sort of . . . well, took my bonus in advance, sir."

For henpecked husbands Mr. Orford had no sympathy; he could well have been the most henpecked husband in England, a role he had repudiated absolutely with the most satisfactory results.

He said, "Bill"—and the use of the Christian name was to Bill Thorley as comforting and reassuring as the lighted window, the warm room, Effie's smile, and the children's prattle, a way of life which he had endangered—"I think we can come to some arrangement. . . ."

It took a little time, several journeys to and fro. What residue of sentiment was left in Anna was about equally divided between Charlie and Bill, but she'd known Bill longer and owed him more. Charlie out of his plenty had been generous, but it was Bill who years ago had saved his scanty 'prentice pocket money to get Anna out of service in Bressford—the strictest possible Methodist household, chosen by her stepfather, and never mind how many stairs. So when Bill stood by the pool in the woods one evening and said, "Anna, if you don't do it, I'm done for. He's only holding his hand. And I'd as soon drown myself as face Effie and tell her I've lost my job," she'd given in. "All right, Bill. I'll do it. But it'll be a hundred."

So it had gone, exactly as arranged.

Outside the stockroom door, smelling of oatmeal and dates and soap, Mr. Orford said, "Next time you're pushed, ask me. Don't go putting a sticky finger in the till. You can repay—that'll make you feel better. A shilling a week."

Bill Thorley looked as though he were about to cry from relief —Effie need never know; a shilling a week would not be missed. Mr. Orford disliked emotional displays, so he said, "Good night," abruptly and went out to his gig.

A ragged little boy slid from his perch on the rail and adopted a busy, important pose.

"I been watching him for you, mister."

Mr. Orford at that age—four? five?—had been a horse watcher, too, not at the station yard, for the station was non-existent then, but at the market or any other place where a horse was left unattended for two minutes. He felt in his pocket and took out twopence, and that brought the small boy's earnings for the day to fivepence. He watched every horse at the rails—that is, any horse not already watched by somebody bigger and stronger. A lot of people said, "Bugger off!"; some gave a farthing; some a ha' penny. Gents were usually good for a penny. But twopence! That was real toff money. He gave Mr. Orford the accolade. "Thank you, sir. You're a toff."

For the convenience of residents in this area there was a stout red pillar box at one corner of the station yard. Mr. Orford checked collection times before pushing the blue envelope into its maw. It was all right; Charlie would receive it by first post tomorrow morning.

For a moment the father's heart followed the letter. Charlie would be hurt, but he'd get over it. Young minds, like young bodies, were resilient. Charlie was young for his age—twenty-one in July—but soft, because he had always been cushioned and protected and provided for. Mr. Orford at the age of fifteen had been a man, hardened and tested by circumstance. And a murderer; no doubt about that! He very seldom thought about it and certainly never regretted it. He'd acted then, as he had always acted, as circumstance dictated.

His father had been a drunkard, a drover when he was sober enough to stand up; his mother had been the provider, scuttling about, haggard and harassed, taking in washing, going out to wash for people who disliked the idea of their laundry being washed with that of others, scrubbing steps, laying out the dead for those who were too squeamish to do it themselves and too poor to give the undertaker a full order.

When Mr. Orford was fifteen, he'd come home to find his father in the most dangerous stage: drunk enough to be witless, sober enough to be active. He was twisting his wife's arm to make her give him a hard-earned sixpence so that he could drink himself into the next stage. The boy, overgrown, gangly, knew that he was no match for his father. Physically. But there was, ready to hand, a poker, slightly bent. One well-aimed blow, with years of hatred behind it. The drover crashed to the ground and did not stir again.

There was no fuss. Drunken men did often fall down and crack their skulls. Old Born Drunk Orford had just happened to do it in his home instead of the street. The son had said to the jubilant widow, "Now maybe we shall have a chance." He'd been ambitious, even then. But reasonable, too.

Mr. Orford drove back through the town, took the turning, and was soon at his own imposing gateway. It was flanked by weather-worn brick columns topped by stone eagles, and just inside were two pretty octagonal lodges from which, in bygone years, alert women and children had emerged to open the gate. Mr. Orford's gardener now lived in one, his stableman in the other, and the gate had been removed; its service was adequately performed by a cattle grid. A large part of Mr. Orford's social success was due to his complete lack of pretension; you simply couldn't help liking a fellow who was so extraordinarily successful and never put on airs. He was still capable, in an emergency, of donning an apron and serving behind one of his own counters. A bit eccentric—and the English upper classes still favoured eccentrics while producing fewer from their own ranks.

Under the freshly budding trees of the spacious park Mr. Orford's prizewinning Southdown sheep and famous herd of Jersey cattle grazed or lay placidly chewing the cud. Mr. Orford would never have communicated the thought to anyone, but it frequently occurred to him that Rose, his wife, bore a marked resemblance to a pretty Jersey cow. And when he entertained this—not entirely denigratory— thought, another invariably followed. Who would believe that Rose had once been a creature of turbulent moods? So petted, so pampered that if her will was crossed in any way, she had a fit of screaming hysteria. In the last twenty-three years she had tried that tactic only twice—once soon after their engagement and once eleven years ago. The final convulsion had been caused by a dispute about this very house, now coming into view.

Just as Mr. Orford never approached one of his three subsidiary stores—Foster's didn't count, it was not of his making—without a feeling of satisfaction, so he never looked at his house without joy. It was a beautiful house, built in the reign of Queen Anne and never tampered with, never "improved." In the evening light the red-brick walls had a mellow glow and took on tinges of other colours, pinkish, purplish, even ochre. At one end the heavy trusses of wistaria were showing blue. The symmetry of the windows, the fan-lighted front door never failed to give delight to the master of the house.

And Rose, poor dear, had wanted a house called Sunnybank in Victoria Avenue.

Mr. Orford had literally fallen in love with Flixton Old Manor the first time he ever saw it—from the high hard seat of a grocery delivery van. A hopeless love then. . . .

The drive curved round to the rear of the house, and having left horse and gig in the charge of another Thorley—no acknowledged relative of the Monkswood family—Mr. Orford entered his house by a side door. This brought him near part of the garden, and he could smell his heavy-headed stocks. In another part of the garden were grown the small so-called bedding-out plants so beloved by Victorian gardeners, but they were for the hanging baskets of the stores; for his own enjoyment Mr. Orford chose larger and scented things, making an exception of the camellia, which made up for its lack of scent by being highly decorative and a little earlier-flowering than the rose.

Once inside the house he could hear voices—those of his wife and three daughters. The sound came from the door, just ajar, of the communal living room, a room furnished and bedecked in exact accord with Rose's taste, which tended towards the cosy.

Ordinarily he joined his family with some such redundant remark as, "Well, here I am." Tonight, put slightly out of his stride, he decided to postpone the moment of reunion, went softly along the bit of corridor which joined the side hall to the front one, and by the dining-room door hesitated. He felt tired, a feeling unfamiliar to him. Now that it was over he was willing to admit that the whole Anna Thorley business had been a bit of a strain. He'd suffered strain before, but he was built to withstand it, both mentally and physically. His mind never indulged in aimless worry; in its cool, logical fashion it separated the possible from the impossible, decided to do what was possible and leave the impossible alone; and his body, spare and still a bit slight, was all whipcord and whalebone. But it was fifty-two years old.

A brandy and soda would soon put him right. He went, still moving quietly, into the dining room, helped himself from the cellarette, and, carrying the glass, climbed the stairs to his own room.

It was his own. He and Rose no longer shared a bed or a room. The separation had been a matter of mutual agreement, facilitated by the move, eleven years ago. Rose's sexual fire, burning hot and fast, had died down; his, never very ardent, but adequate, welcomed retirement; and out of the bed thing, four healthy children the result, not enough remained to override the difference in habit for which the rooms over Foster's in the High Street had offered small accommodation. Rose prepared for bed with all the slow deliberation of a religious rite: fifty strokes of the hairbrush on her pale-gold hair, innumerable applications of lotions and creams for the beautification and later the preservation of her famous complexion. Like every other really respectable woman, Rose faced the day with an honest face, merely correcting a slight shininess of the nose with a brush of *papier-poudre* or on bad, pallid days just a touch of geranium paste. The nighttime ritual was different and could go on for an hour. At the end of it she came to bed and grumbled because Mr. Orford wanted to go on reading. She liked her bedroom warm; he liked his cool. She liked thick blankets, bulky eiderdowns under which she slept snug. Heavy blankets, closely tucked in, provoked his night cramp, and there was something about eiderdowns and down-stuffed pillows which sometimes made him wake up feeling as though he were being choked, made him rush for the window and open it and gasp in the fresh, life-giving air.

Hundreds, thousands of happily married couples faced such problems. Most had no choice, having no room, and

others sacrificed choice to conformity. To most middle-
class people the idea of separate beds, separate rooms hinted at something not quite right with a marriage. In fact,
when the move was first made and Rose's old friends from
Bressford had paid visits of inspection, she had always
shown her own room as "ours," incongruous as it appeared,
all velvet and lace and bows.

In his own room Mr. Orford washed and changed, not
into formal dinner wear but into what he called easy
clothes. As he did so, he took sips from his glass and awaited the feeling of being restored—this evening slow in
arrival.

Like many confirmed drunkards' sons, he'd gone through
a period of devout teetotalism. That had mitigated with the
years, but he was still a temperate man: a glass of sherry
with the family before dinner; a glass of light wine with the
meal; on occasions port to follow. Brandy and soda, taken
very rarely, was a pick-me-up after, or even during, a very
heavy day, and although he did not realise the connection
with his father, it was there. Old Born Drunk Orford, defeated by life from the first, had needed a pick-me-up all
day long.

Mr. Orford was sipping the last of his drink when there
was a tap on the door and a voice asked, "Are you decent?"
Without waiting for an answer, his eldest daughter, secret
favourite of all his children, preferred even beyond Charlie,
opened the door and entered.

"Caught in the very act!" she said. "Secret drinking. Absolutely disastrous!"

There'd been some mild argument about the naming of
this girl. Charlie had, quite naturally, been named for
Rose's father. Old Born Drunk Orford deserved no such
tribute, and had been dead for years, but Rose's father,
Charles Edward Foster, had lived to see and approve of his
grandson. There'd been no dispute about that. Mr. Orford
had wished to pay a similar compliment to his mother when

his first daughter was born. Comfortably installed in one of
the rooms over the shop in the High Street, the ex-washer-
woman was enjoying the autumn of her days, far, far better
days than she in her wildest dreams had imagined.

Her name was Elizabeth, and Mr. Orford wished his
daughter to have that name. Rose said it was old-fashioned
and all too likely to be contracted into Lizzie, a servant's
name. Rose, having learned the futility of throwing fits
where Mr. Orford was concerned, pointed out, rationally,
that Queen Victoria had not seen fit to name any of her
daughters Elizabeth. Rose then, with one of those touches
of sentiment, at once pleasing and slightly deplorable, said,
"Why not after you, dearest? Edwin . . . Edwina. I always
meant, if I had another boy. . . ."

Charlie's young tongue could not manage Edwina; it
could eventually say Edda, and Edda had stuck. In a curious way it suited her, a trifle out the ordinary and reaching
back far beyond what Rose called old times.

"How did you know I was back, Edda? I stole in."

"I always know. If I went to sleep for forty years, like Rip
Van Winkle, and woke up, I'd know whether you were in
the house or not."

"Twenty years." Mr. Orford corrected her.

"As you say. . . ." She gave him a look, the kind of look
he had never received from anybody else: a touch of merriment, mocking the pedantry of his correction, companionable, fond, and a dozen other things which—he knew—few
men ever found in any woman.

From behind her skirts, less voluminous than fashion
dictated, she moved her hand, produced a shell-pink camellia.

"Surprise!" she said. "The first from that tardy bush."

She pushed it into the buttonhole of his lapel and flat-
tened it with the palm of her hand. It was a lover's gesture,
though neither of them recognised it as such.

"There now, you do look handsome."

"So do you, my dear."

The word was apt. Even his fond eye could not regard her as pretty; she was far too like him, even to the crisp hair, more red than brown, which besides being out of favour as a colour, was out of fashion in texture since it could never be smoothed into demure loops or satisfactorily curled. There was nothing actually masculine about her face, no coarse or displeasing feature, but it consisted of planes rather than curves, and the thin mouth and steel-grey eyes made her look severe, except when she smiled. She'd still be handsome at an age where prettiness faded; but that was years ahead, and there were times when her father was concerned about her immediate future. She was nineteen, and so far no offer, however tentative, had been made for her hand. Louise, three years younger, was always the centre of a bevy of young men and was becoming something of a flirt.

"In fact," Edda said, slipping her arm through his and turning him towards the long glass, "we are a handsome pair."

The glass imaged them. His hair, though silvery now, was still plentiful and still crinkled, and he was unfashionably clean-shaven. The growth of facial hair had not been encouraged in grocery counter hands, and the habit of shaving every morning had stuck. He was a tall man, all of six feet, and one of Edda's misfortunes was that she was a mere two inches shorter, and most men were too vain to feel fully at ease with a woman as tall as, or taller than, themselves. In fact, in all their circle of friends and acquaintances, Mr. Orford knew of only one man who was physically a match for Edda, and although modesty had never been one of his drawbacks, reason compelled him to think that such a match was, to say the least of it, unlikely.

"New dress, I see."

"Yes, do you like it? Please say yes. Mamma and the girls absolutely decried it. Louise said it made me look like a horse. The point is I don't mind looking like a horse. I refuse to look like a camel. Which I do with bustles and bows hitched onto my rear."

He said, judicially, "It suits you." And that was true; the severe russet-coloured taffeta, its almost sculptured lines unbroken by bows, flounces, or frills, was somehow right, almost as becoming as the riding clothes in which she looked her best. Until Edda had been old enough to assert her own tastes, Rose had deliberately chosen her dresses to mitigate both her height and a certain lack of the fashionable curves.

"We must go, Papa. Mamma and the girls are sitting there by the sherry, looking like dogs put on trust. What have you been doing today?"

What indeed?

"I went to Wyck-on-Rad. I looked in the Bressford store. Nothing very exciting."

The brandy and soda had done little for him; the feeling of tiredness persisted, and alongside it ran an almost equally unfamiliar feeling, but of the mind, not the body. He would have liked to tell Edda exactly what he had been about that day—seek her approval, as she had sought his over the frock. Unthinkable, of course.

The sitting room, Rose's room, was typical of its time, though fortunately too large to seem really cluttered or claustrophobic. Everything that could be draped was draped, lavishly; everything that could be made to look like something other than it was, was made to look so. Rose's workbox, for instance, was a not bad miniature model of the Taj Mahal. Bamboo was fashionable, therefore Rose had acquired some bamboo tables, but all tables must be clothed, and the bamboo tables wore velvet and plush and, above the more solid materials, mats of lace-edged muslin or of embroidered satin. With every kind of material in great plenty and labour cheap there was no end to the proliferation of uselessness.

Outside the door of this room Edda released her hold on his arm, and he went in and greeted the rest of his family. So pretty, so amiable. He had already noted Rose's likeness to a Jersey cow—her once-golden hair, despite all that conscientious attention, fading now to fawn, but her big brown eyes with their long lashes. . . . She'd been, within a closely drawn circle, quite the prettiest, and the most eligible young woman in Bressford.

He was a man who had always honoured his debts, and he knew exactly what he owed to Rose, who had been Rose Foster, the boss' daughter, remote as the moon.

Edda's remark about dogs on trust was, like so many things that Edda said in her casual way, apt. In their pretty dresses, with their curls, they really did look like King Charles spaniels, waiting for a pat, a kind word—a glass of sweet brown sherry. He poured it. There was another decanter holding a paler, drier beverage, from which Edda poured, for him and for herself. The gentle, trivial domestic chat began and continued as they moved into the dining room and ate a delicious, though by some standards very simple, meal. The Prince of Wales was reported to have said that he didn't consider a dinner of less than seven courses a dinner at all. But look at his paunch! Mr. Orford on really grand occasions conceded and provided five dishes; *en famille,* three were ample.

Much of the talk flowed past him, claiming no more than a moment's attention. He thought of that thin, insolent half-gypsy girl; of the letter now on its way to Charlie; even of the little ragamuffin who had performed the voluntary and utterly redundant service of watching the horse.

(The small boy had scuttled across to the stores and with the confidence of one with wealth at command, said, "Two pennorth of pieces." Pieces were the debris of the day, for no matter how neatly one carved, there were crumbs, odds and ends of fat, gristle. And tonight the small boy had been lucky. Bill Thorley, so relieved that in the end it had hap-

pened, Anna had kept her word—throughout the negotia-
tions he had never been quite sure—and the paying back so
leisurely and easy, felt well disposed to the world. "You can
have the bone, sonny," he said.)

Halfway through the meal Edda said, "Well, now I have
a piece of news for you."

Louise, with a resigned shrug, said, "We lend you our
ears. Topaz cleared a five-foot fence."

"And I still wish you wouldn't, dear," Rose said. "I think
it is dangerous. I always did." She turned her large brown
eyes towards her husband with a reproachful look; he had
always encouraged Edda to ride, bought her for her last
birthday the rangy, golden-brown, unfriendly young horse.

"Absolutely nothing to do with Topaz jumping a fence. I
know who is to take the part of Lady Gytha in the pageant."

Interest sparkled. The Bressford Pageant took place every
twenty-five years, a harmless, wildly inaccurate mime of
Bressford's past. Of those about the table only Rose had
seen the former one, so she could speak with authority.

"Lady Chelsworth, of course. And to think that it is fifty
years . . . I mean since the first. I can well remember
when I saw her all those years ago, everybody said that
she'd taken the part in the former one and hadn't changed at
all. I was young then, and I remember thinking, as I sat
there: It can be done! Age can be fought off. . . . In fact,
the other evening I almost told her that she'd been an in-
spiration to me, but I thought. . . . Well, at seventy-five
any reference to age is not exactly welcome."

Just as nobody could ever accuse Mr. Orford of pretentiousness, nobody could ever accuse his wife of lack of tact.
Within her somewhat-limited range she operated well, and
even the fact that she had three daughters—all likely to be
well dowered and two of them positively pretty—evoked as
little envy and malice as was possible in the circumstances.

"Lady Chelsworth has come to the sad conclusion that
even she, adept as she is at holding the years at bay, cannot

now impersonate a young woman of twenty. That I had straight from the horse's mouth!" As Edda spoke, she laughed and her eyes sparkled. "In truly royal fashion, she has chosen her own successor. You may have one guess each."

Mamma and the girls took this invitation seriously and named three girls of well-known families. Mr. Orford said, "Mrs. Maxwell-Phipps." Then everybody laughed, for that lady weighed close on twenty stones.

"I must give you a clue. Her ladyship chose—I quote— the only girl of suitable age that she knew who didn't sit in a saddle as though she wished it were an armchair and was capable of controlling her wolfhound. Now?"

Mr. Orford was visited by a fantastic idea which he refrained from putting into words for fear that it was not correct and might inflict hurt. It was Maude who said, "Could it be *you*?"

"You clever girl! For that brilliant deduction, dear Maude, you shall be my number one page. Her ladyship has conferred upon me the right of appointing my personal attendants."

"What about me?" Louise asked quickly.

"I think that even at a distance you could hardly pass as a boy. You shall be a lady, Louise. I'll know more about it when I have read the script. After all, I only heard this morning."

"Who told you?"

"Lord Chelsworth himself, no less. I was exercising Topaz, and actually he did jump his five feet. We met his lordship, hastening to deliver the royal command."

Talk—and inner thoughts—ran this way and that way. It was extraordinary and most satisfactory news, Rose thought. She hoped it wouldn't go to Edda's head. She was wilful and sometimes difficult enough already. And there was no doubt about it, the part of the Lady Gytha was *the* leading part—not surprising since the first pageant, half a century ago, had been specifically designed to display the charms and the horsemanship of the third earl's young wife. Rose also hoped that this honour would somehow moderate Edda's attitude towards Lady Chelsworth and her grandson, the present earl; she almost always referred to them in a slightly sarcastic manner. Also, at the back of the mother's mind there was another troubling thought, of which she would speak when her memory cleared a little. . . .

Mr. Orford thought: And of course the old girl was dead right; Edda was the obvious choice. One that would not be questioned either. Lady Chelsworth had effortlessly dominated all social life in the district for fifty years and would continue to do so until she died. Mr. Orford also knew now why Edda had laughed when she said, "straight from the horse's mouth," for Simon Talbot, fifth Earl of Chelsworth did strongly resemble one of the horses of which he was so fond. A handsome horse, dignified, solemn, conscientious.

Unmarried.

Slightly over six feet tall.

Land poor as so many were in these days of free trade, with farming at its nadir. Somebody high in office had said, "Half the land in England would be for sale tomorrow if only there were any effective demand for it." There was no such demand, with frozen meat pouring in from Australia, New Zealand, and the Argentine, cheap corn from Canada and America.

The only suitable match which Mr. Orford had momentarily thought of and prudently shelved as unlikely seemed now to be *just* possible. Not to be counted upon. But that arbitrary and not entirely conventional old lady up at the castle was no fool. She must have realised that her decision over this seemingly trivial matter would bring her grandson and the girl who was a grocer's daughter and granddaughter—let Old Born Drunk rest, unremembered—into close and, for a while, constant proximity.

Mr. Orford's mind, which in more favourable conditions could have developed in other ways because it had both

range and sensitivity, thought what a mercy it was that
chance, coincidence, luck, call it what you would, had ena-
bled him to save Charlie and therefore the whole family.

Rose said, "I have remembered. Edda, I don't think it
would be a good idea for Maude to be that page. Last time it
was another dog, of course. . . . But this is just as big and
just as dangerous. I remember very clearly. . . . I don't
think Maude could manage Shamus. In fact, the last time
we went to the castle for dinner, he lay behind Lady Chelsworth's chair and growled at the footman. It made me positively uneasy."

"Oh," Maude said. "I didn't know that being a page
meant having anything to do with *that*."

"I did," Rose said, enjoying her small triumph. "The
page led the hound in, and it was as big as a donkey."

"Don't worry, Mamma. There is time. By the day of the
pageant Shamus will do what I say and I'll tell him to be
nice to Maude, horrid to everybody else. Very impressive.
You'll see. And although her ladyship"—that sardonic note
again—"wishes to lend me, together with the wolfskins, so
carefully preserved from moth by camphor balls, her own,
her very own horse, Blackbird, I intend to ride Topaz. I
know Gytha was supposed to ride a black horse, but Charlie
said the whole thing was legend. He said there was absolutely no historical proof that there ever was a Lady Gytha.
So whether the mythical lady rode a mythical horse, black
or brown is for me to decide."

"Oh," Rose said, putting a plump, white, well-kept hand
to her mouth, in one of the pretty gestures, so effective in
the past, "Charlie! What with one thing and another, I completely forgot. There was a letter by the second post. He's
snatching a weekend—next weekend."

"He must have changed his mind about the Hospital
Ball," Maude said. "Veronica will be delighted."

"Poor girl," Edda said. "Charlie may be her darling; she
certainly isn't his."

With rather sharper interest than he usually showed in

girlish gossip, Mr. Orford said, "Why do you say that, Edda?" He had completely overlooked the possibility that Charlie might have confided in his eldest sister.

"She's not at all his type. Far too blond and solid. Charlie's darling will have long, long black hair and look as though she never had a square meal in her life."

Too exact a description of Anna Thorley to be guesswork! "Has he ever said—"

"I was going by how crazy he was about Miss Browston. He never really recovered."

"Edda, how ridiculous! She was three times his age." Miss Browston, a vicar's daughter and more scholarly than most in her calling, had been the girls' governess for some years, and Charlie's boyish infatuation had been a family joke.

And oddly enough, Mr. Orford thought, now that he had been reminded, there was a kind of resemblance between the almost-forgotten governess and the girl he'd just bought off. Partly accounted for by the look of ill health. Miss Browston had been consumptive; Mr. Orford had paid for her to go to Switzerland, where she had recovered and married a man who kept an inn high in the Alps.

Maude said with the seriousness of one to whom marriage and everything connected with it was a matter of prime importance, "Claudia Stanton has black hair. If she went on a diet. . . ."

The store opened at seven o'clock in the morning, largely for the benefit of the feckless who were unable to think one meal ahead and were regularly caught off guard by the arrival of breakfast time. Bill Thorley's presence at this time—"Two rashers and a screw of tea"—was not strictly necessary, and usually he came along from his house in Albert Terrace, unlocked, saw that his underlings were present, fed and chained the dog, and then went back to breakfast with his wife and family.

On this Saturday morning, having performed his duty and seen others busy about theirs, he went across to the station, climbed the fish-scented stairs, and waited for the first up train. Anna had promised to leave *immediately* for London. But she might have decided to catch a later, slower one; she'd always been, except when forced by circumstances to be otherwise, a bit of a sluggard in the morning.

However, she'd caught it and was on the lookout for him.

Dear Anna, she'd kept her word, and she bore him no grudge.

The train made quite a halt here, for it began its journey at Radmouth, where fish, fresh and cured, was taken on, some to be unloaded here, some to continue on its way to London, to restaurants and big houses discriminating enough to know that although "Dover soles" were the better known and more plentiful, the Radmouth soles were both rarer and better flavoured. At Bressford, where some fish was discharged, the casks of ale from the Wyck-on-Rad brewery were taken on. It all took time, and the up train stood, hissing impatiently, for ten minutes.

"Sit yourself down, Bill," Anna said, patting the seat of embossed plush, a little worn, a little darkened from its pristine crimson. "Was it all right?"

"All right." His throat thickened. "Anna, I can't tell you how sorry. . . ."

"Don't fret over that. If it hadn't been you, it'd have been something else. I never did have any luck. Except with you—and Dad, in a backhanded sort of way. . . ."

She had arrived, in February, wearing a warm dress and a jacket collared with tired-looking fur and carrying everything else she possessed: a nightdress and a brush and comb wrapped in brown paper. She was wearing the dress now, the jacket lay folded on the rack above her head, and a brown paper parcel, only very slightly larger, lay upon it. There was also a bunch of bluebells, already wilting. Pathetic, Bill Thorley thought, with a pang; she'd always been

such a one for the country, the woods and the wild things.
Now she was going back to London, resuming life in the
millinery place where she'd got so ill earlier in the year.

She really had looked like death in February, when she'd
walked into the store and said, "Hullo, Bill," as though
they'd been parted a week, not eight years. Eight years, and
except for a scrawl on a postcard, in the first week, "I got
here. Thanks bill," never a word.

He dropped everything, ran round the end of the counter,
and hugged her. She said, "I didn't know whether you'd
still be here. But I reckoned somebody'd know where you
were."

He had wasted no time in hustling her home to the prim
little terrace house on the other side of the railway. Her
cough was terrible, and she was thin as a rail. But bed and
proper feeding would set her right.

"Look, Effie, who's here. Anna."

"So I see." In Effie's voice and look there was no welcome, none at all, just the head-to-foot, foot-to-head look
with which women summed each other up—usually un-
favourably.

"Well, now that you *are* here, I hope you'll stay for a bit
of dinner. Lucky I made a good big pudding! Steak and kid-
ney."

Effie defied him to do anything for Anna. Wasn't he already helping out his old father, struck down with rheumat-
ic fever at the turn of the year? And look at it how you liked,
every penny that went to Monkswood was robbing Effie
and her two little girls. With Easter looming up and new
clothes needed.

Anna had never been slow to take a hint. She said, "Yes, I
could manage that. I looked up the trains—just in case I
didn't find Bill—and there's one that goes round the Loop
and stops at the Six Mile Halt. I'll catch that."

It was then, with his father not yet back at work and Anna
fit for nothing, that Bill Thorley had begun pilfering.

Now in the smutty-smelling railway carriage, he said, "I never did much for you, Anna. Not half what I'd have liked."

"Oh, yes, you did. Those two years in Bressford when I was in service. Bill, I'd have starved to death, but for you. Or died, if there hadn't been those Sunday afternoons to live for. *And* you gave me my fare to London. Well, now I can pay you back a bit." She burrowed in her reticule and took out ten sovereigns tied in a grimy little handkerchief. "There, you take that and get yourself clear, love. Anything over, have a drink on me."

"You keep it," he said. "Mr. Orford and I settled things last night. You need all you can get. And don't go vanishing again, Anna. Let us know where you are."

She had explained her silence over all these years by saying she had always been on the move, no settled address to give, so what was the point in writing when you couldn't get an answer? Effie had queried that, not to Anna's face, but to Bill in the connubial bedroom. Anna might have moved about, but she'd been employed, and month's notice was the rule; couldn't she have written from one of her hat-making places?

"I'll let you know," Anna said as the noises preliminary to departure began. Doors slamming at the far end of the train. "Good-bye, Bill." They embraced and kissed. "And don't you give another thought about all this. It ended all right."

He jumped down from the train and said, "Look after yourself, Anna."

"You bet!" He stood there looking so solemn, so married-all-over. Could she make him smile? Leaning from the window, she said, "*You* look out for yourself, Bill. Your boss has got a red aura!"

He managed a grin at that as the train jolted away. It had been one of their youthful jokes. Bill, of course, couldn't see, didn't really believe. But she did and was convinced that on two occasions that special way of seeing had saved her life. Twice, though badly in need of money, she had refused advances from men with blood-red auras. And two girls had had nasty ends.

Charlie did not receive the blue letter first thing in the morning because he had gone out to breakfast before the post was delivered. If you were popular, as Charlie was, it was difficult to squeeze everything in, and breakfast parties were one means of extending the day. Cricket practice and a fitting at his tailor's consumed the morning, rowing the afternoon. No lunch. The captain of the St. John's crew had strong views about loading the stomach before rowing. To make up, an informal, very hearty, though minimally alcoholic dinner at a riverside inn called the Eel and Fork.

A busy, happy day, and to crown it the sight of the blue envelope. The writing which Mr. Orford had thought so deplorable sent his son's heart soaring.

He read the letter with stunned disbelief. It couldn't be true. It was true!

Not dated, of course; her letters never were. But the postmark was of yesterday's date: 8 P.M. and Bressford. Did that indicate that she had posted it on her way to London? Oh, God, let that not be true.

To a degree Charlie, for all his easygoing ways, had a bit of his father's capacity for swift, direct action. There was a railway timetable in the porter's lodge. No train for Bressford or even in that direction this evening. The first tomorrow morning, very slow, leaving Cambridge at eight and for some reason known only to those who compiled railway tables not reaching Bressford until eleven thirty. So it couldn't be at the Six Mile Halt until fifteen minutes after that. But there were other means of transport!

Agitated and short of time as he was, Charlie said, "Thanks, Barker," and made for the entrance. The porter, who, like almost everyone who came into contact with him, had a soft spot for Charlie, jangled his formidable bunch of keys.

"Excuse me, Mr. Orford, sir. I am about to lock up. If you go out now, you won't get back. And one more peccadillo, you'll be gated, sir."

The university authorities operated on a theory that midnight was the magic hour, as in the Cinderella story; prior to midnight any young man committed to their care might be foolish, drunken, even riotous. *After* midnight, obviously a reprobate and a sinner.

Charlie was gone, out into a town which, although during the day and the evening was as lively as any place apart from London, was, because of this midnight rule, a deserted place because the young men who kept it alive were all immured.

Charlie ran through a town as complete and as dead as Pompeii until he came to a livery stable known as Hobson's Choice. Nothing to do with the original Hobson, who had let out horses in the sixteenth century and had, unlike most of his kind, really cared for his horses, letting them out in strict rotation, so that he never hired out a horse except in turn. That reasonable and humane man had gone to his grave four hundred years ago, but John Milton had given him a kind of epitaph, and he had had, over the years, several imitators, the latest in St. Mary's Lane, to which Charlie ran. The place had wide doors, closed, like everything else at this hour, but in response to Charlie's impatient and then frenzied hammering an upper window opened, and a voice, slurred with early sleep, asked, "Whadda a matter?"

"I want a horse, Mr. Hobson." Hobson was not the man's name; he'd taken it over, together with the legend. And the take-it-leave-it attitude.

"Want'll be your master then. Till morning."

"It's urgent, Mr. Hobson." But the window had already

slammed down. Just another undergraduate with a skinful. And out after hours. He'd cop it and serve him damn well right.

Charlie went to wait at the station, at this hour as dismal and deserted as the rest of the town. He walked up and down the platform, sat on a bench, drifted into brief, uncomfortable little slumbers, sought for and failed to find the place where decent men went to relieve their bladders, and even in this extremity felt a certain self-disgust at being obliged to use a wall. An endless night, but even the most endless night must end in a morning, and the dawn came up. Never in his almost twenty-one years of life had Charlie been more glad to see it or more apprehensive of what the day it heralded might bring.

He knew, pretty vaguely, the situation of Anna's home, but he had never been close to it. After their first accidental meeting in the road—Anna walking along in such a dispirited way and looking so like Miss Browston, but younger and even more delicate, and he stopping the gig and offering her a lift—they'd met by appointment either where a ride through the woods met at the highway or by a pool deep amongst the trees. They had always parted by the pool. "We'll say good night here." It was only a step, she said; she wasn't in the least nervous; her father still wasn't very well; her mother was terribly inquisitive. She obviously wished to keep the affair private, and at the beginning, until he was *absolutely* sure, Charlie had been of the same mind. It had naturally occurred to him that she might be ashamed of her home, her parents, or both, and the thought had raised no scorn, only pity. Mr. Orford, in that momentous interview, had told Charlie that in thinking it over, he must ask himself whether he might not be confusing pity with love. "It'd be a mistake to marry a girl simply because she is a gamekeeper's daughter."

Here was the pond, wild irises round its edges, proud

moorhens with their young behind them, threading their way through the water lily pads. All around the bluebells were breaking.

It should have been *next* weekend. He'd fully intended to tell his father that he *had* thought it over, would never change his mind; then he'd break the news to his family and take Anna to his home, all open and aboveboard.

Well, it might not be too late.

What Anna had called only a step was quite a long way following on a walk from what must be called Six Mile Halt because it was six miles from anywhere. The cottage—this must be it!—was a welcome sight and a pleasant surprise, so neat and clean-looking; such a pretty little garden. Charlie, full of youthful sentiment and not immune to the fashionable romanticism, reflected that he wouldn't mind living in a similar place himself. If Papa really cut up rough. . . . Charlie did not doubt his ability to earn a living; he'd been to what was undoubtedly the *best* if not the most famous, school in England; unless he went mad, he was sure of his BA. He was a good athlete. He could always be a schoolmaster. If Papa really. . . . It wasn't likely, but it was just possible. Edda had once said, over some trivial dispute, "Charlie, with Papa it isn't the iron hand in the velvet glove; it's the iron hand in a knuckle-duster."

Charlie walked up the path and tapped on the door. Nothing happened, and he banged.

A voice—Anna's—said, "It won't open. Go round to the back." Oh, God, the relief. Combined with the shock of the letter, the gnawing anxiety, a practically sleepless night, it unmanned him. He blundered around the side of the house as though he were drunk—a thing he never had been because he had such a weak stomach that long before he was even mildly inebriated, he was sick.

There was a yard, a doorway, and in it, oh God! Anna, grown old, ugly.

One of the unacknowledged benefits of a disciplined upbringing was that certain patterns of behaviour became automatic, requiring no thought.

Charlie raised his hat, smiled, asked for Anna, Miss Thorley.

"She ain't here, mister. She took off for London, first thing yesterday morning."

The worst that he had imagined.

Coming round the house, he'd felt drunk, now he felt dead. Struck to the heart for the second time.

"Well," he said, "could you give me her address?"

"She didn't have none. She just took off. For London. First thing yesterday morning."

In ancient panelled rooms, in gay modern places like the Eel and Fork, young men joked about women. Three things you should ask yourself before becoming even mildly serious:

Would you take her into a first-class restaurant?

Would you share a toothbrush with her?

Have you seen her mother?

There was the midnight hair, but greasy, undressed, swinging in a plait between the crooked shoulders; there were the eyes, bright and black still, but set amongst puffs and creases.

"I expect," Charlie said pleasantly, "that you will be hearing."

Rosanna made a scornful sound, half sniff, half snort.

"Not likely! Last time she took off without even saying. Eight years that time. And she only come back because she was broke and ill. Not a word, mind you. Not even at Christmas. Eight years. But we took her in and got her back on her feet. Off again without so much as a thank-you. Talk about ungrateful!" The loss of the pound a week still rankled.

There was a discrepancy between this story and Anna's. Anna had said that she had left a job in order to come home

and help nurse her sick father. Charlie had no time to exam-
ine it, for the thought "job" offered something more worthy
of attention. A girl in a job could be traced.

"Had she a job to go to, Mrs. Thorley?"

"Well. . . ." A glint of cunning and malice made the
dark eyes lose any resemblance to Anna's. "You *might* call
it that! Lately she've been getting letters. Real grand. You
know, stamped on the back as well as the front. Very sly
about them, too. But *I* noticed." In all probability his own.
A dead end. Try again.

"Did she, in the time she was here, mention the name of
the millinery establishment where she had been working?"

"No. And for a very good reason. There wasn't no such
place. I ain't blind, and I do notice hands. Making hats is
needlework. Sewing women show it here." She stuck out
her own dirty left forefinger. Rosanna was still angry
enough over the lost pound not to mind blackening the
character of her own daughter. "If you ask me, Anna's work
was mostly done on her back."

A filthy old woman with a filthy mind.

Rosanna had by this time worked herself round to making some connection between her suspicions of Anna's virtue and this young toff's presence.

"What was your business with her anyway?"

"It was purely business," Charlies said, surprised at his
own cunning. "A friend of mine is starting up in the millinery business, and somehow, I can't actually remember
quite how, I'd heard about Miss Thorley. I offered to get in
touch."

A likely yarn, Rosanna thought. Her resentment at Anna's
behaviour increased. Hadn't she told the little bitch that
there was work here—of both kinds? Didn't the presence of
this young toff prove it? And he'd asked for *Anna*, corrected
as an afterthought to *Miss Thorley*. A pickup in the Brewers' Arms, no doubt. Barmaids had great opportunities. Oh,
why couldn't Anna have stayed here and shared?

By this time Charlie was aware of the kitchen. As filthy as

its owner. It smelt a great worse than the ferret cage fixed on the wall of the yard. Their straw, their drinking water were clean, and they exuded simply the natural ferret odour; the kitchen stank of food carelessly cooked, of stale food, dirty cloths, old clothes. Poor Anna, poor darling, small wonder she'd wanted to get away.

By whatever means?

Think about that later.

Think now about getting himself away. But not too finally.

From an inner pocket he took his wallet, best crocodile skin with gold corners and initials. He extracted a card and held it out, fastidiously between his first and second finger.

"If you should hear, Mrs. Thorley, perhaps you would get in touch—or ask Miss Thorley to get in touch. . . ." He was anxious not to make contact with that dirty, greasy hand. But it touched him.

Anna's mother appeared to have gone mad or taken a fit.

Ignoring the card, staring, she seized his wrist and turned it so that his palm was uppermost. Her voice, her whole manner changed completely.

"Now there's an interesting hand," she said. "Lucky! My God! But touch and go. Talk about by the skin of your teeth! You can't alter what's writ here. But you oughta be careful what company you keep, mister. You're gonna have the narrowest escape any man ever had."

He did not ask from what. Close to, she smelt foul, and he was for the moment concerned only with getting away. And if he had asked she would not have told him. Some things were unlucky even to mention—even to *see*.

She had solved for him the problem of whether or not to give her money. Asking her to get in touch with him was asking her to make some effort, buy a stamp. With his free hand he fumbled in his pocket and found a half sovereign. His other hand he pulled away.

Ingrained good manners resumed control. "Well, thank you very much. Nice to hear one is lucky. Good morning."

She took the card without looking at it. She was looking at him. At an aura as blue as an aura could be. So how could he possibly ever be threatened with *that* particular danger?

And it was odd that the special sight which seemed to have deserted her as she aged should have come back so suddenly. So overwhelmingly. The sight, when she had it most powerfully—and that was before Anna was born—had been quite remarkable and had once saved her whole family from what could have been a disaster. The story had been one of those which, in good moments, she had told to Anna and Bill—the kind of story of which William Thorley so strongly disapproved.

"It was in the West Country somewhere. Lonely part and not very friendly. We was all on short commons. Me dad and me brother hadn't had a job for days, and I hadn't sold nothing. So there's this farmhouse, see. Tidy big place, all on its own, and the peas about ready to pick. Me dad sez, "We'll try here." And we go towards till we're near, and then I see death in the house. Blood, like a butcher's place. And I say, 'Stop. There's death in that house, and blood and ruin.' Me dad believed me. He turned the horse round. There was hoofmarks and wheel marks in the lane, and me brother and me walked behind, with branches, smoothing them out. So we get out of the lane, and presently we see a bit of a village, laying low and with a church steeple. We make for it round from the back. See what I mean, as though we was coming in from the other side. And then me dad, he believed me, took the axle pin outa the wheel and let it run and smash itself against a stone heap, side of the road. Breakdown, you see, and the road blocked. Out come the village constable. 'Can't stop here,' he sez. 'Can't move neether,' sez me dad. 'Take a wheelwright for this job.' So there we all was, well on the wrong side, I mean the *right* side, of the village when the couple at the farm are found in their bed, throats cut from ear to ear and their savings gone. A fine pickle we'd have been in if we'd been near the place. Nobody's gonna take a travelling man's word."

For Bill and Anna a fascinating story. William told them
stories, too, but the only one comparable was about the
bears that came out and ate the children who mocked Eli-
sha—and even that he spoilt by moralising about politeness
to elders. Rosanna's stories he called a lot of old rubbish
and wicked into the bargain.

On this Sunday morning, as William Thorley walked
home from his wayside chapel, the story upmost in his
mind was that of the Prodigal Son. Anna should have been
walking here beside him, as she had done several Sundays
since he had been fully restored to activity and she had recovered her health. Her presence beside him in the pitch
pine pew had somehow justified everything, proof of God's
power and infinite mercy. Now she was gone again, back to
the fleshpots of what he was certain was a wicked city, a
modern Babylon, Sodom and Gomorrah. He was grieved
and irked by his sense of having failed, after all. He'd failed
with Rosanna; but that was understandable, she'd been a
grown woman, set in her ways, long before he met her, but
Anna he'd had since she was knee high. He'd taken her and
treated her as his own, let her reach the full age of fourteen
before placing her out to service, made sure it was a good
Christian home she was entering, and told Bill to keep an
eye on her. Not that Bill needed telling; Bill was a good
boy. Still was, a real rock in a weary land, and they couldn't
have managed in the spring of this year without Bill's help.
From this good Christian home Anna had just vanished.
Walked out, leaving a sinkful of unwashed dishes. Partly
understandable—bad blood; Rosanna's daughter, after all,
even to the unwashed dishes. Eight years and no word.
Then suddenly back, no money at all and a terrible cough.
He'd acted just like the father in the parable, taken her in,
shared what food there was. No fatted calf, but better than
she'd had lately, judging by the look of her. And by the way
she'd improved in health. Well enough, just about Easter

time, to get a job. She'd seemed happy and settled. . . . The parable story ended too soon. What would the father have felt if the son had chosen to go back to his husks? *Thanks, Dad, for all you done. I'm off to London first thing in the morning.*

By the pool the path curved, and rounding the curve, William Thorley caught sight of Charlie. Instinctively he straightened his shoulders, pulled himself together. He did not recognise in this young man—plainly a toff—any member of the syndicate that employed him, but he might be the son of one of them or perhaps a possible new member, studying the place before he joined. In either case it wouldn't do to look old, which he sometimes felt nowadays, or as though his illness had in any way affected him, which it had.

Charlie, as soon as he was free of that terrible woman, had been overcome by a most unmanly, disgraceful, shameful desire to cry.

In his life he had shed singularly few tears and those soon staunched; he had been lucky. Even at Biddle's, during those first inevitable homesick days, he'd been petted by the matron who had had a little brother with just such curls and wide blue eyes, snatched away by scarlet fever. Charlie had been the recipient of many a clandestine cup of cocoa. . . .

But now, disappointed, impotent, and, although he did not yet realise it, horrified, he felt like crying. His throat ached; his eyes stung. But a man of the world, coming up for twenty-one in two months' time, couldn't cry, even in the middle of a wood with nobody to watch his humiliation. Also, though Charlie did not realise it, tears say "Help me!" With no one to see, to sympathise, to help, tears are wasted. So he choked back the lump in his throat and blinked his eyes and was glad that he was master of himself just before, rounding the curve, he saw a man. Biggish, oldish, dressed in decent, dark, Sunday-keeping clothes.

Anna's father? Possibly; this path seemed to lead only to the cottage. And if it was her father, was it just possible that Anna had confided more to this eminently respectable person than to that awful old woman?

Activated by very differing motives, the two men behaved almost identically: halting, touching hats, and saying almost simultaneously, "Good morning, sir." On Charlie Orford's part a gesture towards the man who might be Anna's father; on William Thorley's, a gesture towards some link with the syndicate.

Then the more powerful personality took control.

"I'm William Thorley, if you was looking for me."

"I'd like a word with you. You are Anna's father?"

"Stepfather." There was the rub. If she'd been *his* everything would have been different. It was there in the Bible, plain for all who ran to read: No man gathers figs from thistles. He should have given it more heed.

"I understand," Charlie said, falling back in this extremity on to trite terms—people of culture said "I believe" or "I am informed" or "I am given to understand" particularly when they were not too sure of their facts.

"I understand that Anna left for London yesterday. Did she tell you where she would be staying?"

The man's bleak expression became bleaker. Often enough he'd had to remind himself "Charity thinketh no evil." But there was something mysterious and troubling about Anna. That long silence wasn't satisfactorily explained by the fact that she'd been so much on the move that it wasn't worth writing because she could never get a letter back. To him it looked rather more as though she'd been ashamed of herself, not only for running away as she had done—she'd have got over that in eight years! Something that had *kept* her ashamed. He had never seen London, but his distrust of it was profound and kept lively by the reading of denunciatory pamphlets which were eagerly circulated amongst the godly. He distrusted the move from domestic service to the millinery trade. Stupid girls thought they were improving themselves by taking on shopwork, where they were abominably underpaid, practically driven to vice. Service offered protection; employers were vigilant, and girls knew where their next meal was coming from.

He'd never tackled Anna on the subject; but he had treated her not only as a returned prodigal but as a repentant sinner, and to a degree she had behaved as such, occasionally accompanying him to chapel, and when she did take a job, taking one in the domestic line.

Charlie's appearance, voice, and manner roused suspicion. Such a young toff was unlikely to have any worthy motive in seeking out a girl like Anna.

"No. She didn't say. She just went off." There was something in his look and his manner which seemed to say: And if I did know, I shouldn't tell you!

The implication flicked Charlie's raw nerves, and he said with some warmth, "Didn't you see fit to *ask* where? Or why? Didn't you feel *any* responsibility? After all, she came home to help nurse you."

The man's eyes widened.

"If she told you that, she's a liar. Ask yourself—how would she *know* I was ill? Out of touch all that time. And I was better. She was the one that needed nursing. She was so poorly I nearly got the doctor to her, but my missus can mix up a good dose for a cough."

What William Thorley said carried more conviction than anything his wife had said. Neither of them had irretrievably shattered Anna's image, but the whole thing needed some thinking about. In a slightly peevish voice, Charlie said, "Well, one thing perhaps you *can* tell me. The shortest way to Wyck-on-Rad." The up train in the late afternoon ignored the Six Mile Halt.

"On foot?"

"Yes."

"Then your best way is the shortcut. Through the wood.

You go in there"—he indicated a barely perceptible path—
"and keep straight on till you come to a bit of a stream.
Then there's two paths; take the right, and you'll come out
within half a mile."

The first building on the outskirts of Wyck-on-Rad, a new
town, rapidly outstripping Bressford in all but prestige,
was the bacon factory. The next was the brewery, and on
the opposite side of the road a public house called the
Brewers' Arms.

The bar was deserted. The morning customers had gone
home to their belated dinners; the landlord, one of the
Pryke tribe, was taking his afternoon forty winks which
would last until his wife roused him with a cup of tea; and
the landlady, left in charge, was nodding over her knitting.
No local customer was expected at this hour, but now and
again commercial travellers did arrive ready to be on the job
first thing on Monday morning.

Brought back from a half doze, at first she thought that
Charlie might be such a one, but his request—brandy and
soda, please—enlightened her. A request, not an order.
Commercial travellers drank whisky when business was
good; at other times, beer. Mrs. Pryke didn't know a gentleman when she *saw* one—there were so many imitations
about—but she knew one when she *heard* one.

Charlie chose brandy and soda, partly because it was the
drink which Papa favoured when he was a little tired and
partly because it was one of the things he could drink himself, in tiny quantities, without feeling indisposed. Beer,
drunk by his hearty friends, revolted him, and he'd cultivat-
ed the art of carrying half a pint about with him for an hour
if necessary; whisky was sudden death; so was more than a
thimbleful of sherry, any red wine, and all white, except
champagne. His more intimate friends joked about it and
called him Champagne Charlie, in a fond way. He was rich,
and he was generous, he served champagne at his own par-

ties, and very often at others, when different beverages were circulating, there was champagne for Charlie, served a bit furtively.

The bar was rather dark, and Charlie carried his drink to the farthest corner, drank it carefully, and waited for it to take an effect on his tiredness. Saturday had been a heavy day; he'd slept hardly at all, had no breakfast, travelled for three and a half hours, and then walked miles. He thought—quite sensibly—that his physical condition could be, to a large degree, responsible for his emotional state: the renewed impulse to cry.

The b and s did absolutely nothing for him.

He did not, as most customers did, rap on the table, demanding service. He carried his glass to the bar and said, "The same again, please."

This time the landlady saw him as a person, not as a representative of any particular class, and she saw a charming young man, really golden-haired, really blue-eyed. She was not unread; she knew about King Arthur and his knights, and whereas many a bedroom wall was decorated by pictures of famous actors or soldiers, she had Sir Galahad. She'd never seen anybody in the flesh who more closely resembled that ideal young knight.

"Missed your train, sir?" she asked in a conversational way.

"Yes. I missed my train."

"Half past five, the next. Would you like something to eat? Sunday, not much choice." She glanced at the glass cases which on every day except Sunday, when a hot dinner at home was the rule, held an assortment of easily available, instantly consumable food: fresh-cut sandwiches, ham rolls, pork pies. All that remained now were three pork pies which on the morrow would be served to known and disliked customers. For this good-looking, beautifully mannered, somehow-out-of-place young gentleman, Mrs. Pryke could and would do better.

"Wait," she said, in answer to Charlie's halfhearted "Thank you. That might be a good idea." She went through a doorway and in the time it took him to down his second b and s reappeared, carrying a tray. A plate of cold roast beef, each slice delicately thin, brown at the edges, pink at the centre. A nice bit of crusty bread. A pat of butter. Mustard.

"Real horseradish sauce, sir. I made it myself."

"Thank you very much," Charlie said. "And the same again, please."

Perhaps the food hadn't been such a good idea, after all. Suddenly he felt all the old warning symptoms and looked about for a quick exit. Then he mastered himself. The kind woman couldn't know that he had such a weak stomach; she'd think the food had upset him. So he sat, still as stone, forcing down the nausea. And it passed; passed, although he did not know it, forever. Abruptly his tricky stomach and his tiredness were unimportant. He was left there with his mind which had never been clearer or sharper. It was now capable of seeing the whole problem of Anna, like a kaleidoscope.

Perhaps she had taken him for a sucker at first sight. She hadn't been in the gig beside him five minutes before she was telling the woeful story of her poor sick father and the cessation of the outdoor relief. He'd said, "What hard luck!" and made sympathetic noises and regretted that he had only about two pounds in his pocket and wondered how it could be presented without giving offence.

That was still bothering him when she said, "Put me down by the notice." And there was an entry to the wood— "Private. Trespassers Will Be Prosecuted."

He'd used the sick father as an excuse. "Sick people often need little delicacies," he said.

She did not even look at the money; she looked him full in the face and said, "Oh, no. You got me wrong. I wasn't

trying to cadge. I was feeling a bit blue and wanted somebody to talk to."

He realised that perhaps he had been a bit too ready with
the money; it made the next step rather difficult, made it
look as though he had bad intentions.

"You can talk to me any time. . . . Well, any time I'm
free, that is." He remembered that Mamma and the girls always laid on a lot of things for his vacation and John Walinshaw was coming to spend a long weekend. *He* might be
put off; some other engagements could be dodged.

She made it very easy for him. "When'll that be?"

He was able to say, "Tomorrow," for tomorrow was Good
Friday, a day when even people who took their religion
lightly usually refrained from entertainment.

"When? I mean what time?"

"Say half past eight."

"Where?"

"What's easiest for you?"

"About here."

"I'll be here. And look, I say, do *please* take this. I know
it isn't *much* , but you could get him a little something."

"Well, thanks a lot."

He was already half in love with her, and he became
more so. She was so easy, so undemanding, so gentle and
sweet. He was touched by her trust in him which he attributed to innocence—Evil be to him who evil thinks.

She had thought him innocent, too. In the trade they were
known as cubs—shy, inexperienced boys, who had to have
things made easy for them, who paid, sometimes willingly,
sometimes a bit grudgingly, their initiation fee. There were
good cubs and bad cubs, but even the good cubs had
steered clear of a girl with a cough. It was, in fact, the cough
and feeling so bloody ill with it that had ruined her. It was a
ridiculous state of things, but it was true; men hired you in
order to enjoy themselves, fair enough! But they did not,

unless they were freaks, enjoy themselves unless you enjoyed yourself or put up a good pretence at it, too. And even pretence was impossible when you felt so bloody ill that to get up and dress, go on parade was like heaving a mountain.

There was a doctor with a place just off Leicester Square. Everybody—that is, all the girls—said he was kind and discreet. Anna Thorley had never so far been obliged to test his kindness or his discretion. In eight years she had not needed treatment for syphilis, or an abortion, or even stitches in her head. But she had the cough, more potentially lethal than either the dreaded professional diseases or an unwanted pregnancy. He tapped her chest, listened, used his new stethoscope, said, "Breathe in! Out."

He said, "Miss—ah . . . Thorley, you come from the country?" A wasted question; she did, and he knew it because he had seen dozens of them; they came up to London, with their pretty country faces, with their dreams, perhaps even with their good intentions, and they had absolutely no inborn immunity at all. The toughest of their kind were Londoners born and bred, who'd seldom had a breath of real fresh air in their lives. Next toughest and resilient were girls from the Midlands.

Anna said yes, she came from the country and had been in London eight years. That indicated a singularly tough constitution. Three was usual, five extraordinary. With that history there was *just* a chance for her.

"You have a home to go to? In the country?"

Girls like this one were incapable of giving a straightforward answer; the doctor knew that. They waited four months, trying all sorts of tricks, before they came to him and said they were two months pregnant. Or saying yes, they had noticed something, maybe a fortnight ago. It had not taken the pamphlets of the Salvation Army or others, less authenticated, to inform Dr. Saxham of what was going on. But he not entirely resigned his integrity or indeed his wish to be helpful.

When Anna said yes, she had a home, in the country, in Norfolk, he told her the truth. If she got out of London immediately, went back to Norfolk, breathed her native air, ate good sound country food—she might have a chance. In London she would have none, might well be dead by midsummer.

It was not so easy as Charlie had imagined it would be to escape social and family obligations, so his meetings with Anna had not been nearly as frequent as he would have wished, and all seemed far too brief. He'd told a number of lies, too. Examinations were looming, he said, a little midnight oil must be burned, so better say good-night now and save disturbance later. Mamma took midnight oil literally and suggested a pot of strong coffee at eleven. Charlie said coffee, or tea for that matter, taken so late would keep him awake until two in the morning, and things weren't so urgent *yet*. A glass of hot milk then? He preferred it cold and would take it up with him. It was all very complicated and exciting and delightful.

He decided not to withdraw his invitation to Walinshaw; it would seem natural for two young men to go out together and be late home. Walinshaw would take a hint. It was indeed during Walinshaw's long weekend that Charlie fell from the strict standard of behaviour he had imposed upon himself. Wyck-on-Rad, that comparatively new and quite undignified town, was being entertained by a music hall show—not the kind of thing at which any decent woman would be present—and Walinshaw was happy to while away a whole evening there, and if one of the female performers—"direct from the West End of London," as the posters boasted—should take his fancy, he might ask her to supper, if such a provincial town offered facilities for such entertainment. It did. Nothing grand, rather sleazy, in fact, but gay and easygoing. Originally known as the Victoria Rooms—there was nothing to prevent the Queen's name from being taken in vain—it had not been very prosperous; now it was called Pepper's and was doing well.

That night Mr. Orford, suffering one of his insomniac periods, heard some commotion on the stairs, blundering steps, laughter, what sounded like a fall. He went out.

Charlie seemed to be having difficulties in getting his friend the Honourable John Walinshaw up the stairs because the Hon was extremely drunk. Almost as drunk as Old Born Drunk, but not, as the drover had been, morose, violent, or blasphemous. He kept laughing and saying, "No good, dear boy. Every step is two. So are you. Identical twins. Plain case of dip-diplomia."

Charlie, his father was relieved to see, was sober, steady as a rock. A bit bright-eyed. Slightly flushed from exertion.

Charlie, though Mr. Orford did not know it, was drunk on a headier wine than ever came from the fruit of the vine.

"Let me lend a hand," Mr. Orford said. He knew from sorry experience. You couldn't treat a drunk as an ambulant animal; you treated him like a sack. Deftly, Mr. Orford reversed the position of the Honourable John Walinshaw, so that he was facing, not upstairs, but downstairs; then a firm grasp under the arms and heave.

Not so young as I was, Mr. Orford thought, but I'm as strong as ever. The muscles developed in youth from the carrying, the pushing and pulling, sweeping, clearing the pavement outside Foster's of snow, washing Foster's windows, were still taut and strong. Still served well.

"Lift his legs, Charlie," Mr. Orford said when they reached the bedroom. "And get his boots off." He himself dealt with the collar and the cravat. He pulled the eiderdown over his guest and looked at his son. "He'll do. I wouldn't want *his* head tomorrow."

"Goo'night," this amateur drunk said. "Parting is such sweet sorrow. . . ."He turned his head, nuzzling the pillow, and fell asleep.

"You'd better get to bed, too, Charlie. By the look of it you had a good evening."

A good evening? The most wonderful evening of his life.

They'd kissed, of course, held hands, said fond words. But this evening—and he couldn't remember, was never to remember, exactly how it came about—the ultimate had happened.

Not, in a physical sense, Charlie's first experience. Unlike his father, he was a conformer, and in Cambridge half a sovereign got you a girl, a half-decent girl, too. Charlie had had two. Quite meaningless; no more momentous than taking a drink when you were thirsty or emptying your bladder afterwards. In fact, disappointing, after all the mystery that was made of it and the talk about it.

With Anna completely different. Ineffable joy. A future-looking thing, a need to stake a possession. Almost as soon as he could breathe again, he said, "I'll marry you, Anna, if you'll have me."

She said, almost laughing, "Don't talk so silly. Your sort can't marry mine. What'd your family say?"

Ruthlessly throwing off the comfortable cocoon that had held him snug since the day he was born, Charlie said, "They can say—or do—whatever they like. You and I belong together."

By that time she knew a good deal more about him than he did about her. She knew his name, who his father was, where he lived, what his future held, and she was sceptical. There were known cases, rapidly becoming legends, of such incongruous matches: a girl who had pranced about the music hall stage, wearing tights and a top hat, was now Duchess of Denver; another girl who peddled nicely made buttonhole posies was a countess, somewhere in Northumberland. But they were exceptions; in both cases the men had been of full age—the Duke of Denver, in fact, absolutely senile. Very different from Charlie Orford, not yet twenty-one, entirely dependent on his father.

And yet, and yet. He was quite the *nicest* person she had ever had to deal with, and his plans sounded sensible. He did not delude himself that his parents would love her on sight, as he now claimed that he had done; but they were reasonable people, they were fond of him, they'd want him to be happy. On the other hand, if they proved awkward, he could always earn a living, with his athletic record and the degree of which he was practically certain.

Sitting in the bar of the Brewers' Arms through the dead afternoon, steadily becoming more drunk, for the first time in his life, yet seeing very clearly as he pieced the whole thing together, he saw where he'd gone wrong. He'd been dilatory. He should have tackled Papa the very next day and *told* Anna the result, holding her close to him. "Papa wasn't exactly enthusiastic. He kept harping about my age." That would have sounded better *said* than it looked written.

And he shouldn't have left her here. He had plenty of money. He could have installed her in some snug little lodging and seen her every day. He could even have married her.

Was it a good thing that he had not? Had he had a lucky escape? There were gratuitous lies, and she'd told him one within five minutes of their meeting. But wasn't that understandable? Did you, to a perfect stranger whom you found attractive, immediately talk about your own ill health?

He took out her letter and read it again. Abrupt and callous. But belied by the postcript which seemed to ring true.

Was this letter a fabrication, too? Had she actually had an offer of marriage? If not, what was happening to her now? He'd given her ten pounds when they parted. That wouldn't last long in London.

The thing the filthy old woman had said, the thing he had intended never to think of again, reared up in his mind.

Virginity? He'd never considered it. For all their would-be worldly-wise attitude and almost deliberately lewd talk, he and his friends were ignorant. It was supposed to be specially good with a virgin, and all Charlie knew was that it had been not merely specially good, but out of this world with Anna. Because—disgusting thought—she, unlike his other hirelings, had given him value for money?

Mrs. Pryke watched him with a maternal feeling which would have surprised everybody who knew her—even her husband. He was plainly worried about something. He'd hardly touched her votive offering, and he was becoming intoxicated. She knew all the signs, and although to some degree she made a livelihood out of other people's craving for liquor, in this case she deplored it. He wouldn't look like Sir Galahad for long if he went on like this. That golden look, as though something of the hair's colour had seeped down into the skin, just touched with rose on cheek and mouth, would change. Drunks had two colours: purply red or ashy grey. Eyes went different, too; they either bulged or receded.

No business of hers, but a pity.

She looked at the clacking clock. Half past four. Almost time to make the strong brew that would revive Josh and enable him to face the stew, simmering away at the back of the stove. Managing meals on Sunday when all help must have its day off was a bit of a business. She and her husband, taking turns, had eaten a cut off the joint at midday, and that was enough for her; but Josh needed something more sustaining before the evening rush began.

"I'm just about to make a cup of tea, sir. Would you like one?"

And maybe she had been wrong about his being drunk. Perhaps even wrong about his being bothered about something, for he looked up with those beautiful, almost cornflower-blue eyes and said, without any of the slurring speech she had expected, "That would be most acceptable."

The last b and s had bitten home, and Charlie no longer cared about anything. If he'd had a love and lost her, what did it matter? If he'd been a deluded fool, who cared?

The secretly sentimental woman had been the sole witness to Charlie Orford's graduation as a drunkard.

The telegram, for which Mr. Orford was secretly prepared, said almost exactly what he had anticipated: "Terribly sorry. Weekend off. Work calls. Love to all, Charlie."

"Oh dear," Rose said, "what a disappointment. Poor Charlie. Missing the ball."

But the real pity was Edda. Charlie's presence on such occasions was always such a help. Louise nobody, not even the most anxious mother in England, need bother about. The Hospital Ball, like all the others, was a very formal affair. There were programmes, pretty little cards with pretty little pencils, dangling from pretty little cords. Within a few minutes Louise's programme was full, and she was laughingly dealing out extras. It was not so with Edda, good dancer though she was. Too tall, of course, except for Edwin or Charlie and a very few other men. Very few! Edda spent a good deal of time sitting in what was recognised as the Dowagers' Corner, an alcove full of little, frail gilt chairs, or in another alcove, on a velvet sofa, listening with ill-concealed boredom to some elderly gentleman explaining why his dancing days were done.

Charlie's presence on such occasions made all the difference in the world. He kept an eye on Edda, danced with her—and a handsome couple they made—and he had a curious facility for producing other partners for her. They were generally strangers, lonely men whom Charlie had encountered in the bar upstairs, and they were almost all too short, but they did at least keep Edda on the floor.

Papa was aware of the problem and fully prepared to do his duty, but the sad fact was that he simply couldn't dance. He'd come to it too late. Other things, unknown in his youth, he had mastered with amazing ease; he rode well, played a good game of tennis, was an excellent host and an easy guest, but he could not dance because he had no ear for music and therefore no sense of rhythm. He had tried, had even practised on the marble floor of the hall at home, with Louise or Maude at the piano of the drawing room. Everybody agreed that it was useless. Papa also lacked Charlie's happy knack of striking up acquaintances in a few minutes. He gravitated naturally to men he knew, men whose dancing days were done. But he also kept an eye on Edda and frequently interrupted a conversation which he thought had gone on long enough. Edda's face would then light up, her manner become animated, and the elderly gentleman who had been boring her would take a slight offence, get up, and go away, leaving father and daughter alone together on one of the velvet sofas, a thing which, even to somebody far less socially conscious than Rose was, looked odd.

The one person tall enough, young enough, handsome enough to partner Edda was, Rose reflected sadly, Lord Chelsworth, but his grandmother always had a house party for the three balls in whose success she was interested—the Hospital, the Hunt, and the Central Mission. Such house parties invariably included a number of very attractive young women. Lady Chelsworth made no secret of the fact that she wanted to see Simon married. She would like to see at least one great-grandchild before she died, she said. She was equally frank about his need to marry money. Nobody knew, she said, what Bressford Castle cost to keep up, and to abandon it was unthinkable, the Talbots had been there since the Conquest, plain knights at first, baronets since the reign of James I, and finally earls.

She was too well bred to say that naturally Simon's wife

must be the owner of blue blood; in any case that could be taken for granted. Many of her houseguests had titles of their own; a few were American, which for some obscure reason qualified them.

Thinking these thoughts on the receipt of Charlie's telegram and again as she dressed for the ball, Rose came as near to gloom as her disposition allowed. Her temperament was sanguine. It had once been tempestuous, too, but even then optimistic. The hysterical fits had been thrown with some certainty that they would be effectual. Tonight *might* by different. After all, life for Rose Foster had held some astonishing surprises; there might be another in the offing; some tall, eligible stranger, suitable in every way, *might* appear.

Louise, as befitted her youth—she was only seventeen and had been "out" only a year—wore white, sweetly pretty, with little garlands of artificial rosebuds and forget-me-nots. Edda was in aquamarine blue, which *should,* her mother thought, have made her eyes look blue, but didn't. They looked green. Rose herself was modestly grand in the latest colour—Parma violet.

Maude said, "You *all* look beautiful. I wish I were coming."

"You will, next year, darling," Rose said. Naturally Charlie was her favourite child. Apart from one cataclysmic time in her life Rose had always been a conformer, and *all* mothers loved their boys best. Of the three daughters, Louise was her favourite, the most like her.

Mr. Orford, in his resolute avoidance of pretentiousness, called the man who looked after his horses his stableman, not his groom. The man, asked to define his rank, would have said coachman. And he certainly drove the carriage in great style.

* * *

The older part of Bressford had not changed much since its heyday in the eighteenth century, and the building in which balls, concerts, and even theatrical shows took place had not changed at all. It was called the Athenaeum, was extremely handsome, and was quite unsuited for most of the purposes to which it was put. Nine Ionian columns on each side divided it into three aisles—the central one much wider than the others—which rendered it less than ideal as a ballroom. The many alcoves were an acoustic disaster, visiting singers and actors complained bitterly, and before every ball the committee had spirited arguments about the siting of the band, some holding that the best place was at the far end of the central aisle, others favouring the place between the stairs at the other end. The stairs ran up in two flights which met on a half landing which, it was claimed, formed a roof which acted as a sounding board.

On the night of the Hospital Ball, the under-the-stairs party had won; the sounds of the music were clearly audible in the porticoed entry and in the lobby, where, across an expanse of black and white marble tiles, effigies of Victoria and Albert faced each other. They served a useful purpose for they represented their sexes. Ladies left their wraps in the room whose doorway the Queen guarded; gentlemen skirted His Royal Highness.

On such evenings as this there was always a little crowd outside the Athenaeum. Staring, commenting, enjoying the show. Seldom envious. It was after all a free show, something of colour and glamour.

Edda Orford, following her mother and followed by Louise, stepped into the ballroom and thought: For me this is the last! I will never again subject myself to such humiliation or Mamma and Papa to such anxiety. I'll be Lady Gytha because it suits me, and I'll do it well, and after that I'll never make a public appearance again.

Because Florence Nightingale had with her strong character, strong hands and strong opinions lifted nursing from the Sairey Gamp level to something far higher and much revered, so the dealing out of programmes at Hospital Balls was not done by attendants in eighteenth-century costume, yellow breeches, floured wigs, but by volunteers, all young ladies, dressed as nurses. And the rather stark, designed-to-be-unseductive uniform had the exactly opposite effect; they all looked beautiful. As nuns did.

This was all pretence. Veronica Hepworth, Claudia Stanton, and half a dozen others, all pressed into service by that old autocrat, Lady Chelsworth.

But suppose, just suppose that you took up nursing, not as a pretence, but in reality?

Mamma knew just where she was going. Louise was buoyant as a captive balloon simply waiting for the controlling cords to be severed. She danced away, and Edda prepared to follow Mamma to the alcove.

From behind the nearest of those most awkwardly obstructing pillars, Lord Chelsworth stepped. Bowed. Said, "I have been waiting. . . ."

It was all pretence, of course, and Edda knew it. It was, in fact, part of the pageant, the very words of greeting were from the script—the words with which the hard-pressed king of the mid-Anglians had greeted the arrival of the Lady Gytha and the reinforcements she brought. She gave him back the quoted answer, "My Lord, I came with all the speed and all the men I could muster." He looked slightly startled.

Even when he asked her to dance, she remained sceptical. He was probably using her as an escape from the house party, from some particularly eligible girl who had his grandmother's backing. She could think of no other reason, for though she had known him on and off for a long time and had been "out" for three years, he had never danced with her before. She could well imagine him saying that tonight he *must* pay at least a token attention to the Lady Gytha. His grandmother would have agreed, with a shrug of her still-elegant shoulders, and maybe a murmured "So long as it is a *token*. . . ."

Never mind! He danced very well, and for once she enjoyed dancing as much as she ordinarily did only with Charlie. And at the end of the waltz he did not lead her back to the Dowagers' Alcove, but towards a group of people— all young except for one man, almost Papa's age and just Papa's height.

"I want you to meet Lord Greythorpe. He and my grandmother have just had a terrible row. He is a bit of a historian and had the effrontery to say that Lady Gytha never existed. He'll get a bad breakfast tomorrow!" He tapped the older man on the arm and said, "Hi, Toby. Here she is, in the flesh. Lord Greythorpe—Miss Thorley. Lady Gytha."

Except where the matter of dancing was concerned, Edda did not lack confidence.

"Simon tells me you are a heretic. My brother is another."

"I should like to meet him. Is he here?"

Edda explained about Charlie. The band struck up again, a polka.

Rose, watchful, saw Edda dancing with the tall, dark stranger of her hopes. . . .

Mr. Orford, watchful, saw Edda dancing with Lord Chelsworth, with a man unknown, with Lord Chelsworth, again with the man—now known, for paternal care had made it necessary to know—Lord Greythorpe, plainly reputable, since he was one of the castle house party.

In Mr. Orford's mind there was neither elation nor surprise. Nothing was too good for Edda in his opinion. The only thing that had prevented him from placing any hope on Lord Chelsworth was the matter of money. Mr. Orford was rich but, for that purpose, not rich enough, and Edda was not his only child. Charlie must inherit most, and the two younger girls must be provided for. For the upkeep of Bressford Castle even Mr. Orford could not offer enough and, unless he had one of his fantastic strokes of luck, never would be able to.

It was just possible, the fond father thought, that Lord Greythorpe might not be in such desperate need of money. There were still some rich aristocrats about, men who were not entirely dependent on the tottering economy of the land, men who owned property in London or had some connection with the rapidly expanding midlands, with foreign investments, or with shipping lines. There might well be a man who could afford Edda.

Lady Chelsworth watched with dismay and—a rare feeling with her—some self-blame. It was she who had decreed that the Orford family was *acceptable,* she who had dubbed Mr. Orford a *character,* she who, by electing Edda to be Lady Gytha, had thrown the girl and Simon together. But she had trusted her grandson; he knew, without having it spelled out to him, that his wife must be *suitable.* And he was no silly boy to go losing his head; he was twenty-nine. She would have a talk with him in the morning!

Alongside so great an issue ran the lesser, but still important one: the disruption of her carefully managed party. Every time Simon or Greythorpe—hateful man!—danced with Edda Orford one of her young female guests was consigned to a little gilt chair.

And another thing, too, small, but rankling. Shamus, the wolfhound, upon whose loyalty she would have staked her life, had transferred his allegiance to Edda. It wasn't a question of the girl's being able to control him—one of the arguments in favour of choosing her. He positively fawned, had twice run away, and turned up at Flixton Old Manor and had to be brought back.

Thinking these thoughts, Lady Chelsworth looked about her and studied the group of spare men, either nondancers or temporarily without partners, who always congregated by the door of the supper room. One seemed to be a little apart, out of it, even there. Young Dr. Sapey. She rose and made her majestic way down the nearest aisle. Dancing was supposed to be confined to the central space, but an occasional bold couple ventured behind the pillars, always on the side farther from the Dowagers' Alcove. She gave the young man an imperative tap on the arm with her fan and said in a rallying way, "Good evening, Dr. Sapey. You are shirking your duty." He felt that he was doing it nobly, venturing, for the sake of the hospital, into this hotbed of snobbery and privilege, in a hired dress suit and with only the most elementary experience of dancing. It was customary for the hospital to be represented, and older and wiser doctors planned evasive tactics.

"You must *dance,* " Lady Chelsworth said. Dr. Sapey blenched. For a wild moment he feared that she was about to suggest that he should dance with her. Dowagers did not dance as a rule, but he had been in Bressford long enough to know that this old woman made her own. She was capable of anything! However, all she did on this occasion was to lay her hand on his arm and say, "Come and have a glass of wine with me."

The supper room was large and divided into two by a trellis of trailing greenery studded with flowers. Beyond the trellis, in the larger portion of the room, the supper tables were already laid; the part into which Lady Chelsworth led Dr. Sapey was what, at lesser functions, would have been called the bar. Here men alone could order what they wished; men accompanied by young women drank champagne. Young ladies as a rule indulged in an innocuous tipple called wine-cup; a few very daring ones had champagne. With a dance—another polka—in progress, the place was temporarily deserted; when the vigorous exercise ended, it would be crowded. There was not long to wait, just long enough for Dr. Sapey to revise his opinion of Lady Chelsworth and find her absolutely charming in a maternal way. She asked how he liked Bressford, were his lodgings satisfactory, because if not she knew of an excellent place, and how did he occupy his leisure hours?

The dance ended; the rush for cool liquid refreshment

began. Through the murmurous hubbub of well-bred voices, Lady Chelsworth, without shouting, made herself easily heard.

"Edda, my dear, I have kept a place for you." Lord Greythorpe, who had been dancing the polka with Edda, naturally accompanied her towards the little table near the trellis, and with an abrupt change of manner Lady Chelsworth said, "Go away, you horrible man. I am furious with you. Edda, dear, this is Dr. Sapey—Dr. Sapey, Miss Orford. . . . Now, since all the waiters appear to be lost in the mob, I wonder if you could force your way. . . ." As soon as he had gone on his errand, biddable as a dog; through all the little waiting time he had said nothing except "Yes, your ladyship" or "No," or "Quite" or "I entirely agree," her ladyship turned to Edda and spoke quietly, but incisively. "My dear, I must ask you to deputise for me yet again. That poor young man, such a nice young man, is simply longing to dance. Such a very awkward position. It always happens. I've seen it so often. Because it is a ball in aid of the hospital, some doctor must come as a representative. It is not so bad for a married man—he can always dance with his wife—or for one long established and respected, as Dr. Craig was. But poor Dr. Sapey is out on a limb. Damme, I'd dance with him myself—I often conferred such favours in the old days. But my dancing days are done. If I can *prod* him into asking you, will you be kind?"

Why not? Since she was determined to cast it all off. All the pretence. Dance just once more at Charlie's twenty-first birthday party and then no more.

"Of course I will," Edda said. "Heaven knows I have sympathy with wallflowers, but I never realised until now that some were male." The old woman's heart warmed towards Edda again; so forthright, so different, so unmissish. Oh, if only . . . but no good thinking that way. "I'll see that he gets a dance with Louise, too, and one or two others." Managing, Lady Chelsworth thought, recognising her own quality, one which those who disliked her called masterful, but God knew with so many things to be mastered, and managed, someone must do it. Oh, if only. . . .

Bressford Castle, seat of the Talbot family, did not stand in the town with which it shared a name, but at least two miles upriver, on a site chosen because it was the highest point within a radius of thirty miles. From the top of its stern Norman keep one could, on any reasonably clear day, see downriver as far as Radmouth. Bressford town, which had started as a mere village, had grown up on the lower, more easily cultivatable ground.

The castle had stood, keeping guard, since William the Conqueror's time—and probably even longer. There was a belief, insusceptible to proof, that a high Roman dignitary—the Count of the Saxon Shore—had had a fortress and a residence here. Ignoring this, assuming, as most people did, that 1066 saw the beginning of English history, the castle offered a mute record in its jumble of architecture. Somewhere in the fourteenth century a Talbot had built what he thought of as comfortable living quarters, a half-timbered house, known as the West Wing; it was built to the west of the keep, and every door and window in it faced north because—since the plague was more prevalent in summer—most people believed that it was borne on the south wind. Two centuries later some bold Talbot had defied that idea and built another house, to the east but with great wide windows facing south. And later, another Talbot had reared yet another house in the style known as Queen Anne, but deriving much from the Continental influence introduced by the Restoration of Charles II. After that the Talbots had declined in both wealth and power, and there was no more building.

On this beautiful June evening the castle and the buildings that clung to its sides stood dark and solid against the sky as Mr. Orford, preceded by his wife and daughters, edged into the most privileged department of the covered stand and opened his commemorative programme.

It said, helpfully, "Scene One. The Martyrdom of St. Bress." Not particularly interesting to one who had—again much privileged—seen the full-dress rehearsal. Edda did not appear in it, and it was mercifully short. Even modern Bressfordians and the historically minded schoolmaster who had made slight adjustments to the fifty-year-old script didn't wish to dwell too heavily on the fact that a saintly man had come from Lindisfarne to convert a lot of pagans and been stoned to death for his pains. All in pattern. Farther inland St. Alban had been killed by a casting of ox-bones which, presumably, his unwilling audience had been gnawing at the time.

"Scene Two. The Battle of Bressford" proved that St. Bress and others like him had not laboured in vain. The men of Bressford were all stout Christians, ready to defend their faith and their territory from the Danish invaders. But they were in trouble from the start, outnumbered and, by the look of things, outwitted. Their leader, Egfrid, seemed to be an easily discouraged fellow, just holding out, making gestures of despair, until the Lady Gytha arrived.

Mr. Orford, a strictly practical man, making contact with the pageant for the first time—through Edda—had wondered how Lord Chelsworth could possibly bring himself to play such a pusillanimous role. Tradition, he supposed; the third earl had devised the pageant for the glorification of his young wife, fifty years ago, and not long after had gone off, been very brave and got himself killed somewhere on the northest frontier of India. His son, in turn, had played the part of Egfrid, with his mother as Lady Gytha, and then he had gone off, been very brave, and got himself killed in the Crimean War.

Shifting a bit on his seat, which though privileged was hard, Mr. Orford came to the conclusion that if you came of a family long renowned for courage, you could afford to play the craven. In a pageant.

And all the time he waited for Edda to arrive. As she did, looking wonderful, on the golden brown hunter, so aptly named Topaz, which had cost close on three hundred pounds.

Mr. Orford disliked talk about money, but he could not avoid thinking about it, for it had governed his life, ever since he could earn a ha'penny, watching a horse, running an errand. . . .

He watched Edda ride in and make Lady Gytha's rousing speech. You couldn't hear a word, of course. Edda herself had said, "We might as well say abracadabra," but the gist of it was plain. Next time the Danes came sneaking up the river—real River Rad, which lent itself to such spectacular a display—they were in for their surprise of their lives. . . .

When that scene was over, Mr. Orford leant back and re-laxed his attention. Edda would not appear again until Scene Six and then as a ghost, from behind a vast screen of muslin and cunningly lighted, rallying the men of Bress-ford again. This time to resist the Spanish.

The intervening scenes were twaddle.

He gave himself over to reverie.

Errand boy, not even an apprentice, at Foster's, in the High Street. Ten years old, a bit tall for his age, but gangly.

"I doubt whether you're man enough," Mr. Foster said. "The baskets are heavy."

The boy said, "I can carry anything, sir. Try me, *please.*"

The baskets were heavy. Within a certain radius of the shop in the High Street it was both quicker and cheaper to deliver orders by boy than by van. A boy cost eighteen pence a week; a well-fed horse, with oats and hay at the price they were, cost more. But Mr. Foster was not miserly or a deliberate exploiter of the poor. His boys had, besides the stark wage, certain perquisites: broken biscuits, odds and ends of cheese and bacon, anything scooped up from the floor.

Change the heavy basket from the aching right arm to the left, carry it full front like a pedlar's pack, drop it if all else failed, and push or pull it. At all costs get the job done, the vital money earned.

The boy had survived, and grown, been promoted. Van driver, counter hand, head assistant with a steady wage of eighteen shillings a week. Presently he was twenty-six and on the very verge of realising an ambition.

It was a night in early November. Mr. Foster and his three assistants were preparing the orders for the next day, and these were exceptionally heavy since prudent house-wives and cooks were about to begin on mincemeat, Christmas cakes, and puddings. The master sat in his usual place, a kind of pulpit, raised slightly above the shop floor and surrounded by a wide mahogany ledge, which, with the drawers and cupboards beneath it on the inner side, constituted his office. From this eminence he could supervise all activites. The structure was accessible by a small door at its rear. Orford and Snell—next in seniority—weighed and packed, Orford the groceries, Snell the provisions; Pryke carried the delivery baskets from one counter to the other and then to the desk, where Mr. Foster checked the items, totalled the bill, and entered the amounts in his ledger. The atmosphere was tense with concentration.

The clock in St. John's tower boomed nine. And they were still far from finished. Mr. Foster stirred in his chair and sighed and reflected that he really needed another assistant but could not afford him, for though Foster's supplied the best goods to the best people, some of those people ran up the best debts. They always paid in the end, of course, but extended credit was really money lent out, over a period of time, without interest. Lately Mr. Foster had been increasingly preoccupied with money, for he was in

his seventieth year, and the lady who now impatiently
awaited his coming in the panelled rooms above the shop
was his second wife, twenty years his junior; he had to
think of her future—and of Rose's. . . . Rather dispiritedly
he added the sum of four pounds, two shillings, and two
pence to the account of Sir John Manton, who already owed
one hundred, four shillings, and sevenpence. It didn't do to
press for payment, nothing offended the gentry more, and
whereas in the past there had been in all southwest Norfolk
a kind of monopoly, the coming of the railway had changed
all that. There were huge shops in London only too ready
and willing.

The door which gave access to the stairs leading to the
living quarters opened, and Rose stepped into the shop.
The old man's expression brightened; his only child, the
child of his late middle age, and the prettiest thing he had
ever set eyes on. Foster's had been founded in 1732 and had
passed from father to son ever since, but after one sharp,
unguarded pang, the father had never regretted Rose's sex.
Even as a baby she had been so pretty and, as she grew, had
developed such taking ways.

Tonight she looked even more beautiful than ever, quite
angelic, for she had been washing her hair, and it hung,
curling as it dried, pure gold in colour, over the thick white
towel which might have been the folded wings of an angel.

Her arrival caused no disturbance, no distraction to the
young men in the shop. Of necessity, they saw her often, for
although the living quarters had another access, through
the yard where the horses lived and the vans stood and
goods were delivered, it was some way down Hawk's Lane,
and Rose preferred the shortcut. Rose could sail through
the shop, oblivious to all except a few ladies of her acquaintance—mostly from the Avenues—who did their own
shopping; then, of course, there were effusive greetings.
The counter hands all wore invisible cloaks, and the wear-
ers of those cloaks called her—amongst themselves—Ro-

sy-Posy, with no affection in the term. A high-nosed little
bitch, they all agreed.

The Fosters naturally kept a maid, a competent cook-
housemaid-parlourmaid named Martha, and in the ordinary
way Mrs. Foster would have sent her down with any message that was to be delivered; but Mrs. Foster had a sense of
propriety and felt that such a *strict* communication had better be kept within the family; servants were so apt to misun-
derstand and to exaggerate. So it was Rose who came to the
front of the pulpit cage and said, "Papa, Mamma says that
unless you come *at once,* she will not keep supper for you."

Then it happened. Leaning over the wide ledge, Rose
brushed her hair against one of the candles, and it flared up.
Orford was nearest, quickest, *luckiest.* Snell was behind the
provision counter, cutting cheese; Pryke had just staggered
out with a filled basket to the order room; Mr. Foster was
struggling with the latch of the pulpit door, but Orford was
there. With hands hardened by years of hard labour he beat
out the flames in a trice. Even so enough had burned to
make the shop, ordinarily odorous of coffee, tea, spices,
smell like a smithy.

Rose wept. "Oh my hair, my hair. . . ."

Orford said, "No need to worry, Miss Rose. It was only
the ends."

Mr. Foster, out of his cage, stumbled round and took his
daughter in his arms. "It's all right, my darling . . . thanks
to Orford. Come away now. Let's go up. Orford, I'm much
obliged to you."

Orford said, when they had gone and Pryke had come
back from the order room asking what the noise had been
about and what the funny smell was, "Well, I reckon we'd
better finish up. Only ten to do. . . ."

Of much that went on abovestairs immediately after that
not particularly cataclysmic event, Orford was not much
better informed than Snell or Pryke. Rosy-Posy no longer

went out or came in alone; she was always accompanied by her mother—quite understandable, since there was Christmas shopping to be done. Now and again Orford was aware of the master's eye, lingering, speculative, and hoped that it boded a rise in the New Year. That Rosy-Posy from behind her mother's bulk cast looks in his direction, he attributed to gratitude, no more than his due; after all, but for his quick action, her pretty little face, even her eyes, might have suffered. His hands had not suffered at all, the softer skin on the inside of his wrists had been lightly scorched and developed some tough blisters. They were healed by Christmas, when as head assistant he received his Christmas box—fifteen shillings—the others had ten. Adding it to the little hoard, so painfully accumulated ever since the death of the drunken drover had reduced expenses and inspired hope, Edwin Orford said to his mother, "I think, maybe, by Easter. And we'll be out of this!"

Immediately after Christmas Rosy-Posy went on holiday, to stay with an aunt at Radmouth. Not perhaps the most happy time to choose for a stay by the sea in the extreme east of England, so racked by the wind, straight from Siberia, that even the trees grew lopsided. But no concern of his. And when, after a fortnight, Rosy-Posy came back, a white rose, rather than a pink one, that was no concern of his either. And when, two days after Rosy-Posy's return, Mr. Foster said, "Orford, stay behind for a bit. I have something to say to you," Orford was not much perturbed. At best it might be the expected rise, at worst dismissal, since Tom Snell was competent to take over. In that case his own plans would have to be hastened up a little.

He went and stood before the pulpit, erect, alert, and easy; it was Mr. Foster who seemed to be suffering some embarrassment, darting a glance at his assistant, then looking away, fidgetting with things on the ledge. For the first time the counter hand noticed that his master looked less well than he had done; his firm, plump face had sagged into wattles, his neck had grown thin, and the rosy colour of his cheeks was less evenly disposed. The thought occurred to the young man that Mr. Foster was ill, threatened perhaps by an operation, and was about to hand the shop into his keeping for a time.

"It's about Miss Rose . . . about my daughter," the old grocer managed to say at last. "She's set her heart on marrying you."

(Later that evening Edwin Orford told his mother that you could have knocked him down with a butter patter and that nothing would ever surprise him again. At the moment, however, he gave no sign of any emotion.)

"But she knows nothing about me, sir."

But I do, the old man thought; I know everything that the most careful enquiry could reveal. You are a most excellent young man; sober, thrifty, good to your mother; your name has never been connected with that of any female; you attend classes at the Workman's Institute; you go to every Penny Reading that you have time for. In addition, I know that you know the grocery trade inside out. And you're damned good-looking! That, of course, was the trouble; Rose had, just for once, looked upon a counter hand as a human being and seen a very personable young man.

"She seems to know all she wishes to," said the old man, who for two months had argued, coaxed, persuaded, borne temper and tears and tantrums and hunger strikes, with an occasional self-doubt thrown in for good measure. For what indeed was there against young Orford except his humble status and the fact that daughters of men in a good way of business simply didn't marry counter hands? And they'd had such *high* hopes for Rose, quite the prettiest girl in their circumscribed set. It had indeed once seemed more than likely that she would break out of that set in the opposite direction; young Gordon, the solicitor's son, had been very attentive. In Bressford there was still a heavy demarcation between trade and any profession, and Rose was the girl to cross it, if any girl ever did; her looks were unusual, golden hair and huge dark eyes, a rose-leaf complexion, and an eighteen-inch waist.

Much sought after, largely for herself, but also because her father was known to be a "warm" man, and she was his only child. And Foster's was an old, highly respected business.

There'd been, besides young Gordon, young Quantrill, heir to a good bootmaker's business; young Bradshaw, the corn chandler's son; and young Whittle, who had already inherited the timberyard. Nothing had come of any of these courtships, and Rose was now eighteen and a half years old. Her parents were mildly grieved as chance after chance slipped by. And a little puzzled, not blaming themselves in any way for the fact that Rose was so spoilt as to be unreasonably capricious and that the tantrums which they accepted as part of life—and pandered to—had made many a young man think: Am I to live with *this* all my days?

Edwin Orford had never seen Rose Foster in a tantrum, nor had he heard even the most recent and violent ones, for the old shop was solidly built; he had, however, heard *about* earlier ones from a variety of sources. His mother's work brought her into contact with a good deal of backdoor gossip; Pryke's father was a jobbing gardener. There were many tales about "your Miss Rose" or "our Rosy-Posy." And none to her credit. Now Edwin Orford remembered them all, and thought, as men in far better positions had done: Am I to live with this?

He said, "I'd have to think about it, sir." And he meant *think*. Beyond everything else in the world he wanted, he needed, to be his own man, to be able to apply his agile, inventive brain, his seemingly inexhaustible physical energy to his own cause. He did not want a pampered pretty child hanging round his neck, and by God, if he married her—and the business—she'd have the complete whip hand over him forever.

"*Think* about it!" the old grocer said furiously. "Think about it! Orford, do you realise what I'm offering you? I can't last forever. All this will be yours one day. . . ."

They all did it, the young man reflected; they seemed unable to help themselves, business, money, all they thought about. Even at a moment like this. When he was rich, as he fully intended to be one day, how differently he would behave.

"Marriage," he said, "is a very serious business. It needs thinking over."

He intended, of course, to get married one day. No hurry. When he was thirty, perhaps; some fairly pretty, amiable, placid young woman.

"Don't you *want* to marry my Rose?'

"Sir, how could I? I never even thought about it."

"Well, think about it now. Put on your jacket. I was told to give you the lay of the land and take you up for supper."

Told, by Rose, her mother, or both. No woman is going to tell *me* what to do; and I'm not going up there on these terms, whistled up like a dog.

"I'm sorry, sir, but I cannot accept such a sudden invitation. I have the ironing to do."

Mr. Foster gaped.

"I do most of the ironing nowadays," the astonishing young man said. "It's the most tiring part of the job."

Washing was now comparatively easy, for the first thing he had saved up for was a patent washing machine, a tub in which four paddles rotated when a handle was turned. Nobody had yet invented a device to make ironing easier. "It'll give me a good chance to think, sir."

Orford went home, and Mr. Foster climbed the stairs to face Rose, who was first incredulous and then hysterical. "You didn't ask him properly," she said.

As Orford ironed, he talked to his mother, did some quiet thinking, and then, over a late cup of cocoa, told her what he had decided to do. She said, "It's taking a risk, son. But you know best about that."

The next day Edwin delivered his ultimatum. Three months of ordinary walking out, to get to know each other. Then, if Miss Rose still liked him—and he liked her—he'd propose. Reasonable enough, the old grocer thought. "But," Orford went on, "I can't let this or anything else interfere with my own plans. I've got my eye on that little corner shop at the end of Church Street. It's nothing now, but I could make something of it. My mother and I have been saving for years. Seventy pounds for the goodwill, stock at valuation, five shillings-a-week rent, including the living accommodation. *And that is where we would live.*"

Mr. Foster came perilously near to apoplexy. All the old colour, and more, flooded back into his face; his eyes bulged. The audacity of it! The sheer ingratitude! Then he saw that he and his wife—and indeed Rose—had been saved. For Rose would never agree to that!

He reckoned without taking into consideration the strength of his daughter's infatuation. It was as though the girl had been bewitched. In making up her mind to marry a counter hand, she had defied the rampant small-town snobbery in which she had been born and reared. So what did anything else matter? Life with Edwin, anywhere, would be heaven; life without him, anywhere, would be hell. "I *respect* him for it," she told her horrified parents. "This way nobody can say he was marrying a business."

"But he *is*, however you look at it. Foster's will be his one day."

"You will live to be eighty, Papa. Grandpapa did. And by that time Edwin will be well established."

"Rose, I cannot have you living in Church Street. You simply don't understand. You've been protected all your life. Church Street is rough, and you'd be bang next door to the Queen's Head. A terrible place."

She would not be moved.

The walking out began, and so did the teasing, for which Rose was well prepared. Long pampering had given her a massive self-confidence; what she chose to do was right. When her best friends expostulated, "Darling, you can't possibly! He's a boy from the Pike!" Rose said, "I can, and I will. I hold that it isn't so much where a man comes from as where he is going."

"Church Street! You propose to go and live there?"

"If I can persuade Edwin to propose to me. At the moment I am on probation—sale or return, you know."

"You must be out of your mind."

"I'm in love. Wait till it happens to you."

One of the things that surprised everybody, including the infatuated girl, was that Edwin Orford, born in the Pike, had such beautiful manners. But why not? Alongside the copybooks and *Grammar for Beginners,* there were many books—usually anonymous—written by ladies of quality for the information of the rapidly growing middle classes. Not, naturally, for people born in the Pike. But Edwin Orford, whose busy days always ended with an hour's reading by candlelight, had long before he had any need of such esoteric counsel bought a book coyly titled *Manners Maketh Man.* Most of it made sense to him. He had read and, what was more, absorbed it, so that the precepts were part of him, not something to be put on and off like a hat. Mrs. Foster had cherished a secret hope that brought upstairs, faced with a considerable confusion of cutlery, entirely divorced from his own background, young Orford might behave in such a loutish way that Rose would be shocked out of her infatuation. That did not happen; Orford's manners were as impeccable as his grammar. On the other side of the counter—so to speak—Rose had passed every possible test; she'd accepted Church Street and visited the Pike and been extremely nice to the bowed, gnarled old washerwoman, saying very sweetly that since one of the rooms over the Church Street shop was to be *hers,* she must choose the wallpaper.

So by Easter everybody was resigned, and Rose at least was happy.

Unlike other weather, that of Easter, variable festival as it was, was roughly predictable; early or late, Good Friday was invariably a good day for weather, Easter Sunday horrible, Easter Monday good again. So for many years Easter Monday had been the day when children from places like the Pike or Church Street or from some relatively new, stark, ugly, but hygienic buildings known as Alexandra Row were given their annual treat. Good churchmen like Mr. Foster lent their vans to convey the children to some green meadow, subscribed towards the fund for prizes and fireworks, and contributed edible items for a vast meal.

It was not unusual to see a child being sick, what with the excitement and the mixture, but Mr. Foster, ambling amiably around, saw a little boy who, having been sick, did not revive and prepare to eat again. He cried; he said he felt ill all over.

"Would you like to go home? All right, you shall. You'll miss the fireworks, you know."

The old man was not really averse to the idea of going home himself. Although he was now resigned to his domestic situation, the worry had taken toll of him, and he was more than a year older than he had been last Easter Monday. "Come along then, sonny, we'll go home. Where do you live?"

"Down the Pike."

Mr. Foster took the child by the hand, noticing its dry, burning heat, and went towards one of his own vans, called up its driver.

"Drive us home, Tom. This young fellow doesn't feel well. And I've had about enough. Go to the Pike first."

It was not a long drive, but during its course the child was sick again, soiling Mr. Foster's Easter Monday garb.

By Wednesday Mr. Foster knew what it meant to feel ill all over. He was still in full possession of his senses, however, and said a thing typical of his time. "You and Rose, my dear, stay away from me; this may be catching. Martha can see to me. Tell her to make a good jug of barley water." One's womenfolk must be protected; servants were sexless and presumably immune.

Dr. Craig was summoned and came and said vague, soothing things and prescribed various nostrums. Opium could at least be trusted to ease pain and even, with luck, halt one unpleasant symptom of what he privately believed to be a form of cholera, not now endemic in England, but not unknown.

Mr. Foster, emerging from an opium dream, found just enough strength to ring the bell for Martha. "I want Orford. quick!" It was one of the last occasions for quite a long time that Orford was plain Orford. He became, almost overnight, Mr. Orford and stayed so, until he graduated into a stratum of society in which men naturally addressed one another as they had in their schooldays.

"I think I'm going to die," Mr. Foster said in a weak voice. "You'll look after everything? Mr. Gordon has my will. . . . Don't change Foster's more than . . . you have to . . . it has a . . . long tradition. God . . . bless you . . . my boy."

So the ultimate proof of Rose's loyalty and disregard for convention was never demanded.

The six months of what she had termed probation had not expired; but Mr. Orford thought he knew her well enough now, and since she herself had given the Church Street plan the maximum of publicity, there could be no suspicion that he had any immediately ulterior aim in marrying her. Emotionally they were well suited; he was not in love with her, but he was fond of her, and she was still so deeply in love with him, so very demonstrative that her warmth made up for any deficiency on his part. A deficiency of which she was never aware.

A fortnight after the funeral he proposed and was accepted. As he said, everything was altered now. Not to be disregarded was the fact that the two women were now alone at night, and if Edwin moved in with them, another woman would be left alone in the more dubious surroundings of the Pike. The sooner things were tidied up, the better.

It was the era of the half-hoop engagement ring, and the diamond was *the* fashionable stone; even suitors of very modest means would offer a diamond chip, about the size of half a rice grain, set flat in a gold ring. Mr. Orford bought Rose's ring from the pawnshop in the Pike. The shop was kept by a Jew named Ebenezer whose steadiest source of income was derived from advancing a few pennies on Sunday clothes every Monday and handing them back on Saturday, charging one hundred percent for this service. It *was* a service since most of the houses in the area had no storage space. Clothes that were not reclaimed within a given period were piled in one grimy window and offered for sale at exceedingly low prices—another service to the community. But over the years some strange things had come into the Jew's hands, and in another window, captive in a strong iron cage, he offered for sale articles which he considered of value: a gold locket shaped like a heart with a tiny pearl in the centre; a gold watch and chain; several seals; a silver christening cup; and the ring. It was a single, rather large, very dark-blue stone, set high in a filigree framework. Ebenezer claimed that it was a genuine sapphire, ruined because its surface had been cut to make a seal, a seal so much used that its message was now indecipherable. "If it hadn't been so mutilated, it'd be worth every penny of a hundred pounds. You can have it for fifteen."

Rose showed no sign of dismay at the sight of it and instantly abandoned all thought of the half-hoop of diamonds in Collins', the jeweller's. This was what Edwin had chosen; this was what Edwin was offering. She showed it with pride and told a lie or two about it. "It is exactly what I wanted. After all, anybody can have a diamond half-hoop. This is something different. The marks? It is an Italian sign which says—I love you."

Women discussed the engagement and the odd ring and wondered when the wedding would be. Six months was the very minimum mourning period. So October at the earliest.

Men indulged in the kind of talk which Mr. Orford regarded as abhorrent. Old Foster had "cut up" for far less than might have been expected. Only just over five thousand pounds. Amazing when you considered that he had lived modestly, never kept a carriage, never moved into the Avenues. A lot of bad debts, they concluded. And it was a known fact that the grocer was always the last to be paid. It remained to be seen what that young man would make of it. Mourning did not mean the complete cessation of all social life; arrange a quiet little supper party, and we'll hear what he has in mind. After all, it was July now, and poor old Foster had been in his grave three months.

It was over one of these invitations that Rose and Edwin had their first quarrel.

"Rose, I can't," Mr. Orford said. "Thursday's always a busy evening with orders, and when they're done, there's the bookwork."

On the surface the bookkeeping at Foster's had looked simple and straightforward; to the closer, sharper view it was in a calamitous muddle. Mr. Orford reckoned that it would take him at least three months of overtime to get it straightened out.

"But, darling, I can't go alone."

"You wouldn't have to. Your mother is invited."

"That is not the same thing at all," Rose said. Nor was it. Engaged couples in Bressford were invariably invited together. And she was so proud of him, with his good looks, his beautiful manners; she wanted to show him off. "Mrs. Quantrill said that she was particularly anxious to meet you."

"My dear, Mrs. Quantrill has met me every Tuesday morning for the last six years. Across the counter. She does her own shopping." (And a difficult, bitchy customer she was!)

Something deep inside the spoilt little girl said: Now! This is your last chance. You've given way and given way. Unless you make a stand now, you'll be lost forever.

Everything she had said or done under the force of an infatuation that ran counter to her nature, her upbringing, the approval of her parents, and the admiration of her friends suddenly piled up, a dark, threatening shape which, unless she demolished it *now*, would loom up over her marriage, reducing her to nothing.

She made her stand. "You just don't *want* to please me. You just *try* to be awkward!" Tears first—they usually served. Huge tears welling up so that the dark, agate eyes were enhanced and enlarged, like stones underwater, and then spilling over the rose-petal cheeks.

Unavailing now. And the tantrum that followed was just as futile. No burnt feathers, no smelling salts, no soothing words, no hasty submission. She flung herself, screaming, to the floor, and Mr. Orford jerked her to her feet and shook her until she was so breathless that she could no longer utter a sound.

When she had breath enough, she said, "If you think that I'm going to marry you, after that, Edwin Orford. . . ." She tugged the grotesque ring off, not without difficulty, for it had been made to fit a lean fourth finger, and her hands and fingers were pleasantly plump. Once it was freed, she flung it at him.

He said, "If that's the way you feel . . ." and left it there.

He was not altogether sorry. The Church Street corner shop was still available. Foster's, it was now obvious, would never do more than survive, and he was committed to the dead man, who had been a good master, not to make any radical changes. It would survive, living like a camel on its hump, but it would never be the vital, vibrant business of which he dreamed. Hobbled down by long tradition. . . .

And certainly his mother would be far happier in Church Street than in the High Street.

Maybe all for the best.

Rose held out for four days against Mr. Orford, who was prepared to hold out forever. Then she gave in, and it was a long time before she threw another tantrum, and that not self-induced.

Five thousand pounds was not a huge fortune, but it could be put to work, and for the next few years Mr. Orford had worked it to the utmost. He skipped Church Street and bought the store by the station, a nasty little place where women came and dipped their dirty jugs and jars into the barrels of treacle or vinegar, where sacks of rice or other cereals stood about, an open invitation to leg-lifting dogs—and children. It catered to the poorest, roughest element in the town and was avoided by the decent housewives in the Terraces, who would trudge, often pushing perambulators or hauling toddlers, to the corner shop of their choice. It was these women whom Mr. Orford set himself out to woo with the white paint, the flowers, the higher standards of service and hygiene. At the same time he did nothing to discourage the old clientele, many of whom used the store as a larder, coming in for a screw of tea as often as three times a day. It was self-evident fact that a pound of cheap tea sold at a halfpenny a screw was far more profitable than a pound of the best Su-Chong, bought on credit, delivered to a house ten miles away and then entered, and reentered, account owing.

There was an art in the presentation of bargains: a penny off condensed milk this week, irresistible, and never mind the halfpenny on bacon, butter, biscuits, cocoa. Very soon after its reopening, "under new management," the station store was serving two very differing types of customer, according to the hour of the day. The poor or improvident came early in the morning or towards evening, buying just enough for the next meal; in the middle hours came the women from the Terraces, buying ahead for the week, expecting no credit, providing their own transport by basket or perambulator.

In quick order four corner shops closed down. So did three village stores along the line, for it was soon plain that the prudent housewife could save more than a twopenny fare by taking advantage of the offered bargains—and have a train ride, too.

Mr. Orford had no wish, had never had a wish, to ruin anybody. But people were ruined all the same.

He introduced his cooked meat counter. And what went naturally with cooked meat? Bread. Any baker in his right mind would sooner take one big, regular order than hawk his wares through the streets. Mr. Orford picked his man and struck his bargain. At the station store you did not even have to buy a whole loaf, half of which might be stale tomorrow; you could buy half a loaf. Two slices. . . .

Presently there were buns and a good solid fruitcake.

After two years Mr. Orford saw that what he could do in one place he could do in another. He bought a shop in Radmouth, sixteen miles to the east, and was building a brand-new one in Wyck-on-Rad, fifteen miles inland and growing rapidly.

He had not neglected Foster's, which was actually more prosperous because with bigger orders to wholesalers a man got better terms. All that cheap tea served in a way to subsidise the Su-Chong, just as the cheaper, sweeter biscuits, ordered in vast quantities, subsidised the more expensive kinds.

Four stores, three flourishing and Foster's rather less than a drag than it had been, were, he thought, as much as one man could oversee properly. He began to look about for openings for investment, things near enough to home to be kept under his sharp eye, but not overdemanding of his time. Again he was lucky; the bacon factory at Wyck-on-Rad, and the adjoining brewery were both tottering, both in charge of aging men, only too anxious to hand over to a young man with some money to invest and endless energy to contribute. In what appeared to the outsider merely the blink of an eye, but what to Mr. Orford had meant long hours of work, of concentrated mental activity, he was in control of both businesses; they linked together; the bacon factory supplied the hams, the bacon for his stores and also to the three or four "tied" houses which were linked to the brewery, places which, until he took over, had never thought of offering more than a bit of bread and cheese— and that grudgingly.

Presently he ventured a little farther afield and bought an interest in a three-boat concern at Radmouth and, with their auxiliary, a processing place where fresh herrings were made into kippers. They fitted in, too, because, cutting out all the middlemen, Mr. Orford could offer his growing number of customers kippers at least a penny, sometimes a penny ha' penny less a pair than any other retailer could.

By the time Charlie was walking strong on his feet and Edda was born the men who talked about money, the men Mr. Orford avoided, were talking about his golden touch.

And Rose was talking about a house in one of the Avenues.

She was dead right to say that the accommodation above the shop was overcrowded. Her mother, his mother, and the growing young family. She was honest in saying that a house in one of the Avenues had always been her ultimate ambition. Most of her friends at Miss Gibbs' select little school lived in the Avenues. It was now very old-fashioned to live above your shop; it was horrid to have to approach your home through the shop or through the yard. On this point, however, her father had been immovable. He never said that he couldn't afford a house in the Avenues—to do so would worry Rose and her mother. He fell back upon sentiment; his father, his grandfather had lived here, and he was attached to the old, dignified panelled rooms. Besides there was always the hope that Rose would marry into the Avenues.

Now Edwin was equally stubborn. Rose still visited friends in the select part of town—visits not wholly encouraged by him. She always came back with a lot of chatter about the beauties and the amenities. She knew every time a house in the Avenues was for sale: Sunnybank; Briarbank; Westward Ho. To ignore such hints or downright nagging was easy to him, for he had developed, early in marriage, the habit of listening to her with his ear and the surface of his mind only while devoting his real thoughts to something else. He made sensible answers, though, and when she said that children needed a garden to play in, he pointed out that the public gardens were only just across the square into which the High Street debouched—not five minutes' walk away. They were public in that they were open to any family capable of paying a guinea a year and of passing the scrutiny of the management committee.

Sometimes Mr. Orford wondered what Rose would have said had he told her the truth: *I am waiting for an old woman to die.* And once he gave her a terrible fright. He bought a farm out in the country at a place called Flixton. Home Farm it was called, and she visualised life there: no water in a tap; no gas; no friends. She was so greatly relieved to learn that he had no intention of living there that she did not mention the Avenues for almost a month. After a while he bought another farm, Park Farm, almost adjoining the other.

Then Charlie reached the age when by law he must go to school or receive some alternative form of tuition. Miss

Gibbs catered to little boys until they were eight, but Mr. Orford would have none of that. Charlie was to have a governess, and she was already chosen—a Miss Browston, a clergyman's daughter, taught by her father, and no mean scholar. "But where will she *live?*" Rose asked. "And where will the schoolroom be?" He knew the answer to that. Miss Browston would go into lodgings for the time being and teach in a screened-off corner of the room which Mr. Orford had made into an office for himself.

In fact, before Miss Browston was installed, pressure on space lessened considerably. Old Mrs. Orford died, peacefully and happily, with a blessing for Edwin—the best son a woman ever had. She had enjoyed eight years of almost perfect bliss, adoring her grandchildren, getting on well with Rose and, even more surprisingly, with Rose's mother, to whom she had endeared herself by being so useful on the maid's afternoon off.

But it was not for his mother's death that Mr. Orford was waiting.

Soon after that the household lost another member. Mrs. Foster, just into her fifties, and well preserved, received and accepted a proposal from a widower, many years her senior—history did sometimes repeat itself. She moved into one of the best houses in Victoria Avenue. It even had a tennis court. Miss Browston played the game well, though she grew breathless and tired easily. They all had very happy summer afternoons at White Walls, and sometimes, if he could manage it, Mr. Orford would join them and even receive a little tuition. With his height, his agility, and his long reach, he had the makings of a good player and would have played more frequently had he had time. One could hardly say to Miss Browston, the clergyman's daughter, that one wished one could play on Sundays, but he did say it to Rose, who was shocked. "Good gracious, darling. What would the neighbours think!"

After a visit to White Walls, Rose was usually moody, but

moods needed attention to thrive upon, and Edwin gave hers none.

Charlie was nine when Mr. Orford acted out of character and took a real risk. So far—apart from some railway shares—he had never invested a penny in anything which was not already under his thumb or about to be so. As a result, he was rich, but not rich enough. However, he felt justified in gambling a small sum on a business he knew nothing of, in a place he had never seen, and never would see —a gold mine in Africa, a place called Inangula, not even marked on the map.

On purely monetary investments—that was those into which you merely put cash, not time, sweat and imagination—five percent was a reasonable return; seven and a half very good; ten astonishing. Mr. Orford knew that men joked—not always good-naturedly—about his Midas touch, but really there seemed to be something in it. A hundred percent; a hundred and fifty. And not only the interest; his modest stake in an unknown business, in an unknown place, so increased its capital value that now and then he was stunned.

And still that old woman would not die.

The programme said, "Interval." Badly needed. Even those on the padded privileged benches were getting a bit numb in their behinds, and those who, like Mr. Orford, had long legs, were cramped. Rose gave him an unnecessary nudge and said, "Wake up." Unnecessary because he had not been asleep; he had simply been remembering. Now it was time for refreshments. Badly needed because the pageant, beginning at six o'clock in order to take full advantage of what remained of daylight and bring the last scene into dusk, with dramatic lighting effects, had disturbed all the usual eating habits. Those on the hard benches had forgone their tea; those on the padded ones, their dinner. Lady

Chelsworth had decided that this pageant should make some contribution, however small, to her three pet charities. (Privately she regretted the fact that it was impossible to divert a little to be used for the absolutely necessary repairs on the West Wing. She could see no really logical reason. The pageant was taking place on Chelsworth ground, on the natural amphitheatre between the mound on which the castle stood and the river it had guarded for so many years. The erection of the stands, the trampling of many feet would reduce the turf to a state that it would take a long time to put right. But of course the idea of using any of the money for private purposes was unthinkable. One must face one's obligations.)

It amused Mr. Orford to pay—in the privileged buffet—a shilling for a ham roll which would have sold in his shops or his pubs for twopence. Of drinks there was a choice between lemonade and champagne, very bad champagne, too. Holding a glass of it in his hand, being convivial and modest, he accepted congratulations on Edda's performance. A few people, who had really read their programmes, mentioned Louise and Maude, too.

Lady Chelsworth made her way towards him, saying in the voice which without effort dominated all others, "Was I not absolutely right? Who else could have done it?"

She spoke—it was a trick of hers—as though the selection of Edda had been made in the face of massive opposition.

She could afford to be generous now, for the fears which had momentarily assailed her at the Hospital Ball had proved unfounded. Edda Orford had plainly inherited a full share of her father's sound good sense. Dear girl, she'd never by look or word given Simon the slightest encouragement. In fact, she had snubbed him, and God knew he needed something to bring him to his senses. Twenty-nine years old and flipping about between two attitudes: a young man with not a care in the world and an old man settling into bachelordom. About the disrepair of the West Wing he showed no concern at all. It wasn't lived in, he said, and on the estate there were more urgent proppings up needed: a roof here, a barn, a cowshed. . . . She avoided the thought that she had failed with Simon; after all, she had reared him, and one could hardly find fault with one's own handiwork. And one must be hopeful. Lady Margery Springfield was still in the offing.

"After this," Lady Chelsworth said, "life will seem rather dull. But we are all so much looking forward to Charlie's twenty-first."

All those within earshot—and most were—felt that if they had been invited to celebrate Charles Orford's coming-of-age, they had been honoured; if not, they had been scorned. A man named Babcock, settling back on his eighteen inches of padded seat, nursed his grudge carefully and said to his meek wife, "You must have done or said something to *her*. I've always been very civil to *him*. Gone out of my way, in fact."

In fact, quite a lot of them had gone out of their way.

The entertainment resumed with a vigorous display of Morris dancing.

Mr. Orford fell back into reverie.

Mrs. Cartwright, whose house he wanted, lived to be ninety. Charlie was then between ten and eleven, and Mr. Orford was thinking disconsolately that he would have to content himself with another house, and what a pity that would be, since he had bought the two farms in order to have a compact little estate. Buying the farms had brought him into contact with the old woman's solicitor, Mr. Gordon, who had said that there was really no need for her to sell land at all; she suffered from the delusion that she was poor.

"It's pathetic really, but she's had a sad life. Her husband was killed at Waterloo, her son died in a hunting accident, and her grandson in the Indian Mutiny. Enough to turn anybody a bit queer." Mr. Orford said that when the house came on the market, he would be interested in it.

"Have you ever been inside it?"

"No."

"Well, I have. Believe me, to make it habitable would cost more than the place is worth."

"A house built in 1702 isn't going to fall down through a little neglect."

"How did you know its date?" the solicitor asked, thinking what a curious fellow this was.

"It's on a gutter spout."

Mrs. Cartwright's delusion of poverty extended to food. Her standing order for groceries and provisions for herself and two old servants came to three and sixpence a week— not worth delivering—but ever since he bought the Home Farm, Mr. Orford had taken upon himself to deliver the miserable little parcel, just for the joy of rounding the curve in the drive and coming face to face with the house which had made such an impression on his youthful mind.

Mrs. Cartwright left a vast sum of money, all to a home for aged clergymen whose stipends had never exceeded a hundred and fifty pounds a year. The secretary of this worthy society, himself well advanced in age, came down to inspect Flixton Old Manor with a view to moving the whole concern there. One shuffling walk amongst the cobwebs, the dust, the ominously stained ceilings showed him that this was not a feasible project. He instructed Mr. Gordon, his companion on this dismal tour, to sell it, if possible, before it fell down.

"And the contents, sir?"

Feeling very crafty, the old man said, "If they would attract a buyer, include them, by all means."

So Mr. Orford, who had offered so many bargains to so many people, was in his turn offered one.

And as he had always known, the place was not nearly so

derelict as it appeared to be. One blocked gutter, one loose roof tile could cause a lot of apparent but really superficial damage. The actual structure was sound as a rock.

He said nothing to Rose. Hidden away behind his practical exterior, there was a streak of the artist, wishing to work alone and produce the finished article for inspection. He wanted to surprise her and to show her once and for all that the Avenues were not the ultimate standard of perfection.

Rose was appalled. The idea of living at the Home Farm had been dreadful enough; this was worse, practically half a mile away from the road; far too big, a great, hollow, echoing place. And already almost furnished with stuff that was not to her taste at all. Great, ugly four-poster beds, like tombs. The prospect of *two* bathrooms did not comfort her at all, though she had often talked about the bathroom at White Walls, one of the few in Bressford, even in the Avenues.

She hardly spoke at all; without being fully conscious of it, she was reserving her strength, mustering her resources. On almost every point she had given way to him, because she loved him still and because to fall out with one's husband was a failure. By Avenue standards—hers, although she had never lived in that sacred atmosphere—women bore anything, meanness, infidelity, neglect, and came up smiling.

Mr. Orford showed her the two rooms which would be entirely *hers:* a bedroom, empty, adjoining another, furnished with one of those tomblike beds, and downstairs another, slightly too large to be cosy and with tall french windows looking out onto desolation. A man with a scythe was working there, cutting nettles, a lawn that was like a neglected hayfield.

They were back in the hall again. The spoilt little girl whose ghost had lingered on, dwindling from inanition inside Rose Orford, happy wife and mother, suddenly took charge, but in a surprisingly violent and uncontrollable way. All her fits, even the last one when she'd flung his ring at him, had retained in their core some element of deliberation, something of pretence, a consciousness—I am doing this *to get my own way*.

And always a bit of herself had stood off, watching, estimating.

This was completely different.

She heard herself say, "I won't live here." And then the screaming began, twelve years of frustration finding voice at last. No Rose Foster, Rose Orford standing aside now, watching what this fit would accomplish. Screaming, banging her head, this time not with the carefully measured and quite unhurtful violence of former times, she went down into the dark and came up again to find Edwin shaking her gently and holding a glass of icy cold water to her mouth.

She took a sip, and he said, "Better now?" in a kind way. There was that to be said for him; he was always kind. Over little things. Indeed now he hastened to say what he, no doubt, meant as consolation.

He said, "If you feel so strongly about it, my dear, you don't have to live here. I'll buy Sunnybank for you. That's what you always wanted—as I wanted this."

She tried to find her voice, that trained, confident voice inculcated by Miss Gibbs who believed—and had proof— that in six lessons she could eradicate any accent. (How now, brown cow. Show Rhoda how those roses grow.)

She could only produce a whisper. "You mean—live apart?"

"If that is what you want." An aura seer would have seen his then, red in the darkening hall. Yet he sounded considerate. "You would not be lonely. Your mother and your friends are there. You'd have Louise and Maude. And Miss Browston. I have my eye on a tutor for Charlie, and Edda could share the lessons."

It had all the hallmarks of a plan long prepared.

She feared she might faint again and reached for the glass. Then, still in that muted voice, she said, "People would think our marriage had failed."

"I have never cared about what people think. We could visit each other and make plain that you refuse to live here and I refuse to live at Sunnybank."

She began to retract. "I only said that because I was so *surprised.*"

"But, my dear, it must have been evident that if I'd wanted to live in an Avenue, I should have moved there long ago."

"I couldn't bear it. The scandal." Once, sustained by her love for him, she had been willing to face any amount of unkind talk. Now she realised that her marriage was very vulnerable; people would say, of course, it couldn't last, it had been a mistake from the first. They'd either pity her or gloat.

She mustered her dignity, ventured a tremulous smile. "Then there's no more to be said."

A protest against the house came from an unexpected quarter. The Tom Snell who had worked alongside Mr. Orford was now the trusted manager of the store in Radmouth. In the presence of others they were Mr. Snell and sir; in private they were still Tom and Ed as they had been when they were struggling with the shutters at Foster's.

On his next visit to Radmouth—everything in order and flourishing—Tom said, over the friendly cup of tea in the diminutive office, "There's a tale going round, Ed, that you've bought Flixton Old Manor."

"That's right, Tom. I have." Tom's face darkened. Peculiar, Mr. Orford thought; I've bought a lot of things since we were boys together, and I've never known him to grudge anything before.

"Then I'm sorry. I hoped the fellow who told me that had got it wrong."

"Why?"

"It's a bad house, Ed. Got a curse on it. If I'd known, I'd have warned you. Is it too late? Couldn't you shift it?"

"I could, but I wouldn't. I've had my eye on it for years. Ever since I was on the van." He was intrigued, though. Anything, everything about the beloved house was important to him. "Haunted, is that it?"

"No. Cursed. I used to spend a lot of time there when I was a nipper. My old grandfather kept the Lodge. He was a rare one for old tales."

"Tell me."

"Well, according to him, the house you just bought wasn't the first. There've been two before, one a monks' place, and then another, built round about the time of that king that had all the wives. You know me, Ed. No scholar at the best of times, and the old man was the same, but old tales last. . . ."

"Henry the Eighth. Your grandfather was quite right. It was Flixton Priory. There're some ruins in the orchard. And there are some remains of an earlier house where the stables now are. But go on."

"The Cartwrights had a place somewhere near London, and the king wanted it, so he made them swop. Flixton Abbey for their place. He was turning the monks out. Is that right? Well, naturally, they didn't like it, and some old monk cursed the place, said it'd never go from father to son or be a happy home. Tell you the truth, Ed, if you was to give it to me right this minute, I wouldn't take my lot there."

"That's a very odd story, Tom, considering that the Cartwrights went there three hundred and more years ago, and old Mrs. Cartwright was there till a few months back."

"No arguing. But it never went to son from father. You look into it a bit closer. Cousin to cousin, uncle to nephew. Once, if not twice, it went to daughters who got married but changed the name back. My grandfather was there once when that happened, and a rare old Tatar she was. I should be sorry to see anything happen to Master Charlie."

"The Cartwrights bred a lot of soldiers, Tom. It's a risky trade."

"There's accidents, too. My grandfather saw one that wasn't a soldier, brought home on a gate. Neck broken. There's other things. Not a happy home, that old monk said. Now this my grandfather had firsthand from his. There was a Miss Cartwright, beautiful as an angel. She went gallivanting about in London and came home in the family way. Nobody knew who the man was; she never would say. They treated her shameful, snatched the baby away the moment it was born, and kept her shut up like a prisoner to the day she died. . . . Oh, there're a lot of tales, Ed, some I forget now, but all nasty. You just take my word for once, get rid of it."

"Having hankered after it all these years? Not likely. Don't look like that, Tom. You meant well, I know. I just don't happen to be superstitious."

"You always was a bullheaded chap. I hope you never have cause to regret the move, that's all."

He had never regretted it. Nor, oddly, had Rose. The place did not seem so big once the children and Miss Browston were installed. Their one maid, Edith, was joined by a trim parlourmaid and a housemaid; a woman came from the village to do the washing on Monday, the ironing on Tuesday, some scrubbing and polishing on other days. The living room and Rose's own bedroom contained everything that was fashionable and expensive and cosy. There was, for the first time, a carriage and pair. The garden began to take shape. All Rose's friends came and were properly impressed. It was one thing to hear from one's husband that Orford must be *made* of money; it was another to see just what money could do, once it began to be spent. Flixton Old Manor was a far cry from the rooms over the shop—and a far cry, too, from the Avenues.

It was Rose's mother—made waspish perhaps by the two bathrooms—who put a pointed question.

"Has anyone called?"

"Yes. Mrs. Brooke, the Rector's wife."

"Well, she would have to, wouldn't she?" Not a very nice thing to say, was it?

Rose retorted with spirit. "*She* admired everything very much. She is very interested in gardens, particularly in roses. Apparently some which Pryke has just cleared of rubbish are very old and very rare. One—the buds are showing already—she said was the genuine Tudor rose."

(Almost at that very moment, Mrs. Brooke was telling Lady Hepworth, who shared her interest in flowers, "I am practically certain, though I have never seen one in the flesh, so to speak; only in pictures." "Well," Lady Hepworth said, "I am much relieved to hear that the garden as well as the house is to be preserved. Do you remember what that dreadful man did to the yew walk at Goff's Hall?" "I do indeed. I am sure that Mr. Orford has much more feeling for such things." "What is she like?" "Very pleasant. And the children are charming. Oh, and isn't it a small world! I discovered that their governess is the daughter of the Reverend Browston, under whom my husband served his first curacy. He was such a great scholar, and she seems to be very intellectual." Lady Hepworth tucked that piece of information away in silence.)

Rose's mother, on her second excursion from the snug haven of Victoria Avenue, said, "My dear, it is all very nice and very grand, but I am afraid that you will feel rather cut off when winter sets in and the days shorten. Far be it for me to say anything against Edwin, he always behaved very well to me—and still does—but I think it was an eccentric thing to do, uprooting you all."

Rose fastened on the word. Eccentric: "out of the usual course; not conforming to common rules." It described Edwin exactly. He had always been eccentric.

He continued to be.

Rose was never to know it, but Mr. Orford, who could learn anything, who was not superstitious and yet had a certain belief in luck, when it was allied to good management, had taken careful note of the dreadful man to whom Lady Hepworth had referred. A bustler, a pusher, a man who'd made a fortune building cheap nasty houses in Manchester and come to Norfolk to set up as a country gentleman. No expense spared. Mr. Orford, slicing and packaging cheese for two customers who liked to choose their own, overheard a significant scrap of conversation: "You go to the jamboree at Goff's Hall?" "More or less bound to. It was in a good cause, and the old boy started the subscription list with fifty pounds." "How was it?" "Port wine at four o'clock in the afternoon. And carpet up to your hocks." The point was not missed upon the counter hand.

Now he laid down a few rules for himself and Rose. Approached for subscriptions, they would give exactly what they had always done; she was not to join any committees. "A lot of women are caught that way. They do all the donkey work for the sake of a nod and a smile and a chance to bring Lady this and Sir the other into a conversation. That is not the way to go about it."

To himself he expressed it more bluntly; he had no intention of buying himself in, by either cash or sycophancy. He shelved the problem of social life and gave his attention to Charlie's education.

It would not be pursued at either of the obvious schools—Eton or Harrow. Places *could* be bought there, but hypersensitive where his children were concerned, Mr.

Orford could imagine Charlie's having a bit of a rough time: "What's your father?" "A grocer?" "Ha, I thought I smelt candles!"

If Mr. Orford could possibly manage it, Charlie was going to a far more exclusive school, one to which only brains gained entrance—Biddle's, not far from Radmouth.

As usual, luck and opportunism and a willingness to take risks played into his hands. Haunting one of the Radmouth pubs, one of those tied to the brewery at Wyck-on-Rad and therefore to be visited occasionally, was a broken-down, but plainly well educated man, over whom, one day in Mr. Orford's presence, the landlady and the landlord had a brief, but momentous, altercation. "You could have let him have a stale one, Sam," the landlady said, speaking of sausage rolls. "Why should I? I've got no patience with his sort." Mr. Orford's attention was arrested; why "his sort," why not plain "drunks"?

"Scrounger, Sam?"

"Not exactly; soon will be, though. Got the sack from Biddle's a way back."

"For drinking?"

The publican glanced at his wife, who was occupied, and said, "Worse! Behaviour unbecoming, you might say."

Mr. Orford had grown up in the Pike, where unbecoming behaviour of every kind was rife; little girls were the main victims, but little boys were not exempt—and he'd been good-looking, even then.

It *was* a risk, and it took him a week—for him a long time—to make up his mind. Then he acted.

He did not take Rose into his confidence; he took Miss Browston.

"I've made some very close inquiries into Mr. Webster's record; he had a brilliant career at Oxford and was very successful at Biddle's. But he has one weakness. . . ."

Women, Miss Browston thought, feeling vulnerable.

"I quite understand, Mr. Orford," she said, mentally

girding herself. It was possible that she did; she was extremely well educated, and even his own desultory reading had brought him into contact with some of the peculiarities of the Roman Emperors. However, he must make himself clear.

"I don't want Charlie left alone with him for a minute. Never mind the girls' lessons; they can soon catch up. Just be watchdog."

"That!" For all her learning Miss Browston was shocked. "Excuse me, Mr. Orford, but is it wise?"

"With some help from you, Miss Browston, *possible*. Mr. Webster will lodge with the Adamses at the Park Farm. He will share this schoolroom. The overwhelming consideration, from my point of view, is that he knows precisely what a boy needs to know in order to get into Biddle's."

Mr. Webster knew. Not only that, he managed to produce a sheaf of old examination papers. And even had he not learnt his lesson and been so carefully watched, he would have had no chance with Charlie, who hated him on sight— not for himself but because his arrival had moved Charlie from his beloved Miss Browston's tuition. But not from her company; in fact, he saw more of the governess than he had done in the past. It was partly—but not entirely—because Miss Browston had been such an indefatigable watchdog that when she fell ill, Mr. Orford sent her to Switzerland.

Two hundred boys were competing for eighteen places when Charlie, just before he was eleven, took the test; Biddle's was not only a school of high scholastic reputation, but was very reasonable and indeed in some cases free. Charlie Orford ranked fourth on the list of successful candidates, and the fact that he was really not Biddle material did not emerge for some time, and when it did, Charlie was safe enough. Biddle's could hardly say: Here is a boy who a year ago was brilliant, fourth in a stiff examination, and now he is merely mediocre, take him away. That would have been an indictment of Biddle's! Orford was plain idle;

having got in, he'd slacked off, and Biddle's knew how to deal with such a situation. Orford must be made to work, by brute force, if necessary. This method worked so well that Charlie's first year at Cambridge was mere play, and he had ample time for every kind of athletic sport and social exercise, which, combined with enough money, went a long way towards ensuring popularity. In another way, too, Mr. Orford's plan had worked to Charlie's advantage. There were major public schools, minor ones, even grammar schools, and Cambridge status was decided less by one's father's occupation than by what school one had attended. Biddle's, by Jove; he must be a clever chap! And absolutely no side about it either.

But that was all far ahead. Meantime, Mr. Orford was making, in his eccentric way, steady progress towards his objective.

Has anyone called? Yes, all men, probing the ground. Sir George Hepworth, ostensibly seeking the services of that wonderful little Jersey bull, Flixton Forcible, who had swept the board at the South Norfolk Show.

Mr. Orford said, "If Adams is agreeable, Sir George, I am. He's a bit particular. Your cow is a Jersey?"

"Not purebred," said Sir George, who was an honest man. "My man took the notion that mated with a true bred, like yours. . . ."

"Adams thinks otherwise. He's a bit of a fanatic. Of course, if you can talk him round. . . ."

It was a rebuff, but it was softened by the offer of sherry. Very good sherry, too, in a room with a good many books on the shelves and a big businesslike desk near a window.

"You read a lot?" asked Sir George, who had not willingly opened a book since leaving Eton.

"Less than I'd like. I've hardly had time to look at these yet. Miss Browston tells me that there are several first editions—*Tristam Shandy, Robinson Crusoe*. . . ."

"She's your governess?"

"Yes. A most well-informed woman."

Lady Hepworth, ever since Mrs. Brooke's report, had thought—and often said—how wonderful it would have been if only a different *kind* of family had arrived at the old manor with a decent governess. Veronica would so much have enjoyed taking lessons with other children, and the Hepworth experience with governesses had been most unhappy; but of course, it was unthinkable—the man was a jumped-up grocer! A thousand pities.

Colonel Stanton came, on a selfless errand. He was genuinely interested in the fate of ex-army other ranks who through age or infirmity came to poverty. No real provision was made for them anywhere—except at that place at Chelsea, founded by Nell Gwynne, where wives were not catered for. He visualised something different, beginning in a small way, which would expand and probably be copied. Small bungalows in a group, with a nurse-warden. He explained his scheme and how far it had progressed.

"I was able to obtain the land for almost nothing, Orford. And the first six bungalows went up in no time. Then interest flagged. The point is, the Crimea and the Mutiny have been forgotten, and nowadays missions get the first cut of the cake." He'd been gravely disappointed in old Agatha Cartwright's disposal of her property; one really would have thought that as the last of a military family. . . . And why *clergymen,* when it was a known fact that she had not been to church since she went dotty?

Mr. Orford listened and was prepared to write his usual cheque—five pounds, the sum he judged to be generous, not ostentatious. But Colonel Stanton wanted more. He knew the value of curiosity. There was this house, for so long cut off, the ruins, so long hidden, and the garden, so full of rarities, both old and new.

"If you would make the place available to the public, one Sunday afternoon. . . . Two shillings entry toll."

Mr. Orford said he was sorry, but no, much as he sympathised with the good cause. The lawns, recovered from the wild, had been reseeded and were not ready yet to be trampled on. He wrote his cheque.

And so on and on. Every approach made from a tangent was repulsed. As with Rose, it must be all or nothing, and he was prepared to hold out forever, supported by the secret knowledge that this would not be necessary.

He was right; the nonwooer was always wooed.

Foster's in the High Street still had the rather narrow, many-paned, slightly bowed windows with which it had been born. Useless for any kind of display, such as was possible in the three new stores with their wide windows. Outside, on the edge of the pavement, there were hitching posts for horses, seldom used except by gentlemen who liked to choose their own cheese by tasting at the counter, where samples were displayed, together with a box of small plain biscuits. It was more customary for the gentry doing a bit of shopping to rap on one of the windows with a whip. Everybody, even customers inside the shop and in the process of being served, recognised the fact that horses must not be kept waiting, and the assistant who was nearest the door dropped everything and ran out.

One morning early in December Mr. Orford was his own assistant. He'd dropped in, as he often did, just to see that everything was in order and found one of his men with a heavy cold; he'd sent him home to bed. "Nobody wants their bacon snuffled and sneezed over," he'd said, in a way that in any other man would have sounded brusque and unfeeling but in him was simply sensible and inoffensive. He tied the white apron over the dark, rather formal suit and settled to the cutting of bacon on the recently installed device—a bacon slicer, guaranteed to produce slices of uniform thickness according to how it was set. Some liked it thick, some medium, some thin enough to frizzle at the touch of a hot pan. As he worked, brisk and attentive, he was thinking about the possibility of a modification of such a machine to cut, not ham—there was the bone to contend with, ham would always have to be cut by hand—but from joints of beef, either roast or salted; the bone, being on the edge of the joint, could be removed. And for this completely new commodity, the "corned" beef now coming in from America and becoming extremely popular with the poor at fourpence a pound, a modified bacon slicer would be just the thing. Must think about that, he thought, when a whip rapped the window and he said, "Excuse me, madam," almost automatically and found Lady Chelsworth, poised high in her spider phaeton, a frail, light vehicle. With a young, restive horse.

They knew one another by sight, but she was the one taken by surprise.

"Oh, good morning, Mr. Orford. . . . My cook forgot to put coffee on the order. I said I'd pick it up."

"Jamaican. Blue River. A pound, unground?" He had a good memory.

He wasted no time; there was no need to. Foster's, compared to others of his stores, was old-fashioned, but it was efficient in its own fashion. All dry goods were kept in close-fitting drawers, plainly labelled. It took him no time at all to collect, weigh, pack a pound of Jamaican Blue River coffee beans.

Her ladyship took the package without much attention. "What's that in your buttonhole?" Mr. Orford had completely forgotten that this morning he had set out dressed for a board meeting and that Edda had given him a flower to wear.

"It's a camellia."

"Hothouse?"

"Yes, this one. But there is a variety which is hardy. On a north wall."

"Surely you mean south."

"North. It sounds contradictory, doesn't it? But it has something to do with the sun striking too soon after frost. I'm no expert; I can only do what I'm told."

A spider phaeton, so high, so light, was designed to take

two people; Lady Chelsworth's passenger this morning was the huge, hairy wolfhound, Shamus' predecessor. He wore a wide spiked collar. Mr. Orford did not make the mistake of offering her ladyship the flower in which she was interested; he took it from his lapel and stuck it into the hound's collar. Edda, he thought, would not mind; she was daft about all animals.

The man was a character, no doubt about that. And a man against whom no word had ever been said, despite his spectacular success; that in itself was unusual since envy gave rise to spite. Lady Chelsworth, as she drove home, brooded over Mr. Orford and his singular ways. His cattle and his sheep gained prizes at agricultural shows; *he* never received them personally, he left that to his stockman—very different from the Prince Consort, who had once won a few guineas and pocketed them, in the sight of all, with his stockman standing by. George Hepworth, despite being disappointed over the bull, had spoken approvingly of the way in which Mr. Orford had restored the older manor without messing it about in any way; and though Peter Stanton grumbled about the refusal to open his garden and called it curmudgeonly, it was a refusal that anyone who knew about gardens must surely regard as sensible.

Not least of her ladyship's reflections dealt with her own sense of power and of mischief. She knew that she could, if she wished, make a far less acceptable person than Mr. Orford accepted. She was sixty-four, ready for a new experience.

Long before she died, which she did at a comparatively early age, Rose's mother had seen her prophecy of loneliness utterly refuted. Whom Lady Chelsworth accepted, who could reject? Once again, Mr. Orford, and this time without any visible effort, had obtained his objective. It became possible for Veronica Hepworth to share the Orford girl's lessons, until Miss Browston fell ill. Soon anybody who *was* anybody was offering hospitality and receiving it.

The boy from the Pike was a genial host and an entertaining guest. There was something about him, a new flavour; he was capable of saying, "When I was in my shop this morning . . . " and recounting the amusing incident.

He was, of course, a freak. Invited to join the County Club, about the most exclusive institution outside India, but suffering from the general recession, he said he had no time, but he'd take out a subscription for Charlie. "He looks like being convivial." The same with the Hunt. "I'm not sure that I even approve of it.But my daughter likes to ride and in company. I'll make her a member—and hope she's never in at the kill."

Once Rose said with a slight tone of reproach, "You are so much nicer, Edwin, to the people we know now than you were to those we knew before."

He said, "Yes. Maybe I am. I prefer the company of those who have had money long enough not to be obliged to talk about it."

The difference was that the people with whom he now consorted spoke, when they did talk about money, of the lack, rather than possession. They were mainly people whose families had for generations been land rich, and now they were land poor; but their references to money, even the lack of it, were infrequent and usually lighthearted.

Once, indeed, Lady Chelsworth had asked his advice about an investment, and he'd been honest. "Personally I wouldn't touch it. It doesn't smell right to me."

"You go by your nose?"

"How else? It's a trained nose. I can still sniff anything mouldy—oatmeal, for instance—at ten yards."

That was what was so absolutely endearing about him. What was even more endearing was that he said, in his easy, casual way, "You'd do better with the Wyck-on-Rad gas company."

She had taken that bit of advice and made just enough profit to mend up the West Wing a little. In return she offered to present Edda. "I know I've led a rusticated life lately, and our town house is sold; but I still have connections. If I bestirred myself, I could give your girl a good season." Mr. Orford said that would be for Edda to decide, and Edda said there was nothing she would hate more.

Thursday, June 18, in the Year of Our Lord 1872, would see Charlie's coming-of-age and a breakaway from Mr. Orford's rule about modest, though sound, hospitality. He had only one son, and that son could have only one twenty-first birthday; some slight ostentation was permissible. A great marquee was erected on the lawn upon which the drawing room faced. The sectional floor, already slippery with French chalk, was laid. Since the evening promised to be warm and dry, one side of the marquee was open. There were mounds of flowers everywhere.

A small, very privileged party would dine, eating food cooked by Edith, who had been cook-general over the shop and who would have been terribly hurt if Mr. Charlie's birthday dinner had been prepared by other hands. After that the caterer's men would take over and convert the dining room into a supper room.

Mr. Orford dressed early and quickly and came downstairs to see that all was in order. Behind him he left the sound of gay young masculine voices— Charlie had three houseguests—and the murmur of four women preparing for the dinner and the ball. Rose had decided that Maude, always so anxious to join in and already a bit tall for her age, should make her debut at this party.

Just inside the hall door stood a table, and on it a silver salver, and on the salver lay a letter. The afternoon post had arrived. Mr. Orford went towards it, halted as though he had seen something deadly, snatched it up, and hurried into his library.

It was the same blue envelope, the same erratic mixture of capital letters and small ones. The bitch! he thought. I bought her off! What now? Ordinarily he used a paper knife, but he opened this letter with clumsy haste. One tiny hope flickered. It might merely be a birthday greeting. With a sickening downward jolt of the heart he read:

> dere Charlie i got to see you. im goin to have a baby and its yores i swear there wasnt no other man i was forced into doing wot I done. But this is diffrunt a Baby must have a father and this is yores i wated till i was sure now I am So we must meat. we Must. Charlie dere I dont want to thretten you but i am desprit if you dont come to the pool tomorrer or next day I shall come to yore house

This was shattering news, but it did not stun him. He glanced at his watch and saw that he had twenty-two minutes. He sat down at his handsome desk and opened the drawer in which he kept every letter he had ever received from his son, from that first homesick tear-blotched one from Biddle's to the latest. The round, childish hand had developed over the years into something individual, the *t* crossed slantingly, the dot over the *i* more like a dash. Not difficult to copy, especially for a man self-taught from copy books. Mr. Orford chose a sheet of plain paper, no heading to prove its origin, and wrote: "Tomorrow. Seven o'clock. In haste."

An active life and moderation in eating and drinking had kept him lithe and lively. He sprinted down the long drive and posted the letter in the postbox which stood not far from the gateway. He walked back, but briskly, ready to await his guests, smiling host, proud father.

Anna's letter, so flimsy as to have almost no substance, he had folded and pushed into the rather shallow pocket of his dress trousers. He was aware of it, sometimes as a weight, sometimes as a scorching heat.

Everybody asked to celebrate on this occasion felt privileged, those asked to dine were the elite of the elite, and all but four—Charlie's three friends and Lord Greythorpe—were local.

Ever since the Hospital Ball, Lord Greythorpe had made

what could only be called diplomatic appearances. Edda gave nothing away, nor did Lady Chelsworth, nor did Mr. Orford, but Toby, as they had learned to call him, seemed to Mr. Orford as suitable as a man could be. He had what Mr. Orford thought of as more *mental equipment* than his friend, Lord Chelsworth, now known as Simon, who, on closer acquaintance, had shown himself to be a bit dull, just a glorified squire. Good landlord, that Mr. Orford would concede. But in the end mental contact outlasted the physical, as Mr. Orford had good cause to know, having spent so many years with Rose, with whom he had never shared a thought outside family affairs.

She sat there, gracious and smiling and pretty still, at the other end of the table. She had always dressed well and had chosen for this great occasion a dress of taffeta which gleamed pale buff or warm brown as she moved or the light caught it. And just below her neck, still white and well preserved, a diamond pendant shone. Rose had got her diamonds in the end.

Mr. Orford's thoughts shifted to Charlie, whose day this was. He was unwilling to think that by his action, just after Easter, he had damaged the boy while seeming to rescue him. But the fact remained that Charlie had changed. He hadn't come home once during the summer term; not for the Hospital Ball, not for the pageant. He'd passed his examination, but far less well than was expected, far below any Biddle's student standard. And at the end of the term he had not come home, hotfoot as in the past. A walking-reading holiday, somewhere in Cornwall, then a stay with John Walinshaw. When he did come home, he came with John and two other young men, quite right and proper, but— could one say *guarded?* Extremely gay and boisterous and drinking a bit too much. Charlie seemed to have outgrown the stage when he became sick long before he was even slightly intoxicated.

Amidst all the gaiety and the chatter, Mr. Orford sat and

planned. He knew where Monkswood lay, but of its inner geography he knew nothing. He had, years ago, been asked to join the syndicate but had refused. He had no intention of becoming one of the Saturday Sportsmen, as they were called. When he shot—if he ever did—it would be on his own land, with people of his choosing. Compromise had never been for him.

Moving about amidst the flowers, the music, the champagne, he thought: I must be up early tomorrow, to spy out the land and find where this pool is. I must also go to the bank. The girl had accepted money before and doubtless would again. He must make some excuse for being absent from the family dinner table. He planned without worry—worry, he knew, did nothing except to exhaust.

The open side of the marquee offered the young an escape from the vigilance of their elders; the bleak grey remains of the priory ruins in the orchard offered an excuse. It was, everybody agreed, the most *wonderful* party.

On Friday morning Mr. Orford rose early and breakfasted alone. He was on his way to the stables when Edda called from an upper window, "Can I come with you?"

For the first time in his memory he did not welcome her company.

"It's only to the brewery," he called back. "And I can't wait."

Neither statement deterred her. Before his own horse was saddled, she was there, helping to prepare Topaz.

"You haven't had any breakfast," he said.

"Bother breakfast. I ate enough last night to last for a week. And what a morning!"

They rode side by side in silence, but not, they were both aware, quite the old comfortable, companionable silence.

The main road between Wyck and Bressford; the point where he had met that wretched girl; Monkswood looming. Mr. Orford would have preferred to make his reconnoitre alone. Now he was obliged to say, as the gate, the notice, and the ride through the woods came into view, "I want to take a look at this place."

She showed neither surprise nor curiosity. She merely said, teasingly, "Thinking of buying it?"

He had an answer to that, had been meditating it as they rode.

"Not *it*. Some timber maybe. And, Edda, I'd sooner not have the matter mentioned. Nor this visit. It's a tricky negotiation."

She wasn't a gossip, but she was quite likely to say, in front of Charlie, that she and Papa had had such a lovely ride through Monkswood while everybody else was slugging abed. Then Charlie would be reminded.

It seemed a long way to the pool. Maybe this way through the woods didn't lead to it at all; it might be in that part of the wood reached by that field path along which the girl had sauntered on that spring evening. But that was hardly wide enough for a horse, nor was there anything there to which to tether one, and Charlie could hardly have kept his trysts on foot. These considerations had governed his choice of entry. And now he came to think about it there was a third, a good way along the road, quite near Wyck. He was about to say that he'd seen enough and to turn back, when a turn brought the pool in sight, placid under the blue summer sky, here and there dotted with clumps of water lilies, the yellow ones, called for some reason brandy cups and stinking of rotten eggs. The ride narrowed to a mere footpath after that. He could see the enclosure, the pheasant nursery, and deduced that the gamekeeper's cottage would not be far away.

"I've seen enough," he said, and turned his horse.

After that the outing became more what Edda had visualised when she looked from her bedroom and saw Papa, dressed for riding. Now they could talk.

"I thought Charlie's party was the best ever," she said.

"*So* much nicer than any I remember. Algie Hepworth's, for example. All those tenants, making speeches and presenting that great tray and then being sent off to eat separately."

"That was exactly what I didn't want. And my employees are such a mixed bag and so scattered." What he had done, to mark the occasion, had been to give every man a guinea, to buy what form of festivity suited him best. And last night, when Charlie's health was being drunk, he had thought of all these varying celebrations. Only the dark-skinned men who dug gold in Africa had been excluded. Not forgotten. He had actually thought of them and how pleasant it would have been to give them some kind of festivity. But they were not, strictly speaking, his employees, and the whole thing was too far away and too complicated for even his organising powers to deal with. As the glasses were raised, he had had another thought, too. That *horrible* girl, waiting in the green depths of the wood.

They clattered into Wyck-on-Rad and into the brewery yard.

"Will you be long?"

"No. I just want a word with Stubbs about the labels."

"Bet you sixpence you decided on the King of Hearts."

"You win! Stubbs will take a bit of soothing. He was reared to look upon playing cards as the Devil's playthings."

"I'll wait then and walk the horses. Then, if you don't object, I'll take my sixpence out in goods. Over there." Edda nodded towards the Brewers' Arms. "Half a pint of Radale and a ham roll."

Mr. Orford dismounted, handed Edda his rein, and went into the brewery. There for a moment he forgot everything except this new venture—bottled beer. Like every other innovation, it had cost money, but like all his schemes, it would pay off in the end. Men drank beer in pubs; only women of no reputation brought jugs and carried the stuff away to be drunk at home—and even they tended to use the back doors. A neat little bottle, with a pretty label, and a trade name. . . . He could imagine neat little women saying, "And two bottles of Red King, please," and tucking the neat little bottles into their shopping bags or perambulators. Like a bottle of sauce. And a refund on the empty bottle. From Radale, long famous, to Red King was nothing of a transition; most people called *Rad Red* anyway. Norfolk men were sparing of vocal effort; they called their local brew Red'le.

Stubbs was not pleased by the decision about the label. He was not a Methodist or puritanical in his views; had he been, he would not have been manager of a brewery. It was simply that his grandfather, a man of some substance, had been a crazy gambler and brought ruin on the family, and after his death no cards, not even those of Happy Families, had been allowed in the house.

"Naturally, it is for you to decide, sir, but I still prefer the Red Rose. It would make more appeal to female shoppers."

"I considered that. But it's a bit namby-pamby for beer."

Mrs. Pryke at the Brewers' Arms was accustomed to Mr. Orford's visits; he often looked in. Privately she thought that he did so in order to see that everything was up to scratch. It always was, so she did not fear his inspections. She had not seen Miss Edda for some time, not since she'd grown into a young lady, in fact. As a child she had sometimes come in with her father on a Saturday morning, always to the private bar, and been regaled with a glass of lemonade. Mrs. Pryke was not absolutely sure whether she approved of young ladies who came into the public, downed half a pint of Radale in a markedly unfeminine fashion and ate two ham rolls with gusto. She had a pleasant manner, though, and her likeness to her father was astonishing.

They talked about the pageant, which Mrs. Pryke had

taken an evening off to see; about the bottled beer which should be on the shelves in a fortnight; about how the place called Pepper's was now known as Peppo's and had turned into a den of vice, with Italian waiters. "Gambling now," the landlady said. "People come from far and near. It's a disgrace, really." Her denunciation was largely academic; apart from a commercial traveller or two, her customers were unlikely to be seduced. Peppo's was expensive, and ordinary workingmen didn't like foreigners. Her complaints stemmed from nostalgia; she'd been born and had grown up in Wyck, then no more than a village with a brewery. She resented all change.

Mr. Orford, who had gone to bed late and not slept well, drank a brandy and soda as a restorative. Edda was pleased by his choice; she wanted him in a good mood.

Outside in the sunshine and clear of the town, she said, "Papa, I've been thinking seriously about my future."

"I also give it a thought from time to time." He had not been unobservant of Lord Greythorpe's visits during the past month, of the fact that whenever he was at the castle, he had ridden over to make a call, of another fact, that during his visits Lady Chelsworth always gave a small intimate dinner party which included himself, Rose, and Edda. Plainly *she* approved. Lady Chelsworth had asked, as a favour, that Toby should be included in Charlie's celebratory party, and occupied and preoccupied as he was, Mr. Orford—always conscious of Edda—had noticed how many times the pair had danced together. And he had heard Toby ask to be taken to see the ruins. Edda replied, "But you've seen them. Twice." "But never by moonlight." They'd been absent quite a time.

Dashing his hopes, Edda said, "I'm nineteen. Practically on the shelf. And I'd like to do something *real* with my life."

"Such as?"

Looking at him warily, she said, "Well, I thought nursing. Or perhaps something even more ambitious. There's a woman called Elizabeth Garrett from Leiston in Suffolk; she qualified as a doctor, against immense opposition. But of course, it was largely her father's doing. He was behind her, every step of the way." Diplomatic, surely!

Mr. Orford thought of Edda, his beloved Edda, leaning over fever patients, breathing tainted air, tending horrible wounds.

"He must be crazy. I should *lead* the opposition!"

"Papa, you haven't even *thought* about it."

"I don't need to think. I know how I feel."

Edda reflected upon this statement and realised its truth. For just as he had watched her over the years, she had watched him. He always gave the appearance of being activated by shrewd thinking and reason, a strictly practical man, but in fact many of the things he had done or refused to do were just as much a matter of feeling, of instinct. And whereas reason was open to argument, feeling was not.

Wishing to placate, for a glance at her face showed him that he had hurt her, while wanting only to protect, he said, "All this talk about being on the shelf at nineteen is ridiculous. There is plenty of time for you to find a husband—if you give your mind to it."

"But I *have*. I know that Mamma thinks I stand in Louise's way. This antiquated idea that the younger sister can't marry first. Did you ever hear such nonsense? They're probably holding a wake over it at this very moment. Algie Hepworth practically proposed to Louise last night in the orchard."

"I knew nothing of it."

"There's been no time. You were too busy to notice the heads nodding together. Waiting to hear whether ruins in the moonlight had a similar effect upon Toby."

"Did they?"

She gave him another glance. A trifle defiant.

"I refused him out of hand. I don't even like him. I can't tell you why. I just don't."

"Then you were right, darling. Quite right." Placating again, he who had never placated anybody, not even his brutal old father. "At least, in your choice of husband, you do have my full support."

Edda laughed, not merrily.

"I had another proposal. Think of that! Wouldn't Mamma and Louise be surprised! Simon Talbot. Really, Papa, you should hire those ruins out, on moonlit nights, so much an hour!"

Ignoring the sarcasm, Mr. Orford said, "And what did you say to him?"

"Oh, the absolute correct and formal thing. Taken by surprise, I needed time to think it over. And so I did. You see, I happen to know that her ladyship, dear Grandmamma, has been against me from the beginning. Two years ago, offering to arrange a season for me in London . . . with Toby abroad just then. . . . Nothing personal; in fact, I think she is rather fond of me. But I was not born in quite the right bed. We may as well face the truth. Last night I could have collared him, well and truly. But I thought I'd ask you about . . . the alternative . . . first."

"Have you any liking for *him?*"

"I like him as well as I like any man." Except you! "What I ask myself: Is liking enough? To base a life on?"

He could hardly tell Rose's daughter that even the most lopsided marriage could survive, that he had not even *liked* that disdainful, high-nosed little Rosy-Posy. Instead, he said, "Well, of course, that is for you to decide. You seem to me to share similar tastes."

"Horses," she said. "And dogs. And country life in general. But there again, is it enough? After all, everybody gets old."

"What on earth has that to do with it?"

"Nothing. Except that when I'm past riding a horse or exercising a dog, I'd prefer to spend my time with somebody who recognised a joke or was prepared to discuss a generalisation. . . . I feel that life with him would be rather a solemn affair."

"Safe, too. He may take himself a bit seriously and be inclined to pontificate a little, but he's had the title since he was very young. That has probably had an effect."

"In fact, you're all for it."

"No, no. I shouldn't dream of influencing you on such a serious matter. But. . . ."

"But what?"

"It would bear thinking over."

"Because such a chance is unlikely to come your way again, you lucky girl!" She spoke in her mother's voice. "Well, I am thinking it over. The thing is, is it fair to him? He must be fond of me to have defied that old graven image. It argues a strength of feeling that I know I can't match."

"My dear, at the risk of sounding pontifical myself, it is a thing you know nothing about."

"No? A marriage based on mutual respect outlasts one based on passion. Kindness is the first requisite. Love can come after marriage. I've heard it all!"

From Rose? Less deceived than he liked to think?

Then Edda said, all mockery vanished, "Papa, for God's sake, don't say a word about this. I just couldn't bear it."

"As though I would," he said.

One o'clock luncheon. Six hours to go now. There was a distinctly day-after-the-party air. Even Louise and Maude were heavy-eyed, and Rose, poor dear, looked her full age.

Charlie said, "We just managed to push Ralph and Peter onto the midday train. John stayed on because he's trying to talk me into something. An archaeological expedition to Greece."

Well, Mr. Orford thought, he might as well spend his birthday present—a thousand pounds—on that as on anything else, and it was a gentleman's occupation.

The confusing thing was that although he had wanted, from the first, to give his son privileges and pleasures that he had not enjoyed himself, he had not wanted Charlie to idle his life away. He'd have liked to see Charlie, his status unquestioned, Biddle's and Cambridge behind him, looks well above average, manners not only impeccable but charming, putting the whole thing into reverse as it were and taking to business in however casual a way. Proving something. That business and gentility were not mutually exclusive.

But in fact, Charlie had never cared, never taken any interest; even as a little boy, he'd eat the proffered biscuit, drink the lemonade, begin to fidget—"Papa, can't we go home now?" Edda was an altogether different proposition. "Papa, what is a *gross?* Papa, exactly what is a *cran* of herrings? Papa, do you think Archbishop *Cran*mer had anything to do with herrings?" Taking Edda around had been a joy, and had she been his son, instead of his daughter. . . . A futile thought and one which he had put aside long ago.

Charlie was scholarly. Devoted to Miss Browston, force-fed by that tutor, very good at Biddle's, quite good at Cambridge, he was now taking his logical way. Who could complain?

Charlie said, "Mamma, John and I will be out this evening. We are going to Pepper's."

That called up sharp memories of a former occasion, when John had gone to Pepper's alone and he had gone to Anna. Time wasn't the healer it was reputed to be—or the cure was a damned slow one! He still suffered whenever he thought of her, and that was often when he was sober. Drinking did not entirely obliterate the memory; it simply made it bearable.

Edda said, "Take your cutlasses between your teeth! The

place is now called Peppo's and is a den of vice, with gambling *and* Italian waiters."

"My dear, that reminds me. I also shall be out this evening."

He gave no explanation, and none was expected. Rose said comfortably, "In that case I shall have an early night. A little something on a tray. If you girls are wise, you'll do the same."

The beautiful day moved on into a lovely evening. Mr. Orford was early at the place of appointment. He wanted to be hidden before the girl appeared. She knew him by sight and might refuse even to discuss the matter with him. He posted himself beside the path he expected her to use.

She was early, too.

She looked different. Her dress was of lilac-coloured silk, cut low in front and with the fashionable bustle behind. Her hair was piled high, a coronet of plaits; earrings shone in her ears, and a beaded reticule swung from her arm. Even from a distance he could smell the scent she used, heavy and musky. He thought: Poor silly fool, going to meet Charlie with "tart" stamped all over her. Charlie had lost his heart to something very different.

She seemed, or so he imagined, to be aware of being watched. As she advanced, drew level, passed him, she half halted, turned her head this way and that. A habit, he thought sourly; a woman for sale, displaying her wares, accustomed to being accosted from behind. He watched with the fascination of horror, thinking that had he not taken action, were he not prepared to act now, Charlie would be ruined.

She seated herself on a fallen tree trunk near the pool, took out and lighted a cigarette. Her gaze was now fixed on the curve of the ride along which she expected Charlie to come.

Well, however startled or angered she was, her retreat was cut off. He stepped out of hiding. She turned, jumped to her feet, and said, "You! Again!"

"I only want to talk to you."

"Buy me off again. Well, you can't! You had me cornered last time, but this is different. I gotta see Charlie."

"Hear what I have to say first. I want to make an arrangement that will be best for everybody."

Her whole face was a sneer. "Best for *you!*"

"For everybody. If you'd just listen. . . ."

"There's only one thing *to* do. Charlie's got to marry me."

"Don't talk like a fool! There's no power in the land that can make a man marry a woman. The most you could do would be to cause a scandal. That, I admit, I am anxious to avoid. And what good would it do you or the baby—if indeed there is a baby?"

"There's a baby all right. And it's Charlie's. I only gotta see Charlie and tell him the truth about that other time, what you made me do. Like you say, there's no law to make him marry me; there's nothing to stop me seeing him neither. Once he *know,* he'll do what's right. Charlie got a good heart."

Mr. Orford seldom lied. One of the copybooks over which he had laboured had declared that honesty was the best policy, and so he had found it. But now he lied. "Charlie *does* know. He denies all responsibility. If he'd wanted to see you, would he have sent me here to talk to you?"

"I'll believe that when I see him face to face."

She hadn't given him a chance to offer his terms, show her the money he had brought, speak of the secure future he would provide in return for her signature on a brief statement to the effect that anything she had ever said in the past or might say in the future regarding Mr. Charles Orford was mischievous lies. Invented for the purpose of blackmail.

As a document it had, he knew, little or no legal value, but she was not to know that. Ignorant people, such as she was, attached great significance to their signatures. That, combined with the money and the promises, should hold her off.

"You can't see Charlie. He's off to Greece tomorrow."

That was not only a lie; it was a mistake. As soon as he said it, he knew that he should have said "gone" and "today."

"Then I must see him tonight."

She half turned in the direction of the gateway. He had a second's nightmare vision of her arrival on his doorstep. He reached out and seized her by the wrist, saying as breathlessly as though he had run a mile, "You must listen to me."

She said, "No. I won't. I'm gonna see Charlie."

Mr. Orford did not know that she was showing admirable courage. He did not know about auras or that his own blazed red. The wrist he held was so fragile yet trying to pull away, her whole body seemed to be inspired by a supernatural strength. He tightened his hold, and she with her other hand tried to pry his fingers loose.

It was as though an electrical circuit had been completed.

He had never, even as a young man, been sexually inclined. Never felt the slightest temptation to be unfaithful to Rose, been glad when her demands lessened and then ceased. Now, in the time it took to draw a breath, he wanted, more than he had ever wanted anything in his life, possession of this much-used, scrawny little body. He changed his hold.

Against all the dictates of sense and experience, Anna screamed. A noise like rent calico that disturbed the pheasants, and then the one word, "Dad."

Mr. Orford put his hand over her mouth, and she bit the side of his palm, inflicting pain which he did not even feel. He simply pressed harder, one hand against her mouth, the other between her shoulders. He did not hear the tiny click like a twig snapping. She went limp, and because his hold on her was insecure, she sagged to the ground at his feet.

Women were prone to fainting; he knew what to do. Smelling salts were unavailable, but he dipped a hatful of water from the pool and splashed some on her face; he slapped her wrists; he found a few feathers, set them alight, and held them, smouldering, to her nose.

Presently the truth dawned upon him. He looked at his watch.

Part II

"This time she didn't take nothing," Rosanna said.

"Then she'll be back for her stuff."

And *this* time she'd get her marching orders straightaway. Not another night under his roof. He hadn't given her much of a welcome on Wednesday. It was one thing to pity a poor sick prodigal; a prosperous-looking hussy was a different matter. And the way she'd gone off then, after all the kindness she'd been shown!

"She said only for one night or maybe two," Rosanna said, "but I never thought she'd go off just like that."

There'd never been much communication between them, except in bed, and that for a very short time. Anna's third disappearance did nothing to bring them together, even in talk across the table. Anna was not mentioned again for a full week.

They still shared a bed; to do otherwise was unthinkable; they were *married.* For all Rosanna's slovenliness it was a fairly clean bed because every so often William would change and wash the linen and, once a year, the blankets. Sometimes, in very cold weather, coming back from a night patrol, he had even been momentarily grateful for the warmth which her fat sleeping body provided. In summer

135

he kept his distance, with a good hump of the thick feather bed between him and her.

A week after Anna had walked out of the cottage in such a shameful dress, William Thorley woke, instantly alerted by a noise. It came, he realised, from the other side of the bed. It was Rosanna, whimpering, as though from pain. Even as he asked what was the matter, a thought of which he was ashamed shot through his mind: illness, death, a thorough cleanup in the kitchen.

"I had such a horrible dream," she said, and made some more of the moaning noises. "Oh, it was horrible. . . ." He could feel the tug on the bedclothes as she heaved herself into a sitting position.

He tugged at them angrily and said, "Lay down and be quiet."

"It was Anna. . . ."

"I don't want hear it. Bad enough to be woke up. Lay down and forget it."

"I shan't never forget it. It was so awful."

"Shut up. Let a man get his rest." He turned on his side and slept.

Several times in the days that followed she referred to her dream, evoking no interest, no sympathy. "Sitting about the way you do all day, drinking the way you do, can't expect to sleep well."

When after an interval, she dreamt the same dream again and began saying it was an omen, he came as near striking her as he had ever been. "You'd believe it if you read it in your Bible," she said sullenly. That was coming pretty near blasphemy in his opinion.

In the outer world it was a gay time. Captain Peter Stanton came home, very splendid in his uniform. His regiment was leaving for India at the end of September. And India was now a place to which, since the Mutiny, a man might take his bride without any misgivings. He hesitated briefly between Veronica Hepworth and Louise Orford and then made an unusual, sensible choice of the plainer, less giddy girl. The regiment must come first, and everybody knew what havoc a pretty flirt could cause. That Louise was a flirt was made plain by the fact that though *almost* engaged to Algie Hepworth, she'd tried all her pretty tricks on him.

The engagement—in any other circumstances scandalously brief—was justified by the imminent departure. Louise was comforted by being asked to act as bridesmaid, by the fact that Veronica was unlikely ever to have a title, and by the fact that a little idle dalliance had made Algie see that *almost engaged* was a precarious state. Why not properly? he demanded. Looking at him seductively from behind half-lowered lids, Louise explained, not for the first time, that Mamma thought seventeen rather young. Also— and the infatuated young man ignored the warning— Louise did not wish her engagement to be overshadowed by Veronica's. Let the wedding get over; then Algie could speak to Papa.

Rose decided that it was time to speak to Edda; something she had avoided, as far as possible as was consistent with maternal care and interest, for quite some time. Edda always had an answer for, always made light of, all the arguments which one could produce. But this was unarguable.

"It is worrying Papa, Edda. I can see that. All this coming and going. Simon here nearly every day, or you there. People are bound to talk. Unless you bring him to the point or send him about his business, people will begin to remember how so many of them kept mistresses. In the old days."

Just for once Edda was not flippant.

"Whatever worried Papa, I think it is over now, and he looks better, it wasn't me. As a matter of fact, Simon asked me to marry him. At Charlie's party. I told Papa next morning, and he said think about it. And I have been thinking. It isn't that. I think it's his health, though he would die rather

than admit it. That night he didn't come home. For somebody who'd never had a day's illness in his life an attack
like that must have been a shock. But he's better, and he
certainly has no need to worry about me."

They both loved him. About the only thing they had in
common.

On the evening after Charlie's birthday he'd gone out—as
he explained, when explanations became necessary—to
give poor old Stubbs a good dinner, to recompense for forcing Red King over Red Rose. A sop to hurt feelings. They
had not gone to Peppo's, but one of the tied pubs, four
miles along the London road where the landlady fancied
herself as a cook of sound *good English food.* In hot com-
petition with Peppo's and its knickknacks. And there Papa,
for the first time in living memory, had been taken ill, so ill,
in fact, that he had been obliged to stay the night.

Mr. Orford had claimed that it was a simple bilious attack. Mr. Stubbs, who had seen his gambling old grandfather die in the throes of similar pain and nausea, thought
otherwise, but that was not for him to say.

For a day or two he had looked what Rose thought of as
"poorly" and Edda thought "damned bad." Both, but separately, had urged the advisability of seeing a doctor, and he
had ridiculed them both.

"A digestive upset," he said. "I ate too much at Charlie's
party, and then I tried to give Stubbs a good dinner. Over-
loaded my system."

But he was getting better.

He was telling himself, over and over, that it was an accident. Accident. Accident. It could have happened to anybody. He'd gone there with the best intentions, to pension
her off for life. Accident. Accident.

Something had happened to him, however, something
which both the women who loved him had noticed with
concern. A change in the lively silver of the hair, whitening
and thinning, a stoop of the wide, upright shoulders. Age,

possibly. Perhaps a son's coming-of-age made a landmark in a man's life, made him aware that he was no longer young. That was Edda's explanation, and it saddened her with its hint of mortality. Papa growing old; Papa ailing; Papa dead! A bleak prospect, for in her life there could be no replacement, even if she did marry.

Rose said, "If Simon proposed to you on Charlie's birthday surely you have had time enough to think and realise what an *exceedingly* fortunate girl you are. I have no wish to be unkind, Edda, but such a chance is unlikely to come your way again. And you're getting on for twenty. I simply can't understand what there is to think about. You're as bad as Charlie."

"I'm making the decision of a lifetime. Charlie has only to choose between Greece with John and Egypt with Toby."

It sometimes occurred to Edda to wonder whether her refusal to regard Lord Greythorpe as a suitor had had anything to do with his sudden decision to go abroad. Probably it was mere coincidence, she thought, pushing away the flattery and the responsibility. Edda hoped Charlie would choose Greece, part of Europe, more civilised, more, she imagined, hygienic. "I should like it, Mamma, if you would not tell Louise or anybody else about Simon's proposal. It is a private matter."

"Very well. This I am bound to say, though. Algie is to be best man at the wedding, Louise a bridesmaid. One wedding often leads to another, and if. . . . Well, I shall simply withdraw my objection to seeing Louise married first."

"That idea went out with the crinoline," Edda said.

Lady Chelsworth regarded Edda with eyes which the years had faded from cornflower blue to perwinkle and asked in her direct way, "Is it that you fear all the ceremonial? I know that you have led a quiet country life. I once offered to present you, but your father did not take to the idea. However, I shall be around for some years yet, and under my aegis you would have no difficulty at all."

"I never gave a thought to that side of it."

"Then why so hesitant? In Louise I should have understood it. Offer her a mere earl and she'd look around for a duke! I always thought of you as a girl who knew her own mind."

"So I do as a rule. Marriage is a life sentence. It needs thinking over."

"Are you in love with anybody else?"

"No."

"You appear to be fond of Simon."

"I am."

The two women shared a thought: This is a curious turn of events! The older about to plead for the very thing she had hoped to avoid. (But Simon had finally said that if he didn't marry Edda Orford, he'd abandon the idea of marrying at all. And that was bad hearing for a woman who, while sometimes happily defying convention, was at heart a traditionalist.)

"I'm fond enough of him," Edda said, "to wish to give him a square deal. Is fondness enough? And a few similar tastes. With, in the background, your disapproval. Not open. But there." This was plain, straight talk. Something they both understood.

"I will not conceal from you," Lady Chelsworth said, "that I hoped that Simon would marry somebody with a *vast* fortune. We need it—at least the castle and the estate need it. Yes, I hoped for an heiress."

"And a long pedigree?"

"That also would have been desirable. My dear, I hope you are not taking this personally."

"It is one of the most impersonal conversations I have ever taken part in." What other girl in the world would have said that, in so cool, judicious a voice?

"I will introduce a personal note, Edda. Something I

have never said to anybody, but which may help you resolve at least one of your difficulties. When I was somewhat younger than you are now, I was head over heels in love with a man, entirely unsuitable in every way. For Chelsworth, who had offered his hand halfway through the London season, I had no feeling. Not even fondness. My parents were adamant. My father threatened to ruin the man I loved, and he could have done it. Men had more power then. I went to bed and cried for a week. Tonsilitis, my parents said. Then I got up, became engaged to the satisfaction of everybody. Except myself, of course. And what happened?" The pale-blue eyes sparkled, periwinkle changing to aquamarine. "A most happy marriage. I became very fond of my husband; his infatuation increased. I cannot recall a single occasion when my merest whim was not law."

"And you call that happiness?"

"For God's sake, Edda. It was for *him*. How many people in this wide world can be by any standard considered happy? One in a thousand? If, by giving the right performance, saying the right thing, you can reduce the average to one of a pair, isn't that worth doing? And there is something more. Work for a lifetime." She rose a trifle stiffly, walked to the beautiful oriel window, and said, "Come here. Look out. Hundreds of acres, scores of people to whom I have been for more than half a century the very kingpin of life. In the old days it was run to the castle for shelter; now it is for advice and guidance. Lawyer, doctor, matchmaker, peacemaker. I have been all in my time. And influence, Edda, is not to be despised. Only the other day, for example, I got a silly boy out of the army. He'd had a trivial row with his father and run off to be a soldier. The farm was suffering; so was the young fool."

She waited, and Edda was silent.

A job, make something worthwhile of life.

("And the devil taketh him up into an exceeding high mountain and showeth him all the kingdoms of the world and saith, All these things I will give thee if thou wilt fall down and worship me.")

She thought: All waiting! Papa, Mamma, Louise, Simon. And I, waiting for my own decision. The old woman watching her, waiting too, knowing that she had issued a challenge.

Edda said, with the air of one about to shoulder a load, "All right. I'll try. I'll do my best."

Lady Chelsworth put her hard, thin arm round Edda, embraced her, and gave her a dry, potpourri-scented kiss.

"Bless you, my dear. You'll do it admirably, I know. And remember, you can always count upon me for anything."

Then, with a briskness that rather suggested that she regretted this brief display of emotionalism, she said, "What kind of ring do you desire?"

"I've never thought about it." Edda looked down at her left hand, imagined a ring upon it, thought: Now I've done it! She also thought about the Chelsworth finances, how the West Wing must be allowed to fall down because some farm needed a new house or some cottages must be rethatched, some boy apprenticed, some old person pensioned off. It was well known that nobody who had ever worked at the castle in any capacity was ever allowed to go into the workhouse.

"Something very simple," she said. "I never was very fond of jewellery."

A tactless thing to say to an old lady who on occasions could shimmer and shine like a Christmas tree. And there was a little ache, too. Papa had given her every ornament she owned: a simple string of jagged coral, when she was six; a single row of pearls, when she was sixteen; a gold watch on a pin, seed pearls, and turquoises.

"I asked, not because I wish to be interfering, but because I would like to show you. . . ."

Old devil! Edda thought. She was prepared. She knew.

For there, neatly ranged in little velvet-covered racks, were twenty, thirty rings, glinting in the sunshine of the September afternoon and seeming to belie, absolutely, any kind of financial stress.

As though reading the thought, Lady Chelsworth said, "These and a few other things I have always regarded as Talbot heirlooms. I had trinkets of my own, long since disposed of. These I held in trust as it were. Some of them have interesting histories."

She touched a diamond, very large and bright. "The inevitable relic of Marie Antoinette. Part of that fatal necklace. And of course, considered unlucky. This—she touched a sapphire of moderate size but very blue and clear—"has, on the contrary, a very different reputation. The Prince Regent sent it to the Lady Chelsworth whom he had failed to seduce. The stone he said was as blue as her eyes and as hard as her heart. He could turn a phrase upon occasion."

Edda had already made her choice, not because it was simple, but because with her red hair she usually wore green or brown colours, and an emerald would suit both.

"Has this a history?"

"There are two stories about it, for one of which I can vouch. The Emperor Nero is said to have used a huge emerald as a lorgnette; the ancients believed that an emerald improved eyesight. The Sir Simon Talbot who went on Crusade was told that this was a fragment of Nero's stone. It was always called Nero's ring. When I was staying here, just after my engagement, my mother-in-law happened to read something about the persecution of the Christians, and she said we wanted nothing connected with *him*. So she threw it into the moat. Two days later a boy in the kitchen, preparing ducks, found this in the gizzard of one of them. My father-in-law considered this a great joke and a sign that, like it or not, she was destined to own it. Is that your choice? I should warn you, it has one great disadvantage—

it is practically impossible to pull a glove over it. It is set so high. Not in claws, or flat into the band, but in a framework of delicate filigree goldwork."

"I still like it," Edda said.

"On your hand be it, then. I will tell Simon that this was your choice."

"If I do this badly, sir," Lord Chelsworth said, "it's because I'm a novice." He seemed a bit awkward, and it occurred to Mr. Orford that behind the man's serious and pontifical manner there lurked a shy boy. Reared by a grandmother who had a dominating personality, forced to assume, because of his rank, a public responsibility rather too early. The solemnity and the tendency to pontificate were a form of defence.

"I have spoken to Edda, and she has agreed to marry me. Subject, of course, to your approval."

It was less the attainment of ambition than the fulfilment of a vague hope. The boy from the Pike, the ex-counter hand, gave no sign of elation; he said, "You have it. And I hope that you will be very happy for many years."

"Thank you."

Mr. Orford had been giving some thought to the division of his estate—a thing he had not much considered until that dreadful evening when a mere bilious attack had held the threat of death. He now said, "Would it be entirely unromantic to talk business for a moment? Edda is my eldest daughter. I have a son, as you know, and two other girls. I must be just, within reason."

"Of course, sir."

Some of Mr. Orford's thinking had gone back to Rose. There was some talk of a Married Woman's Property Act, and his reason forced him to think about Rose. If she had married a wastrel, a gambler, a drunkard, or an idler, where would Rose be now? The shop in the High Street, the five thousand pounds would have been the property of that wastrel, gambler, drunkard, idler. The only protection a woman could have was a marriage settlement.

And one of the most potentially valuable of all of Mr. Orford's concerns was the Rad-on-Wyck brewery, for the simple reason that when everything else failed, men drank. In bad times more than in good. And after all, a brewery wasn't all that much of a jump from dealing in wine—always regarded as a gentlemanly business. The brewery; and a fourth share in those gold mines, so far away, so little under his control that if they had vanished overnight, he would hardly have been surprised; and, because Edda was Edda, three thousand pounds in cash.

"Most generous," Lord Chelsworth said. "Not that I ever considered. . . . We've muddled through often enough and shall do again."

Rose, quite wrongly, attributed this satisfactory outcome to her talk with Edda.

Four days later, not to be outdone, Louise became engaged to Algie Hepworth. She'd be married first, though, because with her, there would not be all this business, which she falsely pronounced to be tedious, of presentation upon marriage. Edda would have a June marriage; Louise's would be in April.

Maude must be provided for, too.

With everything firmly tied up, Mr. Orford left Mr. Gordon's office and rode home in the warm glow of the late September sunset. The old house had never looked more beautiful, and he allowed himself a thought, not one of hubris—the self-exaltation which invited immediate vengeance from the gods—but of satisfaction. Who said that this was an unlucky house?

Turning back into his office, Mr. Gordon reflected with pleasure that this was the last of September. On Saturday he and the other members of the syndicate would enjoy the first pheasant shoot of the year.

"All right, then. If you won't, I must," Rosanna said with some faint flash of the spirit which in a fashion had given her the upper hand. "I can't go on like this, night after night." Actually the dreams had not been as regular as the phrase implied, nor had they coincided with overindulgence. Unpredictable, horrible, and always the same. "It's getting," she said, "so that I'm scared to go to sleep."

It mystified her that Anna should haunt her in this way. There'd been no great fondness between them, at least since Anna's very early years. Nor had she ever done Anna any harm, but there it was, always the same.

It began with the unlikely situation of Rosanna helping William in the enclosure where hens were hatching out the pheasants' eggs. He was scattering grain and saw that the drinking trough was dry. He said, "Fetch us a bucket of water, love." The bucket was there by the entry to the enclosure, and she picked it up and wondered which would be easier and quicker, go to the well in the yard or to the pool. She decided upon the pool, dipped in the bucket, and there was Anna: absolutely recognisable, but awful to look at; not only drowned dead, but with her head at an angle as though she'd been hanged as well.

(Rosanna knew how hanged men looked, for a day when somebody was to be "turned off" outside a gaol was always a great occasion for the travelling people, very profitable. Besides an unequalled opportunity to pick pockets, there was a ready sale for "hanging buns," which were supposed to keep forever and to protect their owners from a similar fate. They could be sold on the day itself. A little later and at a little distance, lengths of rope could be sold as souvenirs, a bit of the genuine rope from the gallows, and the more heinous the crime of the dead man, the more eager the demand. There was also a sale—if only they could be obtained—for crudely printed ballads and so-called confessions.)

"Seven times I've dreamt it now. And that must mean something. And if you don't do something about it, I shall."

It was now the morning of Saturday, October 5, and William was up early, savouring the beauty of slight mist which promised a clear sunny day. Ordinarily he got his own breakfast, but this morning, disturbed by her dream, Rosanna had come down, boiled an egg, and made a pot of tea while he fed the ferrets and his old dog. Then she delivered her ultimatum, adding with her loathsome cunning, "and I shall do it when there's company around to brave me up."

He knew what that meant. In the presence of his gentlemen of the syndicate.

There had been a time—Ellen's time—when the pretty cottage and the woman within it had been part of the Saturday shoot ritual. The gentlemen had, naturally, provided the bulk of the food, cold meat of various kinds, but Ellen had always made a great potful of soup, baked a batch of fresh bread, brewed coffee. Her years in good service had taught her how to speak, how to act, and moving between her speckless kitchen and her shining parlour, Ellen had been at ease, a wife to be proud of. Then. . . . The gentlemen of the syndicate had sent a beautiful wreath, and Mr. Gordon, the father of the present, had said at the next shoot, "I speak for us all, Thorley, in saying that we shall miss her."

Now he had a wife to be ashamed of—and nobody to blame but himself. But if one thing could said for her, it was that she was not obtrusive. She'd always been too lame to go to chapel, and although while the fight between them was on, she'd been able-bodied enough to get into Wyck, to the pawnshop and the pubs, these were not places frequented by the gentlemen of the syndicate. Few had ever seen her.

And should not now, if he could prevent it.

He said, "All right," swallowed the last mouthful of his overboiled egg, and went out to the yard where, between the dog's kennel and the place where a bit of wall had fallen down, years ago, there was a lean-to shed in which he kept all the tools of his trade except his gun.

He selected the tool which he kept for the destruction of squirrels' dreys. It was like a pitchfork, but with a very long handle, for squirrels built high, were notorious egg robbers and, when adult, difficult to kill; their nests, however, were vulnerable, and with what he called his drey fork, William Thorley had brought hundreds of the little squirming things, potential enemies, hurtling down.

Now he used the fork for another purpose. He explored the pool, disbelieving, expecting nothing. And then suddenly, there was weight, resistance, he fought it. And out of the water in which she had lain for forty-seven days, Anna came to the surface. Dead and drowned, with her head lolling, just as Rosanna, with a few words here and a few there, had described.

Horrible. Awful. A little less horrible and awful than if she had lain all that time in the open air. The water, excluding air, had made some kind of preservation, but bad enough.

He had a momentary temptation: free the drey fork, drop the horrible thing back into the mud and the water lily roots.

Something forbade that. His horrified eyes had taken in two things which proved that Anna had not just fallen into the pool. Somebody had killed her and weighted her down.

Somebody must be punished.

He hauled on the long handle, brought Anna to the edge of the pool, turned away, and was violently sick. Mixed in with his physical distress was some sentiment: Such a pretty, lively little girl, and however bad she had been later on, ungrateful, flaunting, defiant, she didn't deserve *this*.

Through the clearing mist and the brightening sun he made his way back to the cottage. Stumbling into the kitchen, he said, "You were right. She's there. Just like you said."

"I knew it. I knew she was there." Just for once Rosanna showed a wifely concern.

"You do look bad," she said. "Sit down. I'll make another cup."

By that she meant adding another pinch of tea and some more hot water to a pot already half full of dregs. While she did it, he said, "She was killed. Weighted down by the feet and the neck."

"I knew it," she said. The trouble was that all this time, troubled by dreams of Anna, forcing William to do something, she had not looked ahead. She'd gone on and on about Anna; she'd forced William into action. She hadn't given a thought to what might lie ahead. She'd just wanted to be proved right, and now she was, and here was William, overcome. Looking like death. With the sleight of hand that she had learned as a child she reached the brown stone bottle, tipped a good measure into his cup, and then sugared it well.

"Here you are. It'll pull you together."

Her own cup held, apart from the faint brown remains of her earlier cup of tea, pure gin. Inspired by it, she said, "We gotta think what to do. I been working it out. One time you made such a good little Methody of Anna. I reckon what she been bothering me about was burial in the chapel yard."

"Somebody *killed* her."

"Yes. But we can't do anything about him now. And we don't want a lot of fuss, do we? They're your friends, ain't they, the chapel people? And you're handy. You bring her under the shed and make a coffin. Then you can say she died in London and wanted to be buried at home. Then we could all rest."

"Somebody killed her," William said again. "There's such a thing as justice. . . . Besides, I couldn't *touch* her. Nor I couldn't play such a trick."

"It'll mean the police." Distrust and fear of any form of authority had been bred in her very bones. William had no such feeling.

"So it should. Somebody did it, and he oughta be punished. I'll go and fetch Greatheart." With this police constable, the representative of law and order over a wide area, he was on good terms; they felt alike about poachers. Then he remembered that even by shortcuts it would be quite a walk. And his gentlemen would soon be here. That thought, while changing his plan, brought a grain of comfort, for one of his gentlemen, Mr. Gordon, was a lawyer. He'd know exactly what to do and how to go about it.

The hot sweet tea, though it tasted funny—but then most things that Rosanna made had peculiar flavours—ran about him sustainingly. He felt bold enough to give Rosanna an order. "Fetch me a blanket. A clean one."

She went meekly and, returning with it in her arms, said, "I could do it. I'd wrap her in this and pull her into the shed."

"You ain't seen her." Despite the gin, he shuddered.

"I *have*. Seven times in my dreams. Look, you do like I say, just this once. If you don't, it'll mean the police, and then there'll be no end to it. Likely as not they'll say you did it. Or me."

"That's daft."

He took the blanket, carried it to the pool, and there, carefully not looking, threw the blanket over what lay by the water's edge, obscene in the sun of a beautiful autumn morning.

The Monkswood Syndicate had been formed about thirty years earlier as an answer to, and in imitation of, the snob-

bery of the local landed gentry, not one of whom would
have dreamed of inviting his solicitor, his doctor, his tailor,
or his bootmaker to shoot with him. So a few local men, all
prosperous, largely of the Avenue class, had got together
and bought Monkswood. They then proceeded to operate
the snobbery which in others was so deplorable. The right
to belong passed from father to son; any would-be new
member was subjected to the strictest scrutiny. It had, for
instance, taken a lot of heart searching before a tenant farmer was admitted. He was one of the few in the area who
made more than a bare subsistence, and it irked him to be
allowed only to shoot rabbits on his hired land. Rabbits
were reckoned as vermin. In the end he was accepted, and
nobody regretted it, for the need to distinguish between a
raiding pigeon and a game bird had made him a good shot.
He increased the day's bag.

And that was important, for the syndicate operated on
business lines. Each member took his brace. If he wanted
more, and most did, to give away, a symbol of status, he
paid a token price. Birds left over from this share-out went,
first thing on Monday morning, to the butcher-poulterers or
the fishmonger-poulterers in Bressford or Wyck-on-Rad.

The Saturday Sportsmen might be despised by those who
were free to shoot any day of the week, but they enjoyed
themselves in holiday mood. They came in shared gigs, or
dogcarts, or on horseback; they brought hampers of food,
bottles of wine—slightly competitive in the way that young
Edwin Orford had so much resented: I can afford more
than you can; I earn more than you do; my horse cost so-
and-so, my dog such-and-such.

Traffic stopped short of the pool at a point where the
grassy ride widened out into a cleared space, almost a
meadow. There horses were unhitched or unsaddled and
the food hampers left. Who now remembered Ellen's soup
and home-baked bread? There were attendants and beaters,

regular employees or boys hired for the day, two shillings, and the chance of a pheasant so riddled with shot as to be unacceptable. A happy day for all.

Through the merry crowd, William Thorley, their employee, made his unmerry way.

"Mr. Gordon, sir, may I have a private word with you?"

Mr. Gordon, his mind trained to essentials, supposed that the private word was connected with the nonpayment of wages much earlier in the year when the man was ill. He had been in favour of paying him, but he had been argued down. William Thorley, everybody else said, was well breeched. He had a wage well above average, no dependent children, and if you started *paying* people to stay at home and loll in bed, where would it end?

"It's my stepdaughter, Anna. Sir, somebody drowned her. Would you please come and take a look."

Not only was Mr. Gordon a solicitor, but he had for the last four years been the elected coroner for the area. During that time nobody had killed anybody, and the inquests over which he had presided had been very brief and simple: a man gored by his own bull; a child run over by a gig, the horse uncontrollable, having been stung by a wasp; an old woman, bone thin, and frozen stiff, found dead in the church porch. Misadventure; natural causes. One or two suicides.

This was neither accident nor suicide, Gordon realised at a glance when Thorley, his gaze still averted, twitched away the blanket.

Anna on her last walk had worn little boots with tasselled laces. These had been knotted together and then tied to the draw cord of a canvas bag of the kind and size issued by banks to customers withdrawing large sums in cash. It appeared to be full of stones. A really determined suicide might have done that herself, but she could not have managed the other contraption: both hands secured by the strings of her reticule and the ends then tied behind her head. The reticule also appeared to be filled with stones.

The one thing about the corpse which long immersion in the water had not affected much was the hair. At the back of Mr. Gordon's mind a faint memory stirred. Black! A pretty little girl with black hair, making rounds at the end of the day with a missionary box. "Sir, sir, just a penny please, for the poor black people."

He said, "Thorley, I'm very sorry." He could say that unofficially. The why and the how and the when—but it must be quite a long time ago—must be decided in another place.

"Yes," William Thorley said, "it was a sorry end. And she died unrepentant." That was beginning to bother him. The way Anna had gone out on that last night, to his mind indecently dressed, her face painted, and so much scent on her that it even overcame, for a moment or two, the stink of the kitchen.

"Replace the blanket," Mr. Gordon said. "I'll send my boy into Bressford."

Despite the growth of Wyck-on-Rad and of Radmouth, Bressford had retained its supremacy as the administrative centre. The Shire Hall was there, the assizes were held there; police headquarters were there, ruled over, subject only to the chief constable, or his deputy, by Inspector Gregson—a mild-seeming man, a bachelor in his late forties. In London, in an affray with armed robbers, he had shown conspicuous bravery and been shot through the shoulder, a wound which gave him from some angles a bit of a hunchbacked look. But offered a retirement—with pension—he had refused. So then he had been offered a virtual sinecure. South Norfolk, an area with about the lowest crime rate in the world, partly because of its sparse population, partly because, Gregson sometimes thought, unkindly, everything, everybody was so *slow*. Slow-thinking, slow-speaking, slow-acting. Here as elsewhere men fell out with their wives, but they didn't kill them as they did in other places. They took ten years to think it over, another ten years to act, and by that time the grievance had been forgotten or one of the pair was dead. There had been a few cases of infanticide—an unwanted baby disposed of—and four or five old women ready to declare that it had never drawn breath or died after the first. (They'd learned that trick after the doctor had said firmly that a child had breathed an independent breath.)

For an ordinary man kicked upstairs as the phrase went, meaning a meaningless promotion, life could have been dull, deadly boring. Gregson had never found it so. With little call upon his true profession, here and now, he had turned his eyes to the past, studying and often writing imaginative reconstructions of bygone crimes. A few of his articles, largely fact, with a dash of fiction, had been published in periodicals which specialised in such things. He was still a police officer, so he used a pseudonym and more than once had enjoyed the secret pleasure of hearing his work praised, even recommended to him: "You'd enjoy that story about Eugene Aram. I never looked on it in that way before."

Gregson was indeed an imaginative man, but he had learned to curb his fancy when on his job.

Mr. Gordon, conscientiously forgoing the pleasure to which he had looked forward, had remained by the pool, not too close to the body. In his brief, scribbled note to Gregson he had said nothing except that the inspector was needed urgently at Monkswood. Now, greeting the police officer as he alighted from the wagonette, followed by Sergeant Marsh, a shorthand expert, the solicitor, not given to committing himself, said, "This looks like a bad business."

Marsh withdrew the blanket and revealed what was indeed a bad business.

"Any idea who she was, sir?"

"Positive identification. Our gamekeeper's daughter. Anna Thorley. He, poor man, is quite overcome. He could not remain in the vicinity. His cottage is along there." He nodded in the direction. He then said, "Well," in an indecisive, yet significant way. He had done his part.

None of the others knew; they'd gone tramping off to another part of the wood, from which now came the irregular crack of shots. While waiting for the police to arrive, Mr. Gordon had pondered the question of etiquette. Should they be informed and the whole shoot called off as a token of respect for the dead? He had decided not. Such a gesture would do the dead girl no service, and it would spoil their day. It'd probably be poor old Quantrill's last day out; his breathing was so laboured that each gasp sounded final. It was the first day out for two newly joined members and for young Whipple.

"Nothing more I can do here," Mr. Gordon said firmly, and slipped away.

Marsh was already writing what Gregson sometimes laughingly called Chinese.

Despite some time in the water, the bank bag still bore plainly the bold black *S* which identified it as coming from Spears' Bank, the still fairly local one. Below the *S* were two crossed spears. The bag now contained stones—large flints, the only form of stone which was found in this chalky area. The beaded bag contined more flints, rather smaller.

The drey fork, which had caught in the girl's bodice, lay there at right angles. William Thorley had released his hold on it as soon as he saw what it had dredged up, and it had teetered for a second or two, like a spear; then it had fallen.

William had sought relief during this waiting time in almost frenzied activity. He'd given the ferrets' cage an unnecessary cleanout, put fresh straw in Floss' kennel, briefly remembering the time when despite her lack of pedigree and the fact that she had cost nothing—a mongrel pup in need of a home—she'd been the best, keenest-sighted, keenest-nosed, and gentlest-mouthed of them all. Old, stiff-jointed now.

After that he had begun to dig potatoes.

He greeted the two policemen civilly, led the way through a kitchen so dirty and cluttered that it was a surprise after the neat front and the tidy yard into a parlour which was again a surprise. So almost clinically clean and precise.

In the kitchen Rosanna sat. She gave just one look, heavy with hostility, a look with which, in his time, Gregson had become all too familiar. Even when you went to their aid, slum dwellers looked like that. She appeared to take no interest, and Gregson was glad. One at a time was preferable, and none of this "No, Jim, it wasn't Tuesday, it was Monday. I *know* because I was washing."

The parlour contained a round rosewood table, well polished, and at its centre there was a crocheted mat, a blue and white potholder and a flourishing aspidistra with well-washed leaves. The empty hearth held a fan of white paper; on either side of it was an armchair, with crocheted antimacassar; above was the mantelshelf holding a pretty clock, two matching china ornaments, and two big pink-lined shells, the kind which, held to the ear, gave the sound of unknown seas. Against the wall stood a chiffonier: a few books on its upper shelf, a runner of more crochet work on its cupboard top, a papier-mâché tray set out with what looked like a silver tea service. You could match it in a thousand decent lower-middle-class, upper-working-class homes.

William Thorley pulled out two of the rather elegant little chairs which flanked the table and then seated himself. Marsh, testing the table, decided that it was, like all its kind, wobbly. He eased his chair away and put his notebook on his knee.

"Now," Gregson said, gently, for after all this was a man bereaved, "if you could tell us what you know, Mr. Thorley. For instance, when did you last see your daughter . . . alive?"

"Stepdaughter. Though I always treated her like my own and give her my name. It was back in the summer. July."

Vague, but absolutely acceptable. Gregson always suspected the person who remembered too exactly. Ask any ordinary person what he had done, where he had been, what he had seen even so little as a week ago, and all you got was a blank stare. Only those with something to hide had the story ready; worthless.

While he thought this and that July fitted with what the poor girl looked like, William Thorley stood up.

"Maybe I can tell you the very day." He went to the shelf of the chiffonier and took down a thick well-worn notebook. It contained every bit of information about the syndicate. Thumbing the pages, he said, "Ah, it was Friday, July nineteenth. I know because Mr. Curry came that evening. Taking a look round, deciding whether to join or not. And I didn't want him to see Anna as she was then."

"Why not?"

"Well. You shouldn't speak ill of the dead, I know. But she didn't look . . . respectable. I got it down here, Mr. Curry, half past seven. And Anna went out at about ten to. And I hoped she be well out of the way. She looked as though she was meeting somebody. All dressed up."

"You have no idea whom she was meeting?"

"Anna never said anything. Years ago she took off for London, without so much as a good-bye. We didn't see her or hear from her till early this year. Then she was back, very poorly. A graveyard cough, but her mother was against sending for the doctor; she undertook to cure Anna. And she did. Round about Easter she was a lot better and got herself a job."

"Where?"

"In Wyck. Mrs. Evans' boardinghouse. Evening work, helping out. I thought she'd settled, but she took off for London again. Then, as I say, she was back again. Either Wednesday or Thursday—I couldn't be sure which. What I do know is it was Friday, the nineteenth, when she went out and didn't come back."

"You made no enquiries?"

"No. She'd gone off much the same way twice before."

"I see. Now, what about her . . . friends?"

"None I never knew of. But then, as I say, she wasn't here long. February some time, till just after Easter this year. And she'd been away eight years. In London."

"At what address?"

"She never had a settled one. At least that was what she said. Not worth writing a letter, she said, when she wouldn't know whether she'd ever get one back."

Oh! One of those! Gregson knew. Sometimes their landladies found out about them, and they were chucked out. A bad week, and they were in arrears with their rent. They had a customer whom for some reason they did not wish to entertain again. Constantly on the move.

His imagination, curbed, but not deadened, presented him with a vivid little picture of the shifting population of London's underworld. A bit farfetched, however, he reminded himself, to think that somebody had wanted a girl dead and come all this way to drown her. With the Thames so handy!

Question. Answer. Gregson knew all the tricks. Often enough a question framed in one way evoked an answer in direct contradiction to its fellow. William Thorley, however, stuck to his story and only once evaded a question.

"Your stepdaughter walked out on the evening of July nineteenth, Mr. Thorley. This is October fifth. Why did you search the pool today?"

He had no intention of giving Rosanna credit for ranking with those Biblical characters to whom God had revealed

Himself in dreams. So, with a slight lessening of his honest look, he said, "My wife"—a jerk of his head indicated the old sloven in the kitchen—"kept on and on. Mainly on account of Anna not taking her stuff and not coming back for it. And there was nowhere else to look."

Mrs. Thorley, reeking of gin, but not drunk, plainly an accustomed drinker with a head as hard as her liver, refused to enter the parlour.

"No. I ain't allowed in there. You wanna talk to me, I'm here."

The smell in the kitchen was terrible, but the table was steady.

Rosanna's story fitted almost exactly to her husband's except in one respect. She said that Anna, as soon as she was fit to work, had gone as evening barmaid to the Brewers' Arms.

"Mrs. Thorley, your husband said she worked at a boardinghouse."

"I ain't arguing. She could've done both. Anna was very lively, once she got her health back." In Rosanna's simple code you didn't argue with the police, nor did you proffer information. What they asked you answered with the truth if possible, a lie if necessary. She could say truthfully that she'd never seen Anna with anybody, never heard her talk about any contact she'd made on either visit.

"I would like," Gregson said, "to see the bedroom in which your daughter slept that last night. Without your permission to do so, I should require a search warrant."

"Go where you like." There was only one thing left behind by Anna that had held any interest for her, and that was an almost-untouched bottle of gin. Drunk weeks ago.

It was a little girl's bedroom, prepared long ago by Ellen, with hope and love. The wallpaper, faded in places, held a pattern of pink rosebuds climbing a blue trellis. There were two framed texts done in cross-stitch: "Thou, God, seest me," and "The Lord Is My Shepherd." The valance of the bed, the cover, the skirts that concealed the legs of the little dressing table, the cushion on the single chair were of white muslin, spotted with blue. All very virginal and in sharp contrast with the articles on the table's top: powder, rouge, lip salve, scent. The small white-painted wardrobe held a travelling costume of tan-coloured alpaca, trimmed with braid of a deeper shade, and a hat like a pancake, made of crushed pansies. Below stood a small leather case which held—disappointingly—only a pair of gloves and a few handkerchiefs. Gregson had hoped for a letter. Women tended to hoard such things. And his mind was already at work. The dead girl had come home on the Wednesday or Thursday and gone out, dressed in her best, on the Friday evening. That smacked of an appointment. The room offered no clue, even when the bed had been stripped. Women often put letters—particularly of a sentimental nature—under their pillows. The only thing under *this* pillow was a flimsy lace-trimmed nightdress, not a respectable woman's bedwear.

"Nothing here, Tom," said Gregson, who in private moments did not stand on formality with his assistants. "You'd better get back and arrange the ambulance. And the autopsy. I know it's Saturday, but the state she's in. . . . Then come back for me, and we'll try the places where she worked. I'll hang round and see if I can pry anything else out of the old girl."

For Rosanna the day and the drinking had begun early. It was now only about eleven, and the brown stone bottle was at a level that boded dismal sobriety towards the end of next week. She was angry with William, who'd refused even to consider her sensible suggestion of an easy way out of the bother, so she was taking less trouble than usual about his dinner. He'd have his rabbit stewed, not baked in the oven as he preferred it. The slightly sickly smell of boiling rabbit now overrode the other odours in the kitchen. She did not look up when the two policemen came downstairs. One of them went straight out. The other stayed. More questions. About letters this time.

"Not that I know of, when she was here last. The other time, yes, some. About a job, or so he said."

"Who said?"

"A young toff. Pretty young man and very civil."

"Did you know him?" She gave the easy, meaningless laugh of the half drunk.

"Me? No, my dear. Past it, years ago. Young enough to be my son."

Only half realised and long ago put away was the thought: If she hadn't been lamed, if she hadn't looked for security and kindness, which people like her own did not show to the disabled, she'd have had a very different life. Other men, other children. A son who'd have seen to it that his mother was respected. She'd have now been in the position which her old grandmother had occupied.

Patiently, Gregson went on. "Where did you see this young man?"

"Right there by the door. He came asking for Anna."

"And you didn't know him then? Would you recognise him if you saw him again?"

"Not 'less I saw his hand. I'd know that. Very queer hand it was. That I do remember."

She spoke the last words defiantly, as though somebody had challenged her memory, and in fact, there was something that she should remember and couldn't. Just couldn't.

Mrs. Evans had fallen on hard times, but she had never given in. Widowed early, with a son and a daughter to rear and one of the few old, big houses in Wyck as almost her sole asset, she had made the most of it, taking in boarders, not lodgers. Lodging houses were still places of disrepute.

Clad in black silk—if she ever had a new dress, it was an exact replica of the former one—she ruled her household sternly, did her own careful marketing, gave value for money, and had established an enviable reputation. She accepted male boarders only, decent, sober, well-behaved men.

When her front doorbell rang on that October morning, she had just finished carving and dishing up. Five identical plates: two slices of salt beef, a feather-light dumpling, two tablespoonfuls of mashed potato and the same of cabbage.

"I'll go, Lily. It may be an enquiry. Carry these through."

She had had a room vacant for a week, and now, removing her apron as she went through the hall, she prepared a small professional smile and a mercilessly searching eye.

Two policemen on her doorstep. A hooded cobra would not have startled or dismayed her more. Police didn't call at respectable houses.

"Good morning, madam," Gregson said. "If you could spare a. . . ."

"Come in," she said, and hustled them into her own private parlour while Gregson murmured something about a simple question.

"Well, what is your simple question?"

She stood up, rather tall, very straight, lean in her respectable black dress, with its high collar clasped by a mourning brooch—a strand of a lost loved one's hair, preserved forever under glass and framed in gold. The hard-won battles of the past had marked her face with lines of anxiety, determination, and a degree of grim humour.

"Did you employ, sometime in the spring of this year, a young woman named Anna Thorley?"

"I did *not*. Why should I? I have a maid, Lily Pryke. I have a very reliable woman who helps when called upon. Her name is Snell. Why should I engage *casual* labour?" She made it sound as though it were the lowest device that

any decent woman could be reduced to. Even Gregson had
a momentary, ludicrous feeling that the question needed to
be apologised for.

"We were informed that she had worked here."

"*Mis*informed," she said. An idea occurred to her; the
dining-room window overlooked the steps that led to the
front door; any boarder waiting for his dinner could have
looked out and seen the two policemen. Speculation would
be rife, and her explanation of the visit might not be accepted, it sounded so silly. Men gossipped, she knew, quite as
virulently as women; they'd say amongst themselves that it
was something to do with her family!

"Wait, please." She crossed the hall, opened the dining-
room door, and said, "Mr. Harlow, would you be so good as
to step this way?"

Mr. Harlow was a known and respected figure, he had
been Station Master at Wyck-on-Rad until his retirement
last year, and he had boarded with Mrs. Evans since his
wife died, almost nine years ago. He rose obediently, leaving most of his first course on his plate. Both police officers
recognised him, and he knew them; but Mrs. Evans
allowed no time to be wasted on cordialities.

"Please repeat, Inspector, the question you just asked
me."

It was foolish to feel foolish, but that was how Gregson
felt as he reshaped the question and asked it.

"Can you remember a girl named Anna Thorley working
here, however temporarily, in the spring of this year?"

"No. I do not, Inspector, for the simple reason that she
never did." Mrs. Evans made a gesture which said: There,
you see!

Slightly nettled, Gregson said, "The idea of having your
word corroborated was yours, Mrs. Evans, not mine. I was
quite prepared to accept what you said."

"Yet the name," Mr. Harlow said, "is familiar to me. It is
some time ago. Yes, I have it. Anna Thorley left her situa-

tion in Bressford and disappeared. Her father was anxious—she was very young at the time—and asked whether a
girl answering to her description had been seen alighting
from a train here. Then her brother received word that she
was in London. William Thorley told me so next time we
met."

Mr. Harlow knew that it would be futile to ask of a policeman what this latest enquiry concerning Anna Thorley
was about.

"Thank you, Mr. Harlow," Mrs. Evans said. "You must
not allow your dinner to grow cold."

Mrs. Evans did not slam doors, but as Gregson and
Marsh descended the well-whitened steps, she shut her
front door with great firmness.

Servants gossipped, too, she remembered, and tomorrow
was Sunday, Lily's half day, so when Lily asked diffidently,
"Was it an enquiry, ma'am?" Mrs. Evans replied, "Not concerning a room, Lily. It was the police. They wanted to
know if Anna Thorley ever worked here "

"Well, she never, did she? Leastways not in my time. Me
and Anna went to Sunday school together. Last time I seen
her she was up in a gig."

Mrs. Evans said, "You need more soda in that washing-
up water, Lily. The plates are rather greasy."

"So now, the Brewers' Arms," Gregson said. "We'll get a
bite there, if nothing else."

They went into the private bar. The counter at the Brewers' Arms was a semicircle of which a third served the private section, two-thirds the public. Occupants of the two
bars were not visible to each other, but a clear view of both
sides of the dividing partition was open to anyone within
the semicircle. The sight of two policemen caused Mrs.
Pryke to feel, not apprehension exactly, but the certainty of
bother pending. On the whole, she and Josh kept an orderly

house, but men did get drunk, and quarrels did break out. Josh had been compelled to eject a habitual troublemaker forcibly on Wednesday night. Had he hurt the man more than he intended? If so there were at least twenty witnesses who could say that Alf Roach had been to blame.

Concealing her anxiety well, she lifted the counter flap and went forward, greeting Gregson with professional affability and Marsh with more warmth; she remembered him as the constable on the beat and had thought his promotion fully deserved.

She waited for Wednesday and Alf Roach to be mentioned, so the question, when it came, both relieved and baffled her.

"No. We have never employed any barmaid, Inspector. Josh and I don't hold with them. Simply inviting trouble." And not from customers only. Mrs. Pryke's was a small world, but she knew it very well. She had been a barmaid herself. "Anna Thorley." She repeated the name thoughtfully. "There are so many Thorleys. Which would she belong to?"

"Her father—stepfather is the gamekeeper at Monkswood."

"Oh! Then I know her mother. There was a time when she was what you might call almost a regular. But she got lamer and older. I haven't seen her for years. And I never set eyes on her daughter. And yet. . . ." Mrs. Pryke put the fingers of her left hand to her face, pushing her plump cheek against her teeth. "I seem to remember something. . . . Wait a minute, sit down, take the weight off your feet." She meant it kindly; her own feet were giving way and always calling for the weight to be taken off them, but policemen's feet were the subject of many ill-humoured jests, and both men were standing when Mrs. Pryke reappeared with her husband. Behind the public bar she had snatched time enough to say, "Nothing to do with Roach. They're asking about a girl named Thorley. They seem to think she worked here. Can you remember what you said to me? Easter Monday, I think it was. About a girl in there"—she indicated the private bar—"being like old Mrs. Thorley."

The steady—never excessive, but steady—consumption of his own wares had not much impaired Josh Pryke's physique, partly because he ate huge meals, slept well, whenever he could, and pursued a calling which demanded a good deal of physical exertion; but his mind, never of the first calibre, had declined, and lately he had been more and more inclined to leave any thinking that must be done to Flo, who never grew even tipsy. She had, behind the bar, her own special pewter mug: a mug with a false bottom. When anybody feeling generous offered her a drink, she said, "Thank you," and poured two inches of beer and four inches of foam. That satisfied everybody. Flo had her wits about her.

"We never *employed* a girl called Thorley. But I think I saw her once. In here. There at that table. She was with a young gentleman. What struck me at the time was that she had a tart's drink—port and lemon. But she didn't look like a tart. But she did look a lot like old Mrs. Thorley when she was young. A lot of black hair, big black eyes. I mentioned it to my wife. The likeness."

"Did you take as much notice of the man she was with?"

"No. He looked a bit young to be out with a port and lemon drinker. But they all have to cut their teeth."

"Can you remember the date, roughly, Mr. Pryke?"

"I can," Mrs. Pryke said promptly, replying as much to Josh's helpless look as to the question itself. "It was Easter Monday when it came on to rain so hard about seven o'clock. People got off the train from Radmouth and had to shelter in here for an hour till it stopped. We were run off our feet."

"You didn't see the young couple?"

"No. I was too busy at the other end. Everybody seemed

hungry as well as thirsty. I had to leave the bar to my hus-
band and the boy and go and cut some more sandwiches.
My husband mentioned the girl looking so like old Mrs.
Thorley later on." Trust Josh to have an eye for the girls!

"Were there other people in this room at the same time,
Mr. Pryke?"

"Yes. More'n usual, on account of the rain."

"Anyone you recognised?"

The man obviously made an effort to remember. "No."
The slightly superior people who used the private bar
wouldn't be out mingling with a bank holiday crowd.

"Thank you both, very much," Gregson said. "Now, if
we could have a half pint each and a sandwich."

Policemen, like doctors, learned early not to allow tragic
events or horrible sights to interfere with their appetites.

"What kind of sandwich, sir?"

"Salt beef, if available," Gregson said.

"The same for me." They had both noticed without being
aware of it at the time, the scent of the boiled salt beef
which had come, with Mr. Harlow, out of Mrs. Evans' dining room.

While Mrs. Pryke was preparing rather special sandwiches, the bread slightly thinner and the meat and butter
more generous than the general rule, Marsh remembered
something and sought for a tactful way of drawing his superior's attention to it. The inspector rather prided himself
on his good memory and would occasionally say, half-teas-
ingly, "No need for you to read your scribble back to me,
Sergeant. I'll tell *you*!" and reel off even a complicated
statement practically word for word. If his memory slipped
a detail, as even the best memory must, he seemed to be dis-
pleased—with himself.

Now, with exquisite tact, Marsh said, "Mrs. Pryke seems
to know the family well. She might know the brother, sir."

Missed something there! Of course, Mr. Harlow had said
that the girl's brother had heard that she was in London.

Gregson did not care to think that Mrs. Evans' masterful dismissal of her boarder had interrupted the smooth flow of enquiries or that he had not taken full notice of the words.

"She might," Gregson said. And when Mrs. Pryke came in, bearing with practised ease a large papier-mâché tray laden with what they had ordered and cheese and biscuits in addition, he said, "Anna Thorley had a brother, I understand."

"Half brother, or stepbrother. I never know which is which. Bill Thorley is his father's son by his first wife. Old Mrs. Thorley had Anna before she was married—I mean before she married Mr. Thorley." The last words were added as a safeguard. You had to watch your tongue when talking to policemen, and Josh had already been a bit careless, saying "tart's drink."

"Do you know where he lives?"

"I know where he works. At least, last time I heard. . . . He was manager of the station stores at Bressford, doing well for himself."

Why, she wondered, all this sudden and official interest in Anna Thorley? And who in the world had given them the idea that the girl had ever worked here? Still, thank God, it had nothing to do with Alf Roach.

The horse which drew the police wagonette had been given his nosebag—a thing always carried in case of emergencies—and he had had a bucket of water from which to drink his fill. He made a good pace back into Bressford and, when tied up to the railings in the station yard, arranged himself with resignation.

Half past three on a Saturday afternoon and a bit of a lull before the last evening rush of the week started. Everything was in readiness, even the broken biscuits bagged for quick service; screws of tea already made up and the old woman who cooked distributing cups of tea, well sugared, fortifying Bill Thorley and his minions for the last effort.

Here, as in Mrs. Evans' boardinghouse and in the Brew-

ers' Arms, the arrival of the police caused a certain conster-
nation. Not that anybody felt guilty of any actual breach of
the law; it just meant bother.

"Mr. Thorley?" Gregson said to the man who came forward assuming responsibility.

"Yes. That's me."

As the dead girl's brother the man must be told the truth.
It often fell to the police to break unwelcome news, and it
was a duty which Gregson disliked.

"Is there anywhere private?"

It couldn't be anything to do with the money he had
"borrowed." He was paying it back. He'd done Mr. Orford
a service. It was all done with and forgotten. Nevertheless,
as he led the way towards the stockroom-office, Bill's legs
felt weak and his heart pounded.

"I am afraid that I have bad news for you, Mr. Thorley.
Your sister. . . ."

"Anna!"

"Yes. She is dead."

"My God!" He thought of her cough, which had grown
better in the country air. And he'd really been the cause of
her going back to London, to the smoke and the grime and
the fog, when she might have been. . . . He remembered
how she had offered him the ten pounds; he remembered
the bunch of bluebells and other bluebells that they had
gathered together. No amount of self-control could keep the
tears from his eyes. Two escaped and ran down the sides of
his nose.

"I was fond of Anna," he said, excusing himself.

Gregson had had no sister, Marsh had two, much older
than himself, married and gone away before he was in his
teens; but both men looked at Bill with sympathy.

Directing his gaze to the well-stocked shelves, Gregson
said, "I am afraid the manner of her death will cause you
further distress, Mr. Thorley, but it must be told. Your sister
was drowned."

"In London river?" Oh, maybe she'd been fonder of Master Charlie than she'd ever let on—trying to make things easier for *him*. Pretending that only the money mattered. Oh, God, God! And he'd only taken the money because he felt an obligation to his father and to Anna; and Effie had been so nasty when he'd tried to spare a bit from what he earned, not *easily* spared but not demanding any great sacrifice either.

"No. In the pool not far from your father's house. I am sorry, Mr. Thorley, but facts must be faced. We have reason to suspect foul play. The body had been weighted."

Murdered. Horrible enough. Yet there was slight relief in the thought that he was not to blame; she hadn't died because she'd gone back to London or killed herself because her heart was broken. Bill fumbled out his handkerchief and pressed it to his eyes, blew his nose.

"When?"

"On the nineteenth of July."

"July! I didn't know she was home then."

But of course, after the way Effie had behaved in February, Anna wouldn't feel like. . . . On the other hand, he and Anna had parted on affectionate terms. Why hadn't she looked in at the shop?

Old Mattie blundered in with three cups of tea on a tray. Police, in the office, with Mr. Thorley. The word had gone round, and her curiosity had sparked. The ritual cup of tea was the perfect excuse. And my word! Mr. Thorley looked terrible: white as chalk and his eyes staring. He didn't speak; it was the inspector who said, "Thank you." She had learnt nothing except that it was something very *serious*. Nothing to do with a bit of shoplifting or little boys scribbling rude words on the shopfront.

"Sugar it well," Gregson said, and when Marsh had done so, he said, "Try to drink this, Mr. Thorley. It's a help against shock." People were inclined to jeer about cups of tea being a panacea; but a cup of tea, well sugared, often worked wonders, and there were still questions to be asked.

Bill drank his tea automatically; Marsh enjoyed his, he liked a cup with some body to it; Gregon took a sip or two with distaste—far too strong. He was meditating his next question when Bill spoke.

"You said *July*. This is October."

"Yes. Your father recovered the body this morning."

"Poor old Dad! He was fond of Anna, too. In his way."

Possibly, Gregson reflected, but neither the girl's stepfather nor her mother had shown much emotion; the mother had been drunk—admitted. But drunken people easily became lachrymose. Mrs. Thorley had shed no tear.

"We are trying to find out about any contacts your sister may have made, earlier in the year, when she was home for some weeks. In July she was home for either one night or two—nobody seemed quite certain. I judge it to be just long enough to renew an acquaintanceship. On Friday, the nineteenth, she left the house soon after seven. She did not go far. Just to the pool. This rather suggests to me a meeting by appointment. Can you think of anyone, known to her round Easter, with whom she could have arranged a meeting at rather short notice?"

However faint and faraway a warning bell rings, its message is unmistakable. Be careful, until you have had time to think.

"No, Inspector." Behind the stricken gaze a shutter dropped. "Anna came home in February and stayed till sometime after Easter, but I didn't see much of her. She was ill to start with; so was my father. I went over a time or two then. And twice, I think, after Easter. Then, when she went back to London, I went to the station to see her off. That's all."

"And she never mentioned having made a . . . friend? Been out with anyone?"

"No." In essence it was true. Anna had never volunteered any information. "She wasn't one to say much."

"Did she have any employment during that time?"

"Not to my knowledge. She wasn't really fit for work."

"Mrs. Thorley—your stepmother—made some mention of letters and of a young man calling and saying something about a job. Did your sister say anything about that when you took leave of her?"

"Not a word." That was absolutely true.

Funny how that shutter fell and lifted. He may not know *much*, but he knows *something*, Gregson thought. And he is fundamentally an honest man. What has he to hide? His sister's profession?

"I am always," Gregson said, gently, casually, "interested in money, Mr. Thorley. Your father said that Anna came home early in the year, ill and in rather a poor way. She recovered some measure of health, yet to your knowledge sought no employment. She obtained her fare to London." That was a statement, not a question.

Down came the shutter.

"I gave her that. The same as I did the first time. Maybe," Bill said, looking backwards for a second, "I did wrong there. But she had such a hard place here in Bressford. And I couldn't give her the time I had done—I was walking out. . . ."

"I see. On both occasions you behaved in what could be termed a brotherly fashion; you went to the station to see her off. Yet, when she came back in July, she did not even inform you of her arrival. Can you think of a reason for that?"

The shutter lifted, revealing misery.

"She didn't have time. You said she was home two days at most. Given time, she'd have got in touch. . . . I wish to God she had. She might have told me something, then I'd know more. As it is, I just can't think why anybody'd want to kill Anna. She was the gentlest. . . ." Emotion threatened to overcome him again.

Dr. Clarke had already discovered a possible reason.

He had planned himself a pleasant Saturday afternoon, pottering round his garden, tidying up and preparing for winter's rough weather, but the body had spent some time submerged in the water. The next day was Sunday, and his wife—a very pious woman—disapproved of work on that day, except in the direst emergency.

Deceased was pregnant. Two months at least. She had not died of drowning, but of a broken neck, and in this particular case that did not imply any great violence. She had—this was interesting—an extra vertebra in the cervical region; this had resulted in an overlong and very fragile neck. Her lungs, free of water, were in an advanced state of tuberculosis. Had the poor creature not died in this manner, her life expectation would have been short. Pregnancy, he knew, could often activate a latent tendency towards tuberculosis, but in this subject the disease far predated the pregnancy. In fact, there was positive evidence, from old scarring, that at some time or another the girl had known one of those intermissions of the disease which optimists called cures. Erroneously, for there was no cure.

Dr. Clarke was far from being a sentimental man, but he did notice, in a detached way, the wealth of black hair and reflected on the curious fact that, long after its owner was buried, that hair would go on growing. That was not just myth. Exhumations, some of them undertaken quite a long time after death, had proved it true. It occasionally confused the issue when death by arsenic was under investigation. While the heart pumped and the blood circulated, traces of the poison reached the hair; the after-death growth was unaffected.

He wrote his findings in the proper form, went home, and just managed to hammer in, more firmly, a few of the stakes which would support his rose trees when the wind tried to bow them. Then, as the light faded, he went in and enjoyed his tea, with the first toasted muffins of the season.

Bressford had had its own paper, a weekly, for a very long time; it had been called, correctly, the *Weekly News* and had just about paid its way, largely on advertisements for things for sale or things wanted; the news it carried was almost purely local. But lately it had changed. The old owner had died, and his heir, thinking: Go ahead or bust, had converted it into a daily with at least half its front page devoted to news of national importance. It had been a touch-and-go experiment, and for six months he had teetered on the brink of ruin. Then suddenly the *Daily News* had staggered to its feet and romped ahead. A lot of people found it more readable than the *Times* because it used more arresting headlines and less stately language.

On the Monday after Anna Thorley had been dredged up, the *Daily* announced, in the far right-hand corner of its front page, FOUND DROWNED. The news item was brief and admirably cautious. The *Daily*'s proprietor had learned not to indulge in fancy or speculation in such matters.

Edda and Papa were breakfasting together, as they often did. Looking at him fondly across the table, Edda reflected that Mamma had possibly been right when she said that he was worried about her indecision. Certainly he looked much better lately; hair once white remained so, of course, but his was regaining its springy vitality, and his slight stoop was less marked.

Or again, was it possible that men had something of the change of life which bedevilled women?

He was reading the *Times*, propped up against the coffee pot. Edda took the Bressford *Daily* and propped it against the marmalade jar.

Suddenly she said, "Oh, dear! I do hope this is nothing to do with our nice Bill Thorley. But Monkswood. . . ."

Mr. Orford made a sound which she took to indicate interest, and without looking up, she read out the few lines. Then, when he said nothing, she did look across and jumped up with a cry.

"Papa! What is it?"

He could not speak immediately, but he had the presence of mind to put his hand to his waistcoat. His face was chalk

white, his eyes staring. He thought he was going to die. He
wished he might. But the shocked heart lurched into action
again; he drew a shallow breath and managed to say the one
word "Soda."

For indigestion baking soda, bicarbonate of soda, was a
specific. Edda flew into the kitchen. Alone for a moment, he
knew that he must pull himself together, knew also that this
might be only the beginning. God! What had gone wrong?

Edda was back, a tumbler one-third full of a semiopaque
liquid. He sipped it slowly, putting off the moment when
he must speak, must explain. When the tumbler was empty,
he closed his eyes and leant back.

"Better," he said. He knew how he must look; he'd felt
the blood drain from his face and leave a stiff mask through
which for a moment he could not even speak. Now he
could.

"Poor Edda. I frightened you. I'm sorry."

He still looked ghastly.

"I was scared," she admitted. "Was it a pain?"

"A pang. Mere indigestion. Maybe," he said, looking at
his plate, "I shouldn't eat bacon and eggs." He never would
again. "I've had a warning or two."

"Attacks like this?"

"Much the same."

"Then honestly, Papa, I think you should consult a doctor."

"For something baking soda can cure?"

She'd heard, or read, of an old doctor saying that if a patient came to him complaining of indigestion, he suspected
his heart and vice versa.

She couldn't say *that* to Papa.

"A doctor could prescribe something more readily available. It could happen when baking soda wasn't handy. And
you still don't look like yourself to me."

"So you propose that I ask Dr. Sapey to make me more
recognisable?"

That was Papa, mildly sardonic, and though it was accompanied by a smile like a death's-head grin, Edda responded with a smile.

Both their breakfasts were ruined, bacon congealing, egg yolk set almost solid on the plate.

And she was going cubbing—the trial run for young hounds and their young prey. She'd never been absolutely sure of her attitude towards the sport; but she'd hunted to ride, and Simon was sure, explaining that but for the sport foxes would have been extinct long ago, like bears and wolves, talking about the damage one fox could do in a chicken run or a lambing pen. And—truth must be admitted—kills were few. Everybody said that a few independent farmers, like Mr. MacDonald, simply shot on sight.

"Would a b and s help?"

"It would indeed." She poured two. "Good for shock," she explained. "But you still look pale. You should lie down for a little."

"Heavens alive, Edda! Whoever took to bed for a touch of dyspepsia? Besides I must go see poor Thorley."

"Of course. D'you know, I think I remember his sister. A long time ago, when we lived at the shop. I used to see them on our Sunday afternoon walks. She was rather pretty."

"Really. Well, I must go. Have a nice day. Don't take any unnecessary risks."

Bill Thorley wore a grey, stricken look, he'd been told. He was minding his job, though, supervising and taking a hand in the window display of this week's bargain. Mr. Orford signalled to him to come into the office. There he said, with all sincerity, "I'm extremely sorry, Thorley. It must have been a great shock."

There had been a second one—Effie's behaviour. He hadn't expected Effie to share his grief—she'd never liked Anna—but he was not prepared for what had happened when he staggered home and said, "Effie, Anna's dead. She was murdered."

Effie said, "I always thought she'd come to a bad end." He hadn't bothered to ask why she thought so; he just sat down and gave way to the tears that he had forcibly restrained so far as possible in the presence of the police. Effie then proceeded to regard the whole thing as a personal affront. Think of the scandal, she said. To have somebody murdered in the family was next to having a murderer. She said to the two little girls, "Don't worry your dad. He's a bit upset about something." A *bit!*

Ordinarily she and the children went to church at eleven o'clock, leaving Bill to mind the Sunday joint, the proper job for a heathen. Bill had reacted against his father's Methodism and was too honest to make even a pretence at adopting any other form of faith. On this Sunday morning she gave ominous signs of what her attitude was to be. She stayed at home, saying that by this time the news would be all over the town, and she just couldn't face the stares. Mary, the elder, asked, "*What* will be all over the town, Mum?"

"Never mind. You'll know soon enough." She was annoyed because he couldn't eat his dinner. "No supper last night either. How long do you think you can go on like that? What good will making yourself ill do?"

Never a sympathetic look or a kind word.

In the afternoon he hired a pony and trap and drove over to Monkswood, and Effie sped him on his way with an injunction *not* to go offering to pay for the funeral. "If people like that do have funerals."

At Monkswood he found no one to share his grief. William Thorley had somewhat recovered from the shock of his discovery and was in the process of hardening his heart. Of remembering Anna, not as she had looked as she came out of the water, but as she had passed through the kitchen on that Friday evening, dressed and smelling like a harlot. He regretted ever having taken her in; he knew as well as Effie did what talk was about to begin. In his secret heart he was now half regretting that he hadn't done as Rosanna advised. He had gone to chapel that morning, and glancing round the congregation with whom he regularly worshipped and to whom he sometimes preached, he'd thought: Yes, the chapel people are my friends; they'd have trusted me. . . .

Bill's stepmother regarded him as an audience to whom she could recount her dreams. Somehow, and she couldn't tell exactly why, she'd missed her chance to speak of them yesterday to the police. All she'd done was answer questions.

Bill drove home with the dismal thought that out of all the world he was the only one who truly sorrowed over Anna's fate, because he loved her and she had loved him.

Now, with Mr. Orford speaking so kindly, telling him to sit down, pressing a hand on his shoulder, he broke down entirely. He muttered between sobs, "Why should anybody want to kill Anna? She was the kindest. . . ."

Mr. Orford waited. There was something he needed to know.

Presently he said, "Wait there. I shan't be a minute." He went into the shop and took a bottle of whisky off a shelf, in Mattie's department found some teacups, still unwashed, returned to the storeroom, rinsed a cup under the tap, poured in a good portion of whisky, added a little water.

"Here," he said, "drink this, Thorley. Help to pull you together."

Once, on Sunday evening, having returned the pony trap, Bill had wished that he were a drinking man with drinking friends in whom he could confide, with whom he could get drunk. But he was not; where Methodism had ended, re-

spectability had taken over; a bottle of port wine, measured
out by the thimbleful at Christmas, had been the limit.

He drank, was heartened, pulled himself together, and,
plying his handkerchief, apologised.

"I'm sorry. I was fond of Anna. I'd always looked after
her, as well as I could. As you know."

Straight into Mr. Orford's hands.

"As I know. Not that we need go into *that*, Thorley. I only
hope, *for your own sake,* that you made no mention of it to
the police."

"Of course not. Why should I? That had nothing to
do. . . ."

"Nothing at all. I only mentioned it because. . . . Well,
to do so would brand you as a thief, and me. . . . Exactly
what? A compounder of felony? I believe that one is supposed to report such . . . misdemeanours."

"You never mentioned it to anybody. And I'm grateful.
Effie'd. . . . And I shan't. It'll be bad enough without
that."

This was the assurance which Mr. Orford needed, and for
the first time since Edda read those few lines aloud, he was
able to draw a full, deep breath. That story, once told,
would have established a connection.

"Would you like to take the rest of the day off?"

"No I would not," Bill Thorley said with extraordinary
violence. "Thanks all the same, sir." The less he saw of
Effie just now, the better. "I'm all right, now. Thanks for
the whisky. . . . And everything. I'd better get back."

"You'd better sober yourself and clean yourself up,"
William Thorley said roughly. "An inquest is a serious
business."

The first admonition was unnecessary. Rosanna had been
sober of necessity, the brown bottle emptied untimely.

Cleaned up—she'd even washed her hair—and clad in

the nearest thing to black, dark brown, she made a quite presentable figure. (At the far end of the garden there was a walnut tree, just where the wall was broken, and some nuts had fallen already. Their husks, well boiled and resolutely mashed, had produced the dark dye.)

And now in this quiet, though crowded, room, she was not restrained within the framework of question and answer. She was invited to say what she knew.

What she said converted a fairly ordinary, sordid affair into something more. It gave a touch of the mystical.

The murder, in an area where murders were few, had naturally attracted a good deal of attention, but only local. Murders more spectacular and more important were committed every day. Certainly, through the room, when Dr. Clarke said dispassionately, "between two and three months pregnant," a little ripple ran, a susurration—what did I tell you? What other reason could there be?

Only William Thorley and Bill really minded. William because working back, he realised that at the very time when Anna had seemed to be so meek and repentant, while under his roof, she had been whoring round, and Bill because this revelation would spike Effie's tongue.

The verdict was inevitable: murder by some person or persons unknown. The coroner gave permission for the burial of the body. A chapel member, stoutly supporting an afflicted brother, approached William as soon as the inquest was closed and began to talk about the funeral.

"I don't want anything to do with it. And what I won't have is her laying alongside Ellen."

So in the end not only the expense, but the arrangement of the funeral, fell upon Bill.

Mr. Harlow took the *Daily* and, now that he was a retired man, had read it from end to end before dinnertime, but he did not leave it lying about in the communal sitting room for the benefit of his fellow lodgers. Let them buy their own. He carried it to his bedroom and made a courteous little ceremony of presenting it to Lily when she brought him his presupper can of hot water. He invariably said, "Perhaps you might care to see the paper, Lily." It flattered her that he should assume that she did not regard paper solely as something to be used for the lighting of fires, and quite often, unless she was in a tearing hurry, she'd just glance at the front page and make some remark which proved that she could read. On hurried evenings she simply thanked him and tucked it under her arm. On Wednesday, in the week after Anna had been found, Lily was not hurried.

On Monday Anna's death had been announced in a corner; on Wednesday Tuesday's inquest was fully reported. Two columns.

"Ooh!" Lily said. "Thass what come of riding about in gigs!"

"Where is the connection, Lily?"

"I seen her. Up in a gig, with a young gentleman. Nice-looking he was, too."

"And when was that?"

"Easter Monday." She remembered it well. Easter Monday was a holiday for everybody except servants, and the only time she'd set foot outside the house on that day had been when Mrs. Evans had sent her out to the postbox on the corner, telling her to hurry. She'd hurried there, but she sauntered back. Easter was early that year; but the leaves were just out on the chestnut tree over the postbox, and some front gardens were all a-dance with daffodils. And all in a queer light, sort of purple. Lily Snell, plain, unsought-after, even by the butcher's boy, had felt the immemorial stir of the mating season. She didn't recognise it for what it was; she thought her feeling was discontent because everybody else was on holiday. Then, slowing down a bit to take the corner, came the gig, and in it Anna Thorley, looking up at the handsome young man and laughing. Envy, pure and simple, had replaced the feeling of vague discontent, and later, when the rain came down in torrents, she'd hoped Anna'd got drenched.

"She always was a wild one," Lily said.

"In what way?"

"Well, one for the boys. We went to Sunday school together. Inside she was like a mouse, but outside she never stayed with us girls. She'd go off with her brother and the other boys, climbing trees and such. She'd go in the river with them. They with nothing on and she just with her drawers." Not a garment one should mention to a man, even one so old as Mr. Harlow.

Mr. Harlow had spent a good portion of his life in managing and organising things.

"Did you recognise the young gentleman who was driving the gig, Lily?"

"No. Never seen him before."

"Would you know him if you saw him again?"

"Ooh, yes. He was ever so nice-looking." And indeed the moment, the . . . the everything about that moment was impressed on her memory forever.

Mr. Harlow, whose mind had lately been like a mill without anything to grind, had been thinking deeply. On Saturday the police had come here asking whether Anna Thorley had ever been employed. On Monday the paper had simply said that she had been found drowned; on Wednesday it reported Tuesday's inquest. The police were obviously looking for a man. Rightly so, since women very seldom murdered other women, and when they did, it was usually by poison.

"I think, Lily, that Inspector Gregson would be interested in what you have to say."

"Ooh! No, Mr. Harlow. I couldn't. I dassn't. Not the *police!* Besides, Mrs. Evans wouldn't like it."

"No need to upset yourself." Upset she was; the red colour which had flooded her face when she mentioned Anna's drawers had darkened to crimson. It was unusual for young women to suffer apoplectic strokes, but one never knew. In the firm, soothing, yet authoritative voice which had soothed and directed foolish people who, not noting a change in timetable, found themselves delayed or stranded or farmers who expected cattle trucks to be conjured from the air, platelayers, signalmen, engine drivers with grievances, he said to Lily, "I will look after everything."

For Gregson the most obvious clue was the bank bag. He was wily enough to know that the most obvious clue was not necessarily the right one, but the obvious must be explored first.

Banks were notoriously cagey, secretive, protective of their customers, to death and some while after. Gregson was obliged to say, "After all, Mr. Field, this is a murder investigation," before Mr. Field would reveal a lot of important, possibly vital information.

It was only on the last of June this year that bags had borne the crossed spears as well as the letter *S*. Other banks and insurance companies had taken to symbols: oak trees, eagles, mythical creatures. Spears reluctantly had followed suit and introduced the crossed spears.

"And how many were issued between the first and the nineteenth of July in this area?"

"Would an answer to that help you, Inspector? Spears' Bank is operative as far north as Lynn, as far south as Ipswich."

"I'm beginning here."

With the utmost reluctance Mr. Field summoned an underling and ordered up the books, sacred, now to be defiled. An orthodox Hindu compelled to slaughter a sacred cow could hardly have felt worse.

Only four. So large a bag would be issued only to a customer withdrawing a large sum in cash—a hundred pounds or more—and coming unprepared.

"Wages clerks," Mr. Field said stiffly, "bring their own bags."

Simpson, J. D., had withdrawn a hundred and twenty pounds on July 3. On the same day the South Suffolk Show Committee, per its treasurer, Colonel Freemantle, had taken out four hundred pounds—expenses and prize money. On the fourth MacDonald, A. F., had carried away two hundred and fifty. Then on the nineteenth, Orford, E., had withdrawn five hundred.

Begin with the nearest; eliminate. Simpson, J. D., was the chemist in the High Street. Quickly disposed of.

"Yes," he said, wondering what on earth this had to do with the police. "My wife and I had never had a holiday. A chemist's business demands constant attention, day and night. But our son is now qualified. So he offered, and my wife and I were able to take a holiday and to celebrate our silver wedding at the same time. The bag? Yes, certainly I was given a bag. I have it here somewhere. I intended to take it back." After a bit of fumbling, opening and shutting drawers, he produced his bag, brand-new, and proffered it.

"I don't want it," Gregson said. "Only to locate it. Thanks."

One eliminated.

"We'll work round, Tom," Gregson said, climbing into the wagonette and consulting his mental map. "The MacDonald place first."

Twenty-two years earlier the farm had been called Mockbeggar, an apt name. Then a lean giant of a Scotsman had bought it, very cheaply, renamed it Kilburnie, and set himself, with the aid of his wife and several children, to make it prosper.

Outwardly there were few signs of prosperity; Mr. Mac-Donald wasted no money on show; he stuck to essentials. Under the tattered thatch of his cowsheds and stables stood some of the best animals in the county. He had one of Mr.

Orford's Jersey bulls, several pedigree Frisians, and a number of their progeny, an excellent cross—Jerseys gave rich
milk in small quantities; Frisians yielded poorer milk in
quantity. One of his sons put milk cans on the up train every morning and then did a round in the better part of
Bressford delivering milk, cream, eggs, and butter. The
family dipped their salted porridge into skim milk; they
spread margarine on their bread.

Called from his work, Mr. MacDonald regarded the police dourly, but that was his usual expression; there was
nothing defensive about it.

"I believe, Mr. MacDonald, that you withdrew two hundred and fifty pounds from your bank on the third of July."

"Aye, I did so." Dourness became tinged with affront.
This was an invasion of privacy. "What of it?"

"You received it in a bag?"

"I was away to the show. There were things I needed for
mysel' and I have Angus to set up in his own place."

"Quite so. I'm not interested in the money, Mr. Mac-
Donald. I'm anxious to know what became of the bag."

"That wee bit thing! Why would I be bothering about
that?"

"You took to to the show?"

"Aye, and brought it home. Nigh empty."

"Then it could be somewhere in the house."

The farmer had no intention of letting them over the
doorsill if he could prevent it.

"I'll ask my wife," he said, and went in, closing the kitch-
en door. Gregson and Marsh could hear some indistinct
shouting, then some wailing, and what sounded like a
smart slap. Almost immediately, MacDonald appeared, the
bag in his hand.

"The lassie had it. She's a mind for rubbish."

A little girl, perhaps five years old, came to the doorway
and leant against the lintel, crying, but quietly now. She
was poorly dressed, and her thin legs ended in huge

ploughboy boots, handed down from a brother. Her face was pitiable as she watched her father, who said, "You'll not be wanting this!" He tipped into his palm a bright new penny, two shining conkers, some pebbles, curiously striped, half a comb, and a thimble worn into holes. The treasures of a child who had not much to treasure.

It pleased Gregson to be able to say, "Thank you, Mr. MacDonald. I don't want it. Only to know where it was."

The child's face brightened. "It is my reticule," she said.

With hurtful contempt the father threw the bag and what it had held towards her. She stooped and gathered them together. Gregson wondered what he could add to this pathetic collection. Not a coin; that might savour of patronage and be resented. He had it!

When he was young, poor, and a collector of trifles, he'd won a medal at some sport; he'd forgotten now whether he'd run faster or jumped higher. He'd cherished the thing ever since, first in his pocket, then, when he acquired a watch, on the chain. It was a pretty thing, the Queen's head in silver on a background of blue enamel. He wrenched it free and handed it to the little girl. "Put this with the rest of your pretty things." She rewarded him with a sudden, astonishingly charming smile.

Her father said, "Away and be of help to your mother! Is that all?"

"Yes, thank you." Gregson's voice was cold with distaste.

"Now you've parted with your talisman, sir," Marsh said as they rattled away.

"I hope it's lucky for her. She needs it."

"Nasty character," Marsh agreed.

"Did you notice his hands? Do you know, just for a moment. . . ." Gregson hesitated on the verge of sharing a confidential, fanciful thought. "If that bag hadn't turned up, I should have suspected him. He could break a stronger neck than Anna Thorley's."

"Why would he do it?"

"He's got a son old enough to be set up on his own. I just thought *suppose*. . . . Suppose the boy had been carrying on."

"He's capable of it. But would any son of his strike anybody as a toff, as such a nice young gentleman?"

"To the landlord a toff would mean somebody in the private bar, spending money. To the gamekeeper's wife I should think it'd be anybody who'd had a wash in the last fortnight."

"I see what you mean, sir." Marsh grinned.

"Well, two accounted for. Two to go."

"Of course," Marsh said in a ruminative way, as though talking to himself, not doing his inspector's thinking for him. "It may not be local at all. Spears have a lot of branches."

"Phipps is busy on them at this minute. They'll all be raked over. The *timing* and the place incline me to think local. She was in London. It'd have been just as easy—easier—to kill her off there. She'd been home at most two days. Just time enough for an exchange of letters making the appointment. Well, now for Colonel Freemantle."

Colonel Freemantle, like Colonel Stanton, had spent a good deal of time in India, but, unlike him, had inherited no family house, no estate. So he had bought a smallish cottage and made it, as far as his limited means allowed, into a little bit of India. It had a wide verandah, adding shade to already dark rooms, and a sitting room cluttered with worthless objects of Oriental origin. Half the floor was covered by an enormous tigerskin, complete with head, over which unaccustomed visitors invariably stumbled. It was one of the largest tigers ever shot in the Killapore area—after which the colonel had named his house.

The colonel himself was in sharp contrast with his twilight, nostalgic abode. Cheerful, garrulous. A convivial fellow who could do sums, he had found his niche, taking on a number of jobs which did not bring in the slightly shabby word "salary" but which merited "honorariums." Also,

more farsighted than many of his kind, poor old Stanton for
example, he had taken the precaution of bringing home
with him an Indian servant, an ex-Thug, who, had he
stayed in India, would undoubtedly have been executed.

"Yes," Colonel Freemantle said, "I withdrew the money.
I took it, in the bag, to the Victoria Hotel in Bressford,
where, as is usual, the members of the Show Committee
met to dine and to discuss the allocation of the prize money.
This is, of course, something that must be left to the last
minute. The desire is to be fair—to allot prizes in propor-
tion to entries. You understand?"

"Of course. Could you tell me what happened to the
bag?"

"I am afraid not. It was probably left on the table."

From which anybody could have picked it up.

"Could you name those present, sir?"

"Certainly. Lord Chelsworth was, naturally, in the chair.
Then, I will name them, clockwise. . . ." He did so: the
judge of heavy horses, of cattle, of pigs, of sheep, all with
subsections like "mare with foal at foot." And this year—a
complete innovation—there had been a goat class.

"Of which," Colonel Freemantle said, "I could not fully
approve. Goats should *not* be encouraged. Unless very
strictly controlled, they can deforestate an area in no time at
all. And once the trees go. . . ." He spread his plump
hands. He knew; he had seen it happen. Even a few trees attracted rain; a bare patch, nibbled down into shadelessness,
sent up a cone of quivering heat which defied the clouds.
But say it, blame the goat for making deserts, and everybody thought you a crank.

He chatted himself happily to a standstill, while Gregson
reflected on the scope thus left open. Any one of the twelve
men named, with exception of the judge of heavy horses,
well over seventy years old and only just mobile on two
sticks. Anyone who worked at the Victoria Hotel or even
passed through the yard where the rubbish heap stood.

"It widens the field," Marsh said as they resumed driving.

"Unless the hotel can account for it. We'll try Mr. Orford."

He knew him in a purely professional way and rather liked him. About two years earlier there had been a break-in at the station stores, one of the plate-glass windows smashed and goods to the value of fifty pounds stolen. Mr. Orford had shown none of the vindictiveness usually evinced by those who had been robbed. He'd said, "The point is, Inspector, if I ignore this, it may happen again." He had been helpful, too; careful not to make a downright accusation, he'd said, "I think it could be an act of retaliation. A man from the Pike—Graves is his name—came in yesterday morning, extremely drunk and abusive. My manager refused to serve him—he has orders to that effect—and two of the assistants threw him out. One cannot have decent women—many with children—subjected to that kind of thing." Graves had cut his wrist in breaking the glass, and his squalid cottage contained most of the stolen goods. In view of this fact the magistrates exercised exceptional leniency and committed him to gaol for twelve months. Mr. Orford had then shown remarkable magnanimity, refusing to take the stuff back. "The poor woman and the children can use it," he said. Gregson had been impressed by this gesture and did not know that it derived from Mr. Orford's experience of life in the Pike, where the man of the house drank too much. Nor did he know that Mr. Orford easily recouped his loss; in a shop doing good business a penny on this, twopence on that, the week's bargain just that halfpenny less of a bargain than last week's or next's, soon caught up with the leeway.

Gregson was no snob—slightly the reverse in fact—but the old house turning its weathered face to the fading afternoon light appealed to his suppressed romanticism. As Mr.

Orford's earlier gesture had appealed to his controlled sentiment. Therefore, when the wagonette halted in the yard, he decided against taking Marsh in with him. It savoured too much of an invasion.

Unlike the other takers-out-of-bank-bags, Mr. Orford was prepared. The trim parlourmaid's appearance at the door of Rose's own room, interrupting the sherry drinking, was only to be expected. And it had been guarded against. "Inspector Gregson wishes to see you, sir."

"Show him into the library. And, Snell, light the lamps there."

One of the peculiarities of this household was that no menservants were employed. Mr. Orford in his omnivorous but rather disorganised reading had come across the remark that the employment of any male servant, however diminutive, was a show of affluence. He had not yet worked out, in his own mind, why good parlourmaids liked to be called by their surnames. In the past he had made the mistake of calling this Snell's predecessor Margery.

He left the family to their sherry, went along to the library, and said, "Good evening, Inspector. And what can I do for you?"

Gregson explained.

"Ah, yes. A tragic affair! One of my managers is related to the girl. He is deeply distressed. As for the bag from the bank. Frankly I have no idea. I did withdraw money on the day you mention. As a rule I prefer to settle accounts by cheque, but that happened to be the day following my son's coming-of-age. There were various expenses. Also, I wished to add a little to the sum I had given Charlie for his birthday. During the evening I had some talk with his friends about the expeditions they were planning and reached the conclusion that he might need rather more."

"I'm only concerned with the bag," Gregson said quickly.

"And there, I fear, I cannot help. The most likely thing is that I took it to one of my places of business. But I will just. . . ."

The pain had struck, clamping down like a vise on his chest, sending a sharp probe along his left arm. He needed to turn his back to his visitor and did so by going to an elegant bow-fronted corner cupboard built in between the end of one set of bookshelves and the nearest window. He went through the motions of searching while he counted, waiting for the pain to ease. The lamplight did not reach this corner, and when he turned, he would not be under the scrutiny of a loving daughter's eye, but of a man, interested only in a bank bag. It was a bad attack, but not so bad as the one which had struck him on the night of the murder or the one he had suffered on Monday when Edda read out . . . . Presently he tested his voice, as on Monday he had tested his legs, and like them, it served.

"I hoped," he said, resuming his chair, "that it had been tidied away. Women have such a passion for tidying and anything not immediately relevant goes into that cupboard. I am sorry not to be able to help."

Did he look like himself, in Edda's phrase? Was his face pallid and sweating? Instinct warned him that there might be further ordeals like this ahead. He must do something about it. The lamplight was kinder than the sunshine of a bright autumn morning, and Gregson, preoccupied with other thoughts—another bag which might be anywhere— noticed nothing.

"No luck," he told Marsh. "Now for the Victoria Hotel."

The Victoria Hotel was run by a brisk little woman whose life could have been a catastrophe, had she allowed it to be. She'd made a good marriage, but within a year her husband had begun to forget things, laughable at first. Little muddles, duly sorted out. Then he'd begun to stumble and mumble. Anybody'd think he was drunk, but he wasn't, she knew; he was ill, and nobody could say exactly what ailed him. He was now virtually a cabbage, knowing nothing, apparently feeling nothing, but a well-cared-for cabbage, lying in his bed in the part of the hotel building upon which she had, for a time, looked as home, imagining children. . . . All dust and done for, those hopes, but at least, by energy, by contrivance, she could keep him cared for and cleaned and fed. He hadn't recognised her for years.

"Oh, yes," she said, in reply to Gregson's enquiry, "I remember the dinner before the show. A very busy time." Not only the dinner in the private room upstairs, but every room taken and the dining room crowded. Two servings and a lot of complaints.

Asked about the bag, she said, "Men are very untidy. I will send for my box. You would hardly believe the things men leave about and do not bother even to ask for."

The box was large, made of cardboard, the kind of container in which a dressmaker would deliver a dress, and its contents fully justified the accusation of men being untidy. Pairs of gloves, odd gloves, handkerchiefs, pipes, a cigar case, a silver matchbox, two watches, a signet ring, several seals, a silk scarf.

"I do my best," the capable little woman said, "to keep track of anything valuable, which might be asked for, but an ordinary bank bag. . . ."

It certainly was not there.

Gregson thanked her.

Outside, Marsh said, "Shall I drop you off, sir?"

"No, thanks, Tom. I'll just look in. Something may have cropped up."

Something had, but not what Gregson had expected.

Neatly written, formal, succinct, the letter had taken Mr. Harlow most of the morning to compose, compress, write first in pencil and then with pen and ink.

"A serving maid in this house, one Lily Snell, formerly a schoolmate of the unfortunate girl whose death is now the subject of investigation, says that she saw deceased on Easter Monday, in a gig driven by a young gentleman. He was not known to her, but she claims that she would be able to recognise him."

Easter Monday, the day of the ruined holiday ending in drenching rain, the day when the dead girl had been seen with a young man in the private bar at the Brewers' Arms, a young man, too good, in the landlord's opinion, to be out with a port and lemon drinker. It linked also with the young gentleman, the proper toff, who slightly later had made enquiries for the girl at the gamekeeper's cottage.

Tomorrow, Gregson thought. Sitting up late, beating your head against a seemingly blank wall was a useless and sometimes fatal exercise. He'd seen it happen, inspectors, chief inspectors, superintendents, supported by innumerable cups of strong black coffee and beating themselves to death running up blind avenues. A man owed something to himself. So he went home, and his housekeeper, an adept at making what she called "keepable" meals, served him with a supper that, heated and reheated, would have been edible in a fortnight's time. And the cat—a stray which had somehow wandered in and attached itself to the household—came in, jumped up upon and kneaded his knees, then curled round, purred a little, and fell asleep, while he pondered. For going home, eating his meal did not absolve a man. Mr. Harlow's letter had confirmed his idea of local. "Gig" implied local, too, and the fourth bank bag had yet to be accounted for. Nursing the cat, Gregson closed his eyes, following Colonel Freemantle's clockwise account of the table, following the even more complicated and distant things which Phipps' investigations into the activities of other branches of Spears' Bank might reveal. Waking thoughts and sleeping thoughts so merging together that he did not even know he was asleep until his housekeeper came in and said, "Sorry to disturb you, sir, but Puss must go out."

The new telegraphic means of communication were wonderful. By midday next day Sergeant Phipps, to whom the job had been entrusted, since he was as expert at it as Marsh was in "Chinese," was able to report that no other branch of Spears' Bank had issued a bag of the new kind until July 26. Most of them were bigger than the one at Bressford and had larger reserves of the old kind.

That narrowed the field, and it was narrowed even more by the appearance, halfway through the afternoon, of the brisk little woman from the Victoria Hotel.

"I thought I'd come right away since you seemed anxious about it. Soiled, I am sorry to say. One of the women who helps on occasions took it home and used it as a jelly bag. Black currant jelly." The brown canvas bag bore unmistakable evidence of the usage to which it had been put: deep purple stains which almost, but not quite, obliterated the letter and the symbol.

To the board which said that the wood was private property and that trespassers would be prosecuted William Thorley tacked another: BEWARE OF THE DOG. It was the only remedy he could think of for the publicity which Rosanna had first seemed to shy away from and now seemed deliberately to court. The young reporter on the Bressford *Daily* knew a good story when he saw one, and immediately after the inquest, while William was repudiating all responsibility for Anna's funeral, he had drawn Rosanna aside and said he would like to hear a little more about those dreams. Rosanna said, "I need a drink after all that," and he'd taken her into the nearest pub and treated her as she had not been treated for many a long year. She told him all about the dream which had repeated itself seven times and forced William into action. After four double gins she

mentioned that she could also tell fortunes and offered to
tell his. The hand he extended was unremarkable, nothing
like her handsome young visitor's, so she fell back upon the
patter which first her mother and then she herself had re-
tailed to credulous maidservants at kitchen doors. To his
disappointment she did not mention marriage; he *looked*
young, but he might already be married, so she steered clear
of that, but she told him several pleasant things: he would
be very successful in whatever he did, enjoy good health
until he was forty, when he would have a brief illness, from
which he would recover and be healthier than ever and live
to a good old age.

The young man had a tenuous kind of arrangement with
a London paper to which he often forwarded items which
he considered might be of interest—and all too often were
not. Nobody, for instance, would have given him his half
guinea for reporting a girl drowned in a remote part of
South Norfolk. But this was different. MOTHER'S DREAMS
LEAD TO GRUESOME DISCOVERY *was* news. He duly relayed
it.

To begin with, the morbid sightseers were local people,
wanting to look at the pool in which Anna had lain for so
long. They were bad enough, but at least not cheeky. Some
pushed a little farther, wishing to see the cottage from
which Anna had walked out to her death, and William was
greatly angered, on the Thursday afternoon of the week after his gruesome discovery, to see a knot of women, four or
five, by his garden gate. It was his day for cleaning the window of Ellen's parlour, and to his annoyance at the intru-
sion was the further chagrin of being caught doing work
which a woman should do.

"Be off," he shouted, "or I'll have the law on you."

One woman said, "But we was only looking, Mr. Thorley."

"And how'd you like it if I stood gawping over your garden gate?"

They knew him. In the rural hierarchy the gamekeeper stood high. But there were others, strangers. And it was at them that the notice concerning the dog was directed. (It would deter no local; everybody knew that poor old Floss was old, almost toothless and stiff in her joints.) But he hoped it would scare off people like that saucy young man whom, earlier in the day, William had met by the pool, of whom he demanded, "Can't you read?"

"I am not trespassing. I wish to call upon Mrs. Thorley. Are her visitors supposed to arrive by balloon?"

To that there was no answer.

And there, in the filthy kitchen, Rosanna sat, acting the fool, telling lies, enjoying herself, getting drunk. Plenty of gin now, for the shrewd young reporter, to whom his colleagues went first, asking where was Monkswood and how did one get there, had told them: "Better take some gin with you; she's at her best when she's half slewed."

While their pact held—a limited amount of gin in return for leaving Ellen's things alone—he'd had some control; now he felt it safer to lock the parlour door.

So Rosanna and her visitors sat in the kitchen, and she explained its state by saying that since the terrible happening she'd just had no heart to do anything. "Reeling under the shock . . ." the fools wrote. "Immobilised by grief. . . ."

She'd had no shock; hadn't she said, "I knew it"? She'd felt no grief, shed no tear. She was having the time of her life. Telling other people the stories which once, to his displeasure, she had told Bill and Anna.

William realised that he had disliked her for a long time, deplored everything about her, while blaming himself; he'd lamed her, and then married her, and done his best to be patient, to conceal his shame. To bear his cross. Now he realised that he hated her.

For Rosanna and many like her, the time was ripe. Orthodox faith was declining; Darwin's *Origin of Species* had been a blow to the thoughtful. Into the vacuum of belief thus created, a number of unorthodox beliefs had edged themselves, and none more powerful than the one loosely designated spiritualism. It catered to mankind's immemorial need to believe that the dead were not dead. It imposed little discipline on its followers. Like most other faiths, it offered rewards for the few able to exploit the gullible many.

Dr. Johann Adolphus was one such. He was the son of a Russian baker and had escaped from a life of dull toil by running away and joining a troupe of jugglers. With them he had travelled most of the countries of Europe, acquiring tricks, a smattering of education, a working knowledge of several languages. He was genuinely interested in the occult, and his favourite city was Prague with its Street of the Sorcerers and its link with Dr. Dee. He had no marketable supernatural gifts himself unless an unusual ability to recognise them in others could count as such—no charlatan ever fooled him! He had come to London when he was thirty-five.

He had chosen his name, foreign enough to seem exotic and to explain his accent, but not beyond the capacity of the tongue-tied English to pronounce. His title was self-conferred; there was no law against it unless, falsely claiming to be qualified, one practised medicine.

Within five years he had established himself, and his tall house in a street just off Bloomsbury Square was the centre of a cult, nameless, amorphous, secretive, and varied in its activities. It had recently suffered a setback through the death of its genuine medium, who one summer evening in the darkened room had sat down and said, "This is the last. I am about to join *them*." She had done so. And those whose powers Dr. Adolphus had tested during the interim, eight women and two men, all had been frauds. Clever enough, but frauds.

He had read with avid interest this account of a humble woman in a remote place who had had genuine revelations,

by way of dreams, and who might have other psychic powers, not yet explored.

William Thorley met him and knew—by *his* extra sense—
that this was no gentleman. A coat with a fur lining and collar!

"There's warning about the dog," he said gruffly.

"Had it announced that a tiger was at large, it would not
have perturbed me," the dressed-up dummy said. "Animals
know when harm is intended. They have instincts which in
man atrophied long ago."

What kind of talk was that? Nothing which William
Thorley was equipped to deal with.

As soon as he saw her, Dr. Adolphus knew that Rosanna
was *real* in his sense of the word. A true psychic. She made
no outrageous claims. Asked whether Anna had *appeared*
to her, she said, "Only in dreams. Seven times." And had
she any other experiences which ordinary people would
call unusual? Yes, one or two. She repeated the story of the
house where the dead people lay. "And I can see auras."

"That is very interesting, Mrs. Thorley. What about
mine?"

"Very mixed. Like a rainbow. There's times when I can
see in hands, too. Not regular, just now and again."

"Try mine." He offered it, clean and plump on the filthy
table. (The dirty stinking kitchen did not affect him as it
had some other inquirers. The dead medium, for all her
gifts and despite the fact that she was paid well, had lived
in similar squalor. One could almost believe that they lived
on another plane, ignoring this one where any ordinary
woman could scrub and scour.)

"Well," Rosanna said, "you've come a long way. And
you're going a long way. There'll be a death, too. Not your
fault, but connected. Funny. A lot of money and
then"—she checked herself just in time, for who wanted to
be told such a thing—"rather less."

"Mrs. Thorley, would you be prepared to come to London and tell other people, a number of people, what you have just told me?"

"I never been there. I'd be lost. It ain't like a wood."

She knew about woods, the way moss grew on tree trunks on the north side, so you could always get your bearings.

"And I'd need some money." That was in keeping, too. Unworldly as such people were about such things as personal hygiene, comfortable or pleasant surroundings, they were concerned with money.

"You would not be lost, Mrs. Thorley. You would be given a very warm welcome. Look," he shook out from a netted purse four sovereigns, not too much to risk, and laid them on the table. "At Liverpool Street Station, take a cab and come to this address." From another pocket he produced his card, and she took it and stared.

"If you decide to come," he said.

"I must remember first. Because of Anna. Maybe tomorrow."

That was in keeping, too. Most mediumistic people, even the genuine ones, were prone to *non sequiturs.* Odd remarks which could be interpreted at will.

"I knew there was something. I kept trying and trying, and I just couldn't. But when that man gave me this, then I did remember. And I looked. *And I found it!*"

It was Charlie's card, which she had stuffed into a jam jar, holding several other things: two nails, a screw, a bit of wire, a length of string, a dried rabbit's paw. The jar had not been washed before it had become one of many receptacles on the cluttered dresser, and all its other contents had been dried in. Charlie's card, except for one corner, was unsoiled.

William Thorley took it with mixed feelings: his sense of justice—bad girl as Anna had obviously been, nobody should have killed her—and his desire to let the whole thing go, to think—Vengeance is mine, saith the Lord. And let there be no more fuss. In the end his desire to do what was right outweighed all else.

"I'll take it in to Bressford this afternoon," he said.

Dr. Sapey laid down his stethoscope. No obvious sign of disease, a regular, normal heartbeat. No fibulation, no murmur of a leaky valve. It *could* be angina pectoris. It could be indigestion.

"You say you have suffered three such attacks, Mr. Orford. Have they anything in common? Following a meal, for example?"

"None that I can see. The first, back in the summer, was during a meal. Naturally I blamed what I had eaten and dismissed it as acute indigestion. The second occurred just as I was starting breakfast, and the third while I was waiting for my dinner. I am not *worried* about myself, you understand. But it is an agonising pain, and I'd be grateful for anything that would relieve or, better still, prevent it."

Indigestion could be guarded against, in a way, by avoiding food likely to provoke it. Angina struck at will.

Dr. Sapey studied his patient, singularly healthy-looking for a man nearing his fifties. No surplus fat. A busy man—Dr. Sapey knew of Mr. Orford's many interests—but one who had plenty of fresh air, driving in an open gig or going on horseback from place to place.

"What palliatives have you tried?"

"Baking soda." Mr. Orford smiled slightly. "Brandy and soda. But the truth is, the pain is so short-lived and so paralysing that by the time I take either it is difficult to give credit."

Somewhat ahead of his time, Dr. Sapey considered the possibility of an emotional disturbance. Indigestion could account for a pain during a dinner or at the beginning of breakfast, if a few hasty mouthfuls had been taken, but an attack while waiting for one's dinner was unusual.

"Could worry or anxiety of any kind be a factor?"

"I hardly think so," Mr. Orford said, defying that copybook heading. "I am not a worrier."

"Well, if you will excuse me for a moment. . . ." Dr. Sapey rose and went into his little dispensary. There for a moment or two he continued his mental debate and then returned, carrying two glass phials, one blue. He sat down again.

"It may be simple indigestion, Mr. Orford. In which case one of these, sucked, or chewed and swallowed will give relief." He essayed a playful remark: "They are at least more portable than baking soda." He indicated the plain glass container which held some flat white lozengelike tablets. "But there is another possibility. I have no wish to alarm you, and indeed there is no reason for alarm. You may be suffering from agina pectoris; the brevity of the pain and the fact that it affects your left arm rather indicate the possibility. It is not, or hardly ever, fatal. No reason for worry at all. I should like you, at the first onset of pain, to swallow one of these with a drink of water." He indicated the blue phial. "Relief should be almost immediate. If not, we shall know, for upon indigestion these capsules will have no effect at all. In the meantime. . . ." Earnestly the young man advised against conditions which might provoke either ailment, realising as he did so that they had much in common, except that any undue physical exertion had seldom been known to cause dyspepsia. Rather the reverse.

The "Beware of the Dog" notice had not turned away that man in the fur coat who was prepared to face tigers, but it might do something to put others off, those who were not locals and therefore aware of old Floss' harmlessness, those who were not prepared to brave tigers. So when William Thorley set out on his afternoon errand and the old dog rattled her chain and looked at him hopefully, he decided to take her along just as far as the gate. She'd never had an ordinary leash, never needed one; in her good days a word was enough. So now William released the hook which was attached to her collar at one end and at the other to a staple on the kennel's side and let her free. With a view to tethering her to the gate, he carried the chain looped over his arm. He said, "You can come along. Heel!" Stiff-gaitedly, she followed—by scent rather than sight—the only god she knew. At the gate by the notice board he put an end to her brief freedom, fixing one end of the chain to her collar and the other to the only obvious stay, the latch of the gate. "Guard," he said, and stepped out into the road, where a man so obviously respectable as he was could be certain of a lift.

In the quiet cottage Rosanna sat and fought her own battle. To go or not to go. The four shining coins she had pushed out of sight under the clutter at the end of the table; it had been less the action of stealth than of slovenliness, just clear a bit of the table.

Four pounds; it would buy a lot of gin which William did not know about; she could sit here, gently rocking in the old chair, or she could rouse up and face London. She balanced things in her muddled mind, thought about what a sensation she had made at the inquest, thought about the long years during which William, always right, always righteous, had borne down on her, altering her very nature. She thought of London, of being welcomed, being fussed over for doing what she *could* do, for being what she *was*.

Rebellion, long quiescent in her, stirred again. She'd go. She'd show William. Show them all.

"Mr. Charles Orford." And two addresses, home and college. It established a link between the young man and the dead girl. It was evidence. Circumstantial, of course, but then in murder cases most evidence was of necessity circumstantial; few murders were committed in front of witnesses. And the time fitted. A springtime dalliance. Pregnancy. A return home, with an appeal for marriage, a threat of blackmail.

Steady on now, Gregson said to himself, don't go concocting stories! Give this little white card its *true* value. A reason for interviewing Mr. Charles Orford.

Mr. Orford was aware that things had changed when there were two of them, but his heart seemed to have adjusted itself to shocks. It went about its work steadily even when Gregson asked to see Charlie.

"I am sorry. My son is abroad, Inspector. He went aboard a P and O liner at Tilbury last Thursday. His destination uncertain: possibly Greece; possibly Egypt. He said he would decide at Marseilles."

Not running away because the dead girl had been dragged up.

"Were you aware that your son was acquainted with Anna Thorley?"

"I was not. In fact, I should be strongly inclined to doubt it. Had he the opportunity? Or time. I would not pretend that Charlie's every movement was known to us; but his vacations were pretty fully occupied, and we usually knew where he was and with whom."

Shock tactics! Gregson produced the little oblong of pasteboard.

The pain began.

"Excuse me a moment," Mr. Orford said. "I'm having a little trouble with my digestion." Deliberately, leisurely, he took out the blue phial, shook a transparent capsule into his hand, placed it in his mouth, and poured a little water from the carafe on the table. Rose and Edda had been pleased to know that he had after all decided to consult Dr. Sapey, who had diagnosed dyspepsia.

A test case, he thought to himself.

It worked, almost instantaneously. It was as though the

little thing had exploded, killing the pain, which this time had had no chance to apply the vise or send a shaft down his arm.

"Indubitably my son's card," he said, as though the brief interruption had never happened. "How did you come by it, Inspector?"

Gregson explained. Marsh quietly turned the pages of his notebook. Mr. Orford thought: Fool! I always knew that fundamentally he was a blockhead.

"*That*," he said, "is possible. It is the fashion nowadays to take an interest in what—shall we say the unfortunate? Sometimes misinterpreted, but I think that if my son spoke of a job for the girl, he meant just that. I would hardly call it an acquaintanceship."

Now that he was certain of his heart he felt sure of himself. Firm as rock and ready to withstand Gregson's next sly question.

"Conscious as you were of your son's whereabouts, Mr. Orford, would you know where he was on the evening of July nineteenth?"

"Were I in your profession, Inspector, I should have the gravest doubts about anyone who speaks for his own, leave alone others, three months almost away. But it so happens that I can. It was the day after Charlie's birthday. Most of his friends had departed; one stayed on; and to avoid the letdown feeling after a party, he and Charlie went to Wyck and spent an evening at the place now called, I believe, Peppo's. I have reason to remember it. On a former occasion—around Easter—they did the same thing and returned home in the same state. Shall we say somewhat inebriated? I helped Charlie's friend to bed. On the day after Charlie's birthday I was absent. Smitten down with the start of this trouble." He tapped his chest. "A wholly calamitous evening."

In his cautious, foresighted way, during those nights when the only consoling thought was accident, accident, and his hair had turned white and his shoulders had bowed under the weight of guilt, Mr. Orford had gone round his defences, preparing for what might never happen, but ready if it did. Offering nothing. Deep inside him the little boy from the Pike lurked. Never volunteer too much information.

"Calamitous?" Gregson asked.

"Quite calamitous. To begin with, I was late for an appointment, and I pride myself on punctuality. I was taking Stubbs, the manager of the brewery, out for dinner."

And, meaning no evil, just a bit of talk, a handing over to a girl who had earlier shown herself to be mercenary; it should only have taken half an hour at the very outside.

"My horse picked up a stone. I had to stop by the smithy. Then, as I say, I became indisposed and was obliged to spend the night at the Three Pigeons, and my daughter was obliged to help two intoxicated boys to bed."

Gregson shifted ground.

"Your son's call upon the dead girl's mother and his leaving the card may have a philanthropic reason. But from two other people we have information of Anna Thorley being seen in the company of a young gentleman."

"There are several in the neighbourhood," Mr. Orford said drily. He thought again: Thundering young ass!

"You have a photograph of him?" There were three photographs, silver-framed, on the desk, but their backs were towards Gregson. In silence Mr. Orford handed one over, and Gregson confronted a happy, handsome young face. Even the rigidity characteristic of all photographs had not affected young Orford's charm. He looked young to have had his twenty-first birthday, and Gregson asked, "When was this taken?"

"At Christmas. All three, with the frames, were my family's surprise present to me." His voice changed slightly. "And I must tell you, Inspector, that I have not the slightest intention of allowing you to hawk this around to your informants asking, 'Is this the young man you saw with Anna Thorley?' Inevitably the answer would be yes."

"We're clumsy at times," Gregson said, "but not quite as clumsy as that. We shall"—Mr. Orford noted that he did not say *should*—"offer it for identification with others as similar as possible."

"To that, naturally, I can have no objection." They were brave words, for where could even the police find similar pictures to this one, to Charlie *before* that fatal Easter vacation? Charlie looked different now, older, less radiantly happy. Oh, if only the whole sorry thing had never started!

Make the bold gesture. "I will lend it to you, if that is any help, Inspector. May I have it for a moment?" He pushed back the little silver clips, opened the blue velvet back and removed the photograph.

Charlie might be recognised, even in the end suspected. But Charlie had the alibi of innocence and also of circumstance; he had spent that evening at Peppo's, leaving home so late that next morning Rose had said that she thought that he and John Walinshaw had changed their minds after all and intended to dine at home. And although there was a growing radicalism creeping about, even a courtesy title like the Honourable still carried weight.

When they had gone, the blank frame stared at him. Rose was still there in the matching frame; she wore the meaningless smile, "Smile please!" but pretty. From the other, slightly larger frame, his daughters faced him. Louise at her best, flirting with the camera, Maude impassive, and Edda almost glaring, hating the whole procedure.

Charlie's photograph would be missed. Mr. Orford knocked the empty frame to the floor, and in the contrary way things had, the glass did not break. He hit it with a heavy paperweight, and it smashed, perhaps too thoroughly; he then bent the frame a little.

Across the dinner table he said, "I'm getting clumsy in

my old age. I've knocked over Charlie's photograph. The glass is broken and the frame rather bent."

"And the picture, Papa?" Edda, always one for essentials.

"Ruined, too, I am afraid. Scarred beyond repair."

"Never mind," Edda said. "Baxter has the plate; he can make you another."

And that was the thought which had made Mr. Orford *offer* the photograph. Not to have done so would have seemed obstructive, and Baxter would have supplied one at the command of the police.

William Thorley had not been absent long. He was a known and if not a popular figure, a respected one in the district and, less than half a mile from the main entrance to the wood, had been offered a lift into Bressford. The driver of the trap, a farmer, had evinced an understandable, if undesirable, curiosity, easily repelled by such phrases as "You know as much as I do" and "I don't want to talk about it."

"I'm going to the station," the farmer said. "Where shall I set you down?"

"The station'll suit me well. I want to look in on my boy."

He looked in and felt a pang of distress at Bill's haggard appearance. He looked as though he hadn't eaten a full meal or had a good night's sleep for a week. Moreover, Bill's manner wasn't very friendly. Because of the funeral, William supposed.

"You mustn't take it too much to heart, son. I was sorry enough—but ashamed. I'd brought her up as my own, given her my name. And now I have something that could put the police on the right track. *She* found this, this morning in a jam jar. I'm taking it to the police now, but I didn't want Snape to see me get off there." He showed Bill the little white card. And Bill looked worse than ever.

Then he proceeded to the police station, and, lucky again, got another lift in young MacDonald's milk float, where the

rattling cans and churns made chatter impossible. Young
MacDonald, who had been up since five in the morning,
was half asleep; so was the horse. Every now and then the
boy roused himself, just long enough to hit the horse and
say, "Get up," to which the horse responded by galloping
for a minute before relapsing into the plodding jog-trot
which had already served its masters over so many miles
and would do so over so many more.

"Here," William Thorley said. "And I'm very grateful to
you. Good night."

The gate, the dog attached to it, were not as he had left it.
Even in the fading light, his night-accustomed eyes saw
that immediately. Somebody, daft, morbid sightseer, had
opened the gate about six inches. Floss, told to guard, had
attempted to do so and got entangled in her chain. She lay
in a peculiar posture, whimpering. At the sight of him, her
master for twelve years, she stopped whimpering for a moment, made an attempt to wag her tail, tried to stand. Fell
over, with yelps of pain.

He disentangled her, leaving the chain hanging. Both
forelegs broken. Only one thing to do, and he well
equipped to do it. He had his gun.

"So I'm going to London, first thing tomorrow," Rosanna
said. There was something about her, long absent, of the
wild spirit which had been a challenge to him, long ago, the
thing with which he had been compelled to compromise.

"Oh, no, you ain't," William said. "I shan't allow it."

"You can't stop me," Rosanna said. "The gentleman this
morning give me the money." She showed it. "He said not
to bother about clothes, not to bother about anything. Ladies in London'd see to it all if I just took a cab." She wasn't
quite sure what a cab was. In her present elated mood she
was prepared to find out, and she visualised herself in crimson velvet.

The death of his old dog had affected William more than

he would have believed. Except where Ellen was concerned, he was not a sentimental man, and his job was not calculated to engender tender feelings about animals; but Floss had been a faithful old bitch, and her accident could be directly blamed on Rosanna. If she hadn't gone gabbing about her dreams, none of this would have happened. In fact, but for Rosanna's dreams Anna would still have been at the bottom of the pool. And it was certainly the jabber about dreams at the inquest which had attracted all this horrible fuss.

William Thorley had not lacked kind "friends" who had carefully cut out and passed on to him every printed reference to the case. Mainly lies. A lot about how Rosanna had been so fond of her daughter. That was a lie if ever there was one. Back in February, when Anna came home in such a poor way, Rosanna wouldn't even have taken her in but for him. Lies about dreams, lies about being able to see into the future, being able to tell fortunes. All the old didiki stuff. Lies about *him*, too. Implications that because Anna was only his stepdaughter, not his blood kin, he hadn't bothered about her disappearance, had taken no note of the dreams, until forced to it.

For once he had no appetite for his supper, the invariable bread and cheese, slapped down just anyhow on the corner of the table from which the clutter had been pushed a few inches. The way poor old Floss had tried to give him a wag of her tail, leant her head against him as he carried her, trusted him, up to the very minute when he had taken careful aim, stayed with him. At the same time he could visualise Rosanna in London, flaunting about, telling the truth about her dreams and lies about everything else.

"You can't stop me," she said again. "It's a free country. And it ain't as though you'd miss me. We ain't been company for years, and I never cooked to your liking."

He had tried to teach her once, patiently, resolutely hoping that the mistake of his life—all due to lust—might be redeemed. He'd shown her, to the best of his ability, how to cook, how to clean, how to mend.

He looked around the filthy kitchen and thought how glad he would be if only she would go away—but be quiet. He thought how much better it would have been if at the end of the first year, when failure was obvious, rows almost daily, she'd run away, and taken Anna with her. How much he—and Bill—would have been spared.

Her glance followed his, and she said, breaking out of the gin-purchased apathy, restored to the old mockery, "Yes. Once I'm gone you can make this place look like it did when your precious Ellen was alive." That was the last straw.

Coming in from shooting the old dog, he had propped his gun against the wall. It was within reach of his hand. Holding it by the barrel, he brought the butt crashing down like a club on her head. The first blow probably killed her, but he dealt others, to make certain.

Mr. Orford, by the pool, had been shocked and shaken, obliged to pull himself together and improvise as best as he could and hastily. With William Thorley it was different. The act itself had been on impulse, the result of accumulated strain, triggered off by a few incautious words. But it seemed almost as though he had known, had planned, prepared.

Earlier in the week, believing that despite everything, life must go on, routine be adhered to, he had lifted his main-crop potatoes. Soft, friable soil.

The thing was, he knew, to dig deep enough, down, down, down. Through the subsoil which no spade had ever touched. Down to the chalk with a few flints here and there. When he had reached a depth out of which he could not easily clamber, he fetched a ladder and dug deeper. The October moon, the hunter's moon, came to aid and to blanch the light of his lantern. And to aid his memory came the recollection of the time when he had tried to dig out a fox hole and struck what was indisputably the floor of a house, ages old, silted over and forgotten. With a good layer of chalk and flint, well rammed back into its former substance, he arranged the bricks of the broken wall which he had always intended to mend and never had time for. Some were mortared together still, in sections; loose ones he fitted together and stamped well down. Then he replaced the subsoil, stamping that, too, and then the black, well-tilled stuff, with—cunning touch—the withering, yellowing haulms of the potatoes scattered here and there.

The thick candle in the lantern guttered out, and the moon waned. He still had a lot to do, and he did it in the bleak light of morning. Like Mrs. Evans, he had belief in the virtue of soda, the ordinary washing kind, and by the time that full morning light came in at the window not a blood spot remained.

As Mr. Orford had surmised, it had not been easy for Gregson to match Charlie, but the photographer had been very helpful. When one of his pictures particularly pleased him, he would ask leave to exhibit a copy of it in his window as an advertisement, and he had a store of such works. The trouble was that men seemed to be photographed less often than women and that the camera tended to magnify any idiosyncrasy—especially loutishness. Then, while Gregson and Marsh compared and discarded, Mr. Baxter remembered the family photographs in the parlour: his eldest son, reckoned handsome, and his brother-in-law, taken just before he left for Canada. In the end they had six, all young, all clean-shaven, all with curly hair, all with amiable expressions and with some claim to toffishness.

"We'll try the parents first," Gregson said.

"My wife ain't here," William Thorley said. "She's gone off to London, and I'm having a bit of a cleanup. Bit of a bonfire, too. She's a hoarder, never throw anything out."

One thing she had hoarded, Gregson thought, had provided a firm clue which must, of course, be substantiated.

"You spoke to the young man that morning, Mr. Thorley.
Could you identify him from these?"

On the now bare and freshly scrubbed table Marsh laid
out the photographs, and William Thorley said, "I can't see
what this is all about. That card I took you yesterday identified him sure enough."

"All the same, if you would. . . ."

"Thass him," William said, without hesitation, putting a
finger on the photographer's brother-in-law, who had left,
smiling, for Canada two years ago and died there, which
was why his photograph was so precious and must be returned as soon as possible.

William Thorley had taken little note of Charlie, and anyway, the police knew, so why mess about? The whitewash
was already mixed and waiting to be applied.

"When do you expect your wife back?"

"Hard to say. Some fool come here, crazing her to go to
London and tell about dreams and such. I was against it,
and I said so. So she didn't tell me much. Just that she was
off."

"Do you know where she is?"

"No. The fellow who crazed her to go—I told you yesterday, it was his card made her remember the other one—he
was foreign. At least his name was. Naturally she took the
card with her. As to when she'll be back—when they're
tired of her up there, I reckon."

Mrs. Evans wouldn't like it, was an understatement. Mrs.
Evans was infuriated.

Lily, told not to be frightened and to take her time, pointed as unhesitatingly and as certainly to Charlie Orford as
William Thorley had done to the photographer's brother-in-
law.

"Thass him! I'd know him in a thousand."

"Why?"

"By the look. Something. I dunno. Sort of special. Up in the gig, with Anna, he had more of a smile, like. But no mistaking. Yes, thass him."

"Now," Mrs. Evans said, "I should like to know what this is all about."

"It wasn't me, ma'am. All I did was tell Mr. Harlow I'd seen Anna up in a gig. With a young gentleman. I didn't know he'd go and tell anybody."

"You will leave, at once, with a week's wages in lieu of notice. This is a boardinghouse, not a police station."

Lily burst into tears. No job in domestic service was easy, but she knew that she was better off than thousands of her kind in one-servant households. Mrs. Evans pulled her weight of the load, rose early, made the first pot of tea, brought a cup to Lily, saying, "Here's your tea, Lily. Time to wake up." Mrs. Evans did the shopping and the bulk of the cooking. Lily knew dozens of girls who in similar-sized houses, occupied by one family, were expected to do everything: cooking, shopping, cleaning, tidying up after the mistress and the daughters of the house.

So she wept. And said again, "It wasn't me, ma'am. It was Mr. Harlow."

"That will do. I will deal with Mr. Harlow."

Mrs. Evans could afford to dispense thus summarily with Lily's services. An advertisement in the Bressford *Daily* would bring her at least ten applicants. As for Mr. Harlow, she need not advertise at all. There was a waiting list.

"As from Saturday, I shall require your room, Mr. Harlow."

It was a ritual phrase, and during his long residence here he had known it to be addressed to a few people. He was stunned.

"Why? Why, what have I done, Mrs. Evans?"

"You allowed your desire to draw attention to yourself to

override your consideration for the good name of this house."

"I only did my duty as I saw it."

"I hope that will be a consolation, Mr. Harlow," Mrs. Evans said. "I believe Mrs. Harris has a vacant room."

"Yes, that's him," the landlord of the Brewers' Arms said. "To the very life." He selected Charlie, too. "I told you he looked a bit, well, too nice to be out with a tart."

Mrs. Pryke, whose opinion had not been asked for on that rain-drenched evening she had been in the background, had, without being invited to look, peeped over the husband's shoulder. After a bit she said, "I didn't see him then. But I've seen him since. Right here, in the public. And very upset, I did feel sorry for him."

"When, Mrs. Pryke? Could you give even an approximate date?"

She couldn't. Once her days had been governed by natural seasons: primroses, bluebells, wild roses, blackberries, the first cuckoo's call, the stuttering farewell. Now she moved to a differing rhythm: payday—busy and sometimes rowdy—middle-week day, when customers said, "On the slate, please." About the only time most of them said please. Days when empty casks were wheeled away and full ones delivered. She'd tried at one time, years ago, to keep up with the seasons by making a bit of a garden, but Josh had argued, with justification, that the space could be better employed as standing room for vehicles and horses. She'd tried a window box, with disappointing results.

"It was summer," she said, at last. "I know because I was knitting this." She touched the garment she wore over her dress, a modified kind of cape. In cold weather they always kept a good fire in the bar, but with the door always opening and shutting draughts were inevitable, and a shawl hampered one's movements and tended to catch on things, so she wore what was called a hug-me-tight, a woollen protection for neck and shoulders, close-buttoned at the waist.

"Tell me about it," Gregson said.

"Well, the bar was empty, and he went and sat over there, and he looked real upset. Nearly as though he'd cry. And he did a lot of drinking, one brandy and soda after another. I got a mite worried and got him some food, but he hardly touched it."

"You are quite positive that this is the young man. Not this one?"

He drew her attention to the photograph William Thorley had selected.

"All the difference in the world. I mean apart from the looks."

Ignoring this illogicality, Gregson said, "What time of day would it be?"

"Afternoon. The bar was empty, except for him."

The afternoon preceding the crime? Drinking to whip up Dutch courage.

"And apart from the fact that it was summer, you can give no indication of the date, Mrs. Pryke?"

"No. I'm sorry, Inspector."

Steve Pepper was a Cockney and sharp-witted enough to make a pretence of earnest scrutiny of each photograph before saying, "No, Inspector, never saw none of them in my life."

"You are certain?"

"In a plice like this, you *do* notice. 'Ave to. I 'ave me regulars, of course. Anybody new I tike a good look at. Exercise discretion, you might sye."

He had recognised Charlie instantly and wondered about the other one. And he remembered the evening of their visit because that had been real trouble. Of which this might well be the echo.

Despite the fact that Peppo's had a reputation as a rather disorderly place, with all sorts of goings-on, Pepper had the establishment well in hand. He had the cauliflower ears, the broken and badly set nose, the lumpy jaw of an old prizefighter, and few people ever tried conclusions with him. Rows were inevitable where drinking and gambling met, but they seldom came to anything. "I ain't looking for trouble. Are you?" was enough to quell most people.

He had a mixed clientele: people who came simply in order to have a good meal, gracefully served in romantic surroundings, people who came to gamble and who, on the whole, took their losses in the right spirit; other people who came to enjoy the pleasures of the upstairs rooms. On the whole, people of little sophistication; on the whole, out on the sly. Easy to manage.

July 19 had been different. There'd been a real row, but real nobs involved, and they were not so easily quelled. The slightly shorter one, with the big nose—the one who had first detected the fact that the roulette wheel was rigged— had not been in the least intimidated. Asked if he wanted trouble, he had said, "I'm ready for it," and he looked ready, a useful man with his maulers. *This* one, more of a gentleman, had intervened and said, "Oh, come on, John. What does it matter? I'll pay." But that was not the end of it. One of the upstairs girls, sister to the croupier, had accused him of being clumsy and stupid, he'd hit her, and she'd knifed him. All the other Italians—excitable lot—had joined in, taking sides. The kitchen was a shambles. He'd sacked the lot of them, put "Closed for redecoration. Reopen next Friday," on the door, and gone off to Soho to recruit more staff. He remembered July 19, all right, but he said, "No. No. None of 'em was ever 'ere."

"What I am asking about, Mr. Pepper, in no way reflects upon your establishment." Gregson was patience personified.

"I should 'ope not!"

"I am merely trying to ascertain the whereabouts of one of these young men. The one who claims. . . ." No, that was not true. "Who is said to have spent an evening here, on a given date."

"Then I can't 'elp you? can I?—never 'aving set eyes on one of 'em till this minute."

For reasons not dissimilar to Mrs. Evans', Mr. Pepper was not pleased to have police on his premises. Get the place a bad name in no time.

"If you can't take me word, take me oath. I swear on me old mother's grive."

Safe enough. His mother was hale and hearty and greatly enjoying life on the regular money he sent her. Good for twenty years.

For Gregson the oath had validity. Men like Pepper, respectful of few things, generally did respect their mothers. At a certain level the mother was the provider. Fathers—so called—came and went; child and sire could pass in the street, unknowing; mother, though rough of tongue and sometimes hand, was the bulwark. Only children with really bad mothers or disabled or dead ones found their way into the workhouse or the charitable institutions.

"It wouldn't have been much of an alibi, anyway, sir," Marsh said. "I wouldn't trust him to tell me the time of day."

They were under a kind of pressure now. Not from their masters—the magistrates and the chief constable, all sensible men who did not expect miracles—but from the idiot press, who but for Rosanna's dreams would never have paid any attention to the case. Gregson had no need of friends to send him cuttings; he could read it firsthand, sly innuendoes: What are the police doing? Nothing libellous, just nasty with a hint, framed as a question: Whether had Anna Thorley been less humble would her killer still be at large? The press and the people it influenced thought that all a policeman had to do was go out and arrest somebody, clap on the handcuffs, and go home to tea.

Suspicion certainly pointed to Charlie Orford, and Gregson felt that given a chance to question him and to watch his demeanour under the questioning, he would feel himself on firmer ground.

Bill Thorley at least was handy and might provide one further crumb of information—when shown that little white card.

Bill had not got over his shock and his loss as Effie had heartlessly predicted, saying, "After all, it isn't as though you ever saw her!" And Effie lost no opportunity of rubbing in the salt. She wouldn't go near any shop; she couldn't bear being stared at. She had tried the butcher's once, and there'd been sudden dead silence as she went in, so she'd walked out again without buying anything. Bill must do all the shopping. And what about the girls going to school? Children could be very cruel, and after all, Anna, not only murdered but pregnant, had been their *aunt!* On the second Sunday, mindful of her obligations, she had gone to early mass; fewer people to gape at her, she said. Neighbours who had tried to act as they would have done to anyone suffering an ordinary bereavement, bringing little gifts, evoked hatred rather than gratitude. They were simply nosey parkers, trying to find out a bit more about Anna. "If we're ever going to live an ordinary life again," Effie said, "we shall have to move to some place where our name doesn't stink."

Through all his years in Bressford Bill Thorley had kept his country-boy colour. It had drained away during Gregson's first visit, when the terrible news was broken, and it had not returned. He was now the colour of tallow, and he had lost flesh. For one thing he had no appetite, and for another the future worried him. It was easy enough for Effie to speak of making a move; he knew that jobs like his were not easily come by. Plenty of room at the bottom, little at the top.

"Mr. Thorley," Gregson said, "we now have positive proof of your sister's association with Mr. Charles Orford."

He exhibited the card and spoke of the two people who had seen the pair together.

Bill licked his dry lips with a dry tongue and said, "If you say so, I suppose it's true. But I didn't know about it."

"Tell me again what you *do* know."

People often contradicted themselves when required to repeat.

Bill stuck to his story exactly. Anna's homecoming in February, ill, with a terrible cough; her recovery and return to London. His seeing her off at the station. Her next homecoming, when he hadn't even seen her.

He omitted the vital information, all that supported Gregson's talk about an association. For one thing his good character was now more important than ever, when, urged by Effie, he was seeking a new job. He couldn't hope even for a post of assistant counter hand without impeccable references.

Nothing new, nothing gained, Gregson thought as he went away. Bill Thorley sat in the office-*cum*-storeroom and propped his haggard face in his hands. His mind whirled madly. A new job, at best only halfway up the ladder, in a new place, with Effie, with Mary and Margaret, miniature Effies in the making. Giving up the trim little house in the Terraces and his garden and his good neighbours. He had no drinking pals—they could be picked up in any pub—but he had neighbours, men who had simply said, "I'm sorry about your trouble, Bill. Could you lend me a spade? Mine came apart yesterday; it'll need a new handle."

No more of that. He surveyed a grim future and shrank from it.

He lacked what his father enjoyed, a complete, if demented, faith in the approval and support of God Almighty. William's conscience had not given him a pang; he had done what was to be done, what he had been inspired to do. Whitewashing the kitchen, unlocking the parlour door, and watering the aspidistra, he enjoyed a kind of happiness, unknown for many years. The cottage smelt clean and fresh. *If thine eye offend thee, pluck it out.* And he had done just that. The wonder was that he hadn't done it before.

Dr. Adolphus had made much of his find, giving Rosanna the kind of advance publicity ordinarily accorded only to circuses. He managed to convey that in seeking out this natural, unspoilt medium, he had been guided by something less mundane than a few lines in a daily paper. This was all the more convincing to his circle because he half believed it himself. He had been inspired to make a tiresome journey in order to see the woman, had immediately recognised her gifts, offered her a chance to use them. Something more than mere chance seemed to be involved.

Enemies of spiritualism often hinted that only a few credulous old women believed in it, but this was far from true. The circle which met in a softly lighted house, with the painted or embroidered mystic symbols on the walls, included several men, the majority of them recently bereaved by the death of a wife, child, or mother, but some interested for less personal reasons. There was a well-known archaeologist who had had strange experiences while excavating a tomb in Egypt; there was a genuine, qualified doctor who had become converted to faith healing; there was the son of an earl—a second son—destined for the family living who, halfway through his theology studies at Oxford, had suffered a severe attack of agnosticism which had left him like a ship without helm or compass.

Dr. Adolphus had explained that Rosanna was a woman of humble background, possibly with some gypsy or other exotic blood in her, that she was completely unsophisticated, had never lived in a town, had been discovered by him in the middle of a remote wood. Ladies of the circle competed with one another in offers to house her, provide clothes. When she arrived. Which she did not. She'd said,

"Perhaps tomorrow," but there was tomorrow and tomorrow, and still no Rosanna.

It was puzzling. She'd seemed willing enough—a trifle scared of a big city, but he'd told her exactly what to do. She could have had very little to pack. No family, except the husband of whom she had spoken with little fondness, to arrange for. On the third day Dr. Adolphus sent a telegram, a prepaid one which must bring an answer.

In the now clean and orderly cottage, William Thorley was undergoing an experience which would have interested the more perceptive members of Dr. Adolphus' circle. Every day, as the place more resembled the home that Ellen had made it, Ellen seemed to come nearer, to be keeping him company again. He was anything but a fanciful man, but often as he shifted a shining plate, a clean cup to another place on the dresser, more as they had once been in the old days, Ellen seemed to be there. It was as though first his grief and then his lustful, disastrous association with Rosanna had stood between him and Ellen, and with the doing away of the intruder and of the mess she made, he had removed a barrier.

Once, sitting lonely at his supper table, eating the kind of meal which Ellen had made and which he had tried to show Rosanna how to make and, failing in that, had often made himself when the children were young and needed good nourishment, and the silence bore in, a voice, Ellen's voice, sounded in his head. *You need a new dog, a puppy.* And the very next morning one of his farmer friends had said, "My old bitch did it again! We reckoned she was past it, but she wasn't. As nice a litter as you ever saw. And homes to be found for them all. You know anybody want a good dog to a good home?"

Then the telegram arrived, giving him less of a jerk than it would have done most country people to whom this new form of communication still meant death or disaster. He had had telegrams before, cancelling a Saturday shoot or ordering this or that. He did not even need to take the pencil which the telegram boy proffered. He wrote, with his own pencil, in clear print, "R. Thorley left for London morning after your visit."

So she had come, as promised, tomorrow, and gone and got herself lost, Dr. Adolphus concluded. And with his circle all so expectant, so hopeful, so prepared, he must do something. Very slightly he blamed himself; he should have forced from her a given date and time and met her himself. Had she been younger, more attractive, Dr. Adolphus would have been more careful, knowing, as everybody did, the danger of a young girl, up from the country, getting off the train, bewildered, lost, ready to accept the first friendly gesture. It had not occurred to him that a fat, middle-aged, poorly dressed woman without luggage would have run any danger beyond that of being overcharged by the cabdriver. And for that she was adequately provided. Still, in a way, he had been remiss and must try to amend.

Liverpool Street Station, like all the other big termini, had its parasites, beggars, prostitutes, tricksters of every variety, as well as poor, honest men who, seeing a cab load, would run behind it, keeping pace with the horse, ready to arrive at the destination, "Help with the luggage, sir?" and glad of sixpence when the heavy trunks, the valises had been carried up three flights of stairs. Somebody might have noticed a woman with very black hair, very black eyes looking round, lost. He'd said, "Take a cab." It now occurred to him that perhaps that very ordinary word had meant nothing to the woman in the middle of a wild wood.

He went to Liverpool Street Station and began to ask about. Fruitlessly. No porter, no beggar boy, no flower seller, no cab chaser, and no prostitute had a word of information to offer. If Rosanna Thorley had ever been here, she had left no mark. And then it happened. Turning away, defeated, he came face to face with a woman so like Mrs. Thorley that for a moment he thought that she had come to London after all and spent what remained of his money on gaudy, fourth-hand clothing, cheap cosmetics, cheap scent. He realised his mistake before she spoke; Rosanna was lame and crooked and did not wear the stamp of hunger and anxiety this woman did.

Aware of his stare, of his interest, the poor drab perked up and said with a horrible attempt at gay familiarity, "I'm what you're looking for, ain't I, dearie?" Her voice, though a trifle hoarse, was not unpleasant.

"Yes," he said. He summoned a hansom by lifting his hand, hustled the woman inside, and told the cabbie to drive to Hyde Park and there just drive round and round until given further orders. "No need to hurry," he said. A nice job, the cabdriver reflected, easy on the horse. A practical, not a humane, thought; the horse had already been on the job for twelve hours, eight of them with another driver, and on second shifts horses did tend to fall down. Very bothersome. Dr. Adolphus' clothes, which had not impressed William Thorley, had impressed the cabdriver. His accent, too. A foreign gentleman and bloody ignorant; otherwise he'd have known that there were far more attractive women to be picked up than that old cow and places where *it* could be done far more easily and comfortably than in a cab. But the great thing about foreigners was that they didn't understand about money. Easily diddled and dead scared of the police. You could end any argument about a fare by saying, "All right then, we'll call a bobby. He'll settle it."

This little amble round and round the park was going to cost that foreign gentleman ten bob.

Inside the cab, Dr. Adolphus explained what he wanted—a substitute for a woman who had failed him. And again he seemed to be under guidance, for the woman understood instantly. "Like the Fox girls," she said, "and that man called Home and a boy, Rashbrooke."

"You are well informed."

"I was interested once. I could do it—tell fortunes, I mean. All that kind of thing. Stare at a candle and go off into a trance. It'd just happen, like it or not. But you can overdo it. I did, nearly as soon as I tried to make a business of it. I'd got married, you see, two children to keep and my husband gone off with a bareback circus rider. Lola Montez her name was, and she ended up with a king. Bavaria. She's dead now. . . . I kept going, though what gift I ever had was gone. But I still had some looks, and I went on the stage. But once you've struck forty, you're done there, too. Nothing left but to take to the streets. Funny," she said, "this evening I didn't feel like getting up at all. I just thought: Lay down and die, who'd care? But death ain't all that easy. In the end you get up—if you can—and make a fight for it. Life, I mean. Just another day, another meal, another night. Born in us, I reckon."

Such a meeting could hardly be looked upon as fortuitous. The woman was accommodating as well as knowledgeable. "Would you mind adopting the name of Mrs. Rosanna?" Dr. Adolphus asked.

"Lord love you, no. I've had half a dozen in my time."

He described the most important members of the circle, offering little guidelines about their characters and their desires. In this he was not actuated by a wholehearted design to cheat, just so that she should know something of them and be a success from the first. She had the sharp wits of the street-bred and missed nothing. It occurred to him that she'd be easier to manage and to handle than the gamekeeper's wife. He spoke of the hospitality that had been offered and said, "I have decided to start with Mrs. Frisby. She is well-to-do and has a very comfortable establishment in Soho Square."

To this the woman responded by mentioning a matter that had been troubling him a little. She said, "I don't look right, do I? Not for a woman straight up from the country. Don't you worry. Just tell him Brewer Street, near the kosher butcher's. It won't take a minute."

Liverpool Street, Hyde Park, a long slow drive round, now Brewer Street and wait. Add half a crown to the ten bob, the cabman thought, as the tired horse let its head droop and rested one leg after another.

It took slightly more than the promised minute, just long enough for Dr. Adolphus to wonder if yet another promising subject had slipped away. Then the woman emerged again from the little opening into which she had vanished, and she was transformed. Gone all the pitiable gaudy clothes, the weary feathers, the face paint. A simple countrywoman to the life.

"Soho Square, now. The big houses in the corner," Dr. Adolphus said. The cabman had had some peculiar customers in his time, but this was an odd lot. So odd as to arouse suspicion, and when at the corner house, brightly lighted, plainly the home of somebody rich, the gentleman alighted too and said, "Wait, please," the cabbie protested. Dr. Adolphus gave him a sovereign and said, "If you care to wait, you can drive me to my home. If not, it is only a step to Oxford Street."

The cab waited, and not for too long. Just long enough for Dr. Adolphus to say, "Mrs. Frisby, this is Mrs. Rosanna. She has had a long journey and is tired. I would suggest bed and a light supper on a tray."

Mrs. Frisby was flattered to have been chosen. The woman who had so unwillingly risen, dressed herself, painted her face, and made for the nearest market, where more attractive wares were on offer, was conducted to a luxurious bedroom, sank down into a soft feather bed, against soft down-filled pillows, was served with a light supper, quite the best meal she had ever enjoyed, even in her good days.

Three pounds a week guaranteed, with more to come if this last enterprise was successful. It might, of course, like everything else she had tried, end in catastrophe, but in the meantime it was wonderful. Breakfast in bed tomorrow morning, and did she prefer tea or coffee, eggs boiled, fried, poached, or scrambled? If nothing else came of it, it was a rest and a change.

Dr. Adolphus climbed into the cab again and said, "Bloomsbury Square. You need not turn in; a little walk will be beneficial." And at the corner, half a sovereign, which meant that the man and the horse could go home, not bothering about the turning out of the theatres.

Everybody was very happy, except, for one moment, in the middle of the night when the woman who had agreed to impersonate Rosanna Thorley had a disagreeable dream. Muddled. A girl coming up out of some water, all dripping and saying, "It wasn't Charlie! It wasn't Charlie!"

Without context the dream and the words were meaningless; the woman attributed it to rich, unaccustomed food, turned over, and snuggled down into comfort and sleep again.

The agent of the Security Insurance Company had been established in Wyck-on-Rad long enough to know that he hated the place and that the job which had sounded so promising looked like being a failure. "Virgin soil, Forbes," his superior had told him. "No rival nearer than Bressford." The company had hired the little house, the parlour of which was to be his office, and paid the rent and the rates; he was paid eighteen shillings a week and a percentage which sounded all right, a move up from twenty-five shillings a week, no percentage, and pay your own overheads. But business, like the seasons, like the people in this outlandish place, was slow. Anybody who wanted insurance had it already with the rival firm in Bressford. Virgin soil proved to be the same old deadly round, coaxing people to pay twopence a week to ensure themselves of a decent funeral. They called it "paying in for death." Mr. Forbes was worse off than the workers in the brewery or the bacon factory who could get along with one decent suit which, worn only on occasions, lasted forever. He had to look spruce every day, all the time. He was disillusioned, almost despairing, when suddenly his luck appeared to change. A man who owned and hired out threshing tackle actually came to the office and insured his whole outfit: threshing machines, steam engines, and the men who worked them. A percentage on that deal was more than a quarter's salary.

And now here was a man wishing to insure his life for three thousand pounds. An ideal subject: a man still under thirty and bringing with him—sensible fellow—a certificate affirming that he suffered from no disease. A man in a good job, too. And he had come from Bressford! It was like a sunrise. Security was actually stealing custom from the older-established firm.

"And it starts now?" Bill asked.

"Mr. Thorley, once these papers are signed and the first premium paid, you could walk out of this office and be run over in the street and die happy in the knowledge that your wife and children would be secure. Security means exactly what it says." Had Bill paid his first instalment by cheque, the policy would not have been effective until the cheque was cleared, but he put down ready cash.

"And may I ask you one question, Mr. Thorley," the agent asked when the transaction was completed. "Why did you choose Security rather than Coverall?"

"The terms seemed better," Bill said. After all, what was a lie? When he'd been acting, living a lie, ever since the day Anna had been found. He'd come to Wyck-on-Rad to do this bit of business because he was known in Bressford, and Coverall's office was in the High Street. He could have been seen.

Summed up on a single sheet of paper, the evidence against Charlie seemed conclusive at one moment, contemptible the next. One moment it seemed to justify Charlie's recall for questioning at least; the next it looked as though such positive action might prove to be ridiculous. The most damning thing was the bag from the bank, and even about that one could not be absolutely certain; it could, like the one used as a jelly strainer, have passed through other hands. Even in the short time that had elapsed between its issue and its final use.

Gregson sat brooding, telling himself that Charlie Orford was guilty as hell, telling himself that Charlie was a suspect in default of another. And all the time knowing that he couldn't afford a slip in either direction.

It was at this point that Bill Thorley arrived asking to speak to Inspector Gregson, in private.

He began by saying that he had told a lie and had come to make a clean breast of it. Then he told his tale, every detail. His own borrowing, his actions as a go-between, everything. "I'm to blame for it all," he said. "I was in such a fix. I stood there by the pool, and I said to Anna, 'If you don't give way, I might as well chuck myself in there and have done with it.'"

Gregson listened without interrupting; then he asked about the letters.

"Did they contain definite promises of marriage?"

"So Anna said. If they didn't, why should Mr. Orford think they were worth a hundred pounds? And the minute they were in his hands burn them on the cook-shed stove?"

"You saw him do that?"

"I saw the flakes; you know how burnt paper'll go. Besides, I saw him post the other letter, the one he told Anna

what to write—at least he told me what to tell her to. If marriage hadn't been on the cards, I mean there'd have been no
call for her to write that way. 'S funny," Bill said miserably,
"but I thought then—Mr. Charlie'll be upset to get that. I
felt sorry for him *then*. Once you loved Anna, she took a bit
of getting over. All I did was try to help out a bit; then I got
so trapped I had to crucify Anna *and* Mr. Charlie. Even
now I feel like Judas, but I thought it ought to be said. I
mean, everybody saying Anna was so loose. It's different if
marriage is *promised*, as in this case it was."

There was, Gregson knew, all the difference in the world.
At a certain social level to a bride who was pregnant, to the
baby born too soon after the nuptials no obloquy was attached. The loose woman was one who lifted her petticoats
without any thought of marriage.

"You have acted rightly in telling me this, Mr. Thorley,"
Gregson said. "You should have told me before, but we
won't go into that." He felt sorry for the man down whose
slightly hollowed temple a single thread of sweat wormed
its way. But the pity was peripheral, for he was thinking
that this tale greatly supported the evidence against Charlie
Orford and that it had been made in private, no witness, no
statement. Gregson knew that the force of which he was a
member was open to more than the open hostility of the
slum-dwellers; there was plenty of other, subtler opposition. The very people who were now yelping because Anna
Thorley's killer had not been arrested would be the first to
yelp on another note if he took any action which in part
took motive from a private interview such as he had just
held with this rather unstable fellow who, when faced with
the *results* of his talking—and they would include, at the
very least, the loss of his job—might well recant and deny
that he had ever said anything of the sort, that the inspector
had put words into his mouth, threatened him, or even
bribed him.

"It would be helpful, Mr. Thorley, if you would repeat your statement. Sergeant Marsh could then note down salient points."

There was also the consideration that unreliable people contradicted themselves when asked to repeat.

Bill Thorley took out his watch and looked at it. A pang. It was a present from Mr. Orford at the end of ten years' service, and here he was. . . . But he was beyond such considerations now.

"I ought to get back to the stores," he said. "Friday— some people get paid, and it's busy. I'd better write it myself; it'll be quicker."

"Just a plain statement of facts will do," Gregson said. So, under Gregson's mildly sympathetic eye and Marsh's impartial one, Bill wrote and signed what he considered to be Anna's vindication. What else it was mattered only to him. Walking the short distance between police station and store, in the crisping evening air, he had an astonishing sense of freedom. He'd shed his burden. He was his own man once more.

"And what do you make of that, Tom?"

"I'd say it strengthens the case against Mr. Charles Orford. But, sir, I doubt whether it can ever be brought home. He may be in Greece or Egypt, and he'd be safe if he'd killed six people. I've been looking it up; the only country with which at this minute we have a mutual extradition treaty is Brazil."

"Full marks for research, Tom. I did not know that. But it might be worked round. I'll give it some thought."

In the store, business as usual. With a hand as steady and as delicate as it had ever been Bill sliced the cooked meats; with an eye as sharp as usual he surveyed his little domain. "Pryke, push the stale rolls a bit nearer the corned beef. Make a *cheap* corner. With some of those pickles nobody took to. What we don't shift tonight, we'll shift tomorrow. And I think a new bag of potatoes. Pete could begin to weigh them out; two pounds to a bag—it'll all help tomorrow."

Bustling about, he cut six ounces of the best ham and folded it in paper.

"I'll just run home with this, Pryke. They'll be waiting for their supper. I shan't be ten minutes."

"Take your time, sir," Pryke said. He and everybody else behind the counter, as well as a good many on the other side, felt sorry for Mr. Thorley, decent man that he was, and for his wife, who had taken the whole thing so hard that she now never did any shopping. And really no relation to him at all. Some amateur genealogist had worked the whole thing out—your stepmother's daughter, sired by another man, couldn't possibly be regarded as blood kin. No relationship at all. (Had this correct pontification been made earlier, Bill's life and Anna's would have taken another course.)

Pryke liked being left in charge; it was a preparation for the managership which must surely come—given time. But on this evening he knew that his reign would be brief because if Mr. Thorley said ten minutes, he meant ten minutes and was about to take the shortcut.

Coming into Bressford, the railroad ran high over an arch. But under the arch the road, far older than the railway, took two curves, wasteful of time. So despite the notices, DANGER; BEWARE OF TRAINS; PRIVATE, TRESPASSERS WILL BE PROSECUTED, a lot of people took the shortcut. The well-worn tracks on each bank proved that. The proper road, under the arch and round the curves, was mainly used by women with perambulators, or with shopping baskets, or with dignity to consider.

At first the up train from Radmouth was a vibration rather than a noise. He had time to think and to be glad that soon it would all be over, this life throughout which he had always done his best and gained so little—except in a material sphere. He'd loved Anna, who had come into his home as his little sister and always been so regarded. He'd married Effie, who'd never looked on him as more than a provider, a father of children. Effie'd be all right; she'd have the insurance money; she could sell the house, move away, marry again, most likely. And he would be dead before Mr. Orford discovered that he had been robbed, this time of a larger sum and in a less simple manner. He would be dead before Mr. Orford discovered that he'd betrayed Mr. Charlie. Death was the refuge of the defeated.

The vibration became a rumble, and then, just rounding the curve, the train became visible. It was lights and a red glow. Then, as he flung himself forward, it was Anna, smiling amongst the bluebells.

"Ran straight into me," the shaken engine driver said. He always kept a sharp lookout for obstacles, for stray animals, on the line. But this was no obstacle; it was some bloody fool taking the shortcut, misjudging the train's speed and his own.

He was even more shaken when he realised that the dead man was his own good neighbour, a lender of garden tools, the man who, when he himself was, as this evening, on the night run, would call in on his way from work, "Everything all right, Mrs. Wicks?"

"God Himself couldn't've saved him," he said. "Ran straight into me."

Rose had taken Mr. Orford's indigestion seriously and on this Saturday, although Lord Chelsworth and Algie Hepworth were expected to dinner, had ordered food unlikely to disturb the weakest stomach. Clear soup, really a sophisticated version of that well-known restorative beef tea; fillets of sole, poached, not fried, and served with an innocuous cream sauce; roast partridges, young and tender; and one of Edith's simple sweets, amber apple.

Over the sunny skies of the postengagements period a few small clouds had drifted. Charlie's absence, and the uncertainty of whether he would decide upon Greece or Egypt. Louise's jealousy because her marriage settlement was less than Edda's. With his usual frankness, Edwin had told both girls exactly what he had arranged; Louise was to have five thousand pounds and a quarter share of his interest in Inangula. Louise had complained first to her mother, who had said, "Papa knows best," but had secretly sympathised, thinking not that Louise had too little, but Edda too much. The Wyck-on-Rad brewery was no mean gift! Privately, Rose decided that she would do her best to make up to her favourite daughter. A woman's jewels were her own, and one day Rose would leave hers to Louise. One day. A distant day. Rose was as incapable of facing the idea of her own extinction as she was of facing the ravages of age.

Then one day Louise had been indiscreet at table. Edwin had not lost his temper—he never did—but he had spoken with cold incisiveness.

"My dear, if my arrangements are displeasing, they can be changed. Simon once professed himself willing to take Edda in her petticoat. I have no doubt that Algie would be equally unmercenary."

Edda blushed bright red, and Louise turned pale; but she stuck to her point.

"The Talbots already have so much."

"They own more land, yes; but all on the wrong side of the river, poor acres. If Simon raised his rents by so little as five pounds a year, most of his tenants would be ruined, the farms left derelict. Algie will inherit a smaller estate, but compact and profitable. You will be very comfortable."

"But Edda will be *grand!*"

"Edda," Mr. Orford said, "will carry a tumbledown castle on her back to the end of her days."

With more percipience than anybody would have given her credit for, Rose thought: Yes, that was always his way; he likes old things. This house, for instance. And it pleases him to think that his horrid smelly brewery will help support Bressford Castle.

Rose still felt more at ease in the velvet-hung bebobbled room that was her very own than in the drawing room which conspicuously lacked the quality of cosiness, and since Simon and Algie were now practically part of the family, sherry was being drunk as usual on informal occasions in Mamma's room. Algie had brought along another young—a very young—very shy young man. "I don't know whether you have met Mr. Tony Babcock, Mrs. Orford." Rose, murmuring pleasant words, thought that Edwin would not be pleased at this. "I told him you kept open house and that we'd be welcome. He's house-trained—he was my fag at Eton." The boy blushed wildly; but he smiled, and his smile was agreeable. Rose thought the inevitable maternal thought: Just the right age for Maude, if only Edwin can overcome his prejudices. After all, one cannot hold the boy responsible for his father.

Papa was a trifle late, very late considering that this was Saturday, when as a rule he came home for lunch and then rested from business. A stroll around the farms perhaps, no more. But today he had sent a message that he would not be home for lunch; something had cropped up.

When he did arrive and looked in, saying, "Sorry to be late. I'll be with you in a minute," only Edda noticed that something was wrong *before* Tony Babcock was named. He looked tired and sad. She always knew.

And then, before he could join them, the bell rang, and the parlourmaid said, "It's the police again, madam."

Edda, not Rose, said, "Show them into the library." She held her skirts high and took the stairs two at a time, gave the peremptory little tap on the dressing-room door.

"It's that Gregson man again," she said. "Shall I send him away? Even you surely cannot be expected to attend to business on a Saturday evening."

"My dear," Mr. Orford said, "this is hardly business. It is tragedy. I couldn't say anything in the face of the general merriment, but I will tell you. Poor Bill Thorley was killed last evening on the railway line."

"Accident?"

"That is still to be decided. Nobody knows yet. Look, darling, don't mention it this evening. Just run down and tell Mamma not to wait dinner. If I can get rid of him quickly, I will, and I'll join you. If not, Edith can cut me a sandwich or something."

"Did you have a proper lunch, Papa?"

For once her solicitude irked him.

"Of course. I know that for a tricky digestion a long fast is as bad as a heavy meal. Run along now and give your mamma my message."

He finished changing into his easy clothes, sipped a brandy and soda as he did it, and went at a leisurely pace down the stairs.

He knew, or suspected so sharply that it was almost as good as knowing, what Gregson would have to say.

And he was armed. At the end of this horrible day he was tired, he was sad, but strong and prepared.

The horrible day had begun when he looked in at Foster's. He often did it on Saturday, just to prove that he was not growing slack. There he had heard about Bill Thorley's death on the line the previous evening. He was genuinely sorry, for Bill had been a likeable fellow and apart from his one little slip—which had worked to Mr. Orford's advantage—absolutely honest and reliable. Hard to replace.

He tied his horse to the rail, and the same little boy, or another so like him as to be identical, sprang out of the ground and said, "Watch him, mister?" Mr. Orford nodded and crossed over to the store, where old Mattie was washing paint. And crying. She looked as though she had been crying for a long time. And emotion had overridden her awe.

"Oh, sir, ain't it awful? Poor Mr. Thorley! And to think that I was one of the last to see him. Coming out of the police station, just as I went home. Having finished up. Looking as right as rain he was, too. Better than lately. I mean, since his sister. . . ."

She mopped her nose and eyes with the cloth known as a dwile.

The police station! Mr. Orford's extra sense, intuition, imagination, had always known that the weak link in his, in Charlie's defence, lay with Bill Thorley.

"Did you speak to him, Mattie?"

"I was on the other side of the road. I did call good-night, but something went past. He didn't hear. But to the end of my days I'll never never forget how he looked. Happy. Happier than he had done since. . . ."

"Yes. Very sad," Mr. Orford said, cutting her short.

Inside the store, Pryke said, "Mr. Thorley'd been out for a bit, sir. He come back looking cheerful, like his old self. He carved enough meat to keep us going for half an hour and rearranged the counter a bit. Then he said he'd just run home with some ham for the family and would be back in ten minutes. I knew that meant taking the shortcut, but he knew the train times." They all did; the train times punctuated their days and for those without watches acted as time markers. "But then he didn't come back, and he didn't come back, so I carved and took over generally."

Pryke paused to allow that statement to hit its target. He had liked Bill Thorley and served under him happily, but here was a chance, a vacancy—and who better suited than himself? "Then somebody come in and said there'd been a accident on the line. They didn't know who then. So I thought I'd lock up and take him the keys. But by that time they knew who was on the rail, and I knew he wouldn't be wanting the keys no more."

Even at this moment some remote part of Mr. Orford's mind made a note that if Pryke were to be promoted, he must learn to speak more grammatically.

Pryke did not think it necessary to mention that he had not done everything as usual; he had not released the dog; he was afraid of it.

"Well, you carry on, Pryke," Mr. Orford said, and though that was not a firm appointment, it was halfway there.

Mr. Orford went into the office, where it took him a very short time to discover another *possible* reason for Bill Thorley's visit to the police station and coming away looking happier, more like himself. He then set out to pay a call of condolence on the widow.

Effie had wept bitterly, tears of self-pity outnumbering those of grief. She'd lost her breadwinner. Mr. Orford might give her a small pension, but it would be *small*, nothing like enough to keep her and the girls as they had been kept, well dressed, well fed, comfortable, and occupying this desirable Terrace house. She might even have to go back to work!

She blamed Anna. Bill had never been the same since his wretched sister's death, always brooding over it, not thinking about what he was doing or looking where he was going. She had taken him to task about it—as she had over his lack of zest for food: "If you mope about at the store the way you do here, you'll get yourself the sack!"

Neighbours had rallied round and tried to comfort her by making cups of tea. Not Mrs. Wicks; she was too busy administering to her husband, whose nerve had been so shattered that he was incapable of continuing the journey to London.

One neighbour, unintentionally, led the way to real comfort. When Effie asked, for the tenth time, "What will become of us all?" the neighbour replied, "Well, you're better off than many. The house is your own. I know that because Bill told Jim when he'd paid off the last of the mortgage. You and the girls could squeeze in together, and you'd have two rooms to let."

Effie remembered that last mortgage, too. Bill had said,

"Well, the house is ours, Effie. We'll be better off, with only the rates to bother us."

Bill had what he called a business drawer, and Effie thought it might comfort her a little to see the deeds of the house. Also, there might be money, too. Bill always saved up for Christmas. Now she'd need money for the funeral.

The business drawer was kept locked against the children's meddling. The key lay snug in the bottom of the little case in which, at night, Bill put his watch.

The last thing to be placed in the drawer, and therefore the first to her hand, was the insurance policy. Good provider to the end, Bill had insured himself against death. Three thousand pounds! Effie, who looked so feminine and helpless, had a good head for figures. Three thousand pounds at five percent meant a steady income of one hundred and fifty pounds a year—and no man to feed or clothe. They'd be all right. And Mr. Orford was bound to give something. She need not go to work or take lodgers. Comfort indeed.

Effie cried again at the sight of Mr. Orford, who took her hand and said what a good manager and what a good man Bill had been. Despite everything, the words were not insincere. Bill Thorley had his faults—but then who had not? For most of his time he had, however, been a splendid manager, absolutely devoted to his duty. And even his "borrowing" had been done because he was a good man and felt responsible for his father and sister. There were, of course, two ways of looking at *that*; had Thorley not helped in February, the wretched girl might have gone back to London and never met Charlie at all.

When Effie had calmed down a little, Mr. Orford said, "What about money, Mrs. Thorley? It may seem a trifle heartless to think about it at such a time, but it is an essential."

Effie's unguarded gaze went to the business drawer. It was only half closed, and the stiff paper of the policy had opened of its own accord. Security believed in display, and the name stood out clear and black. She hoped Mr. Orford wouldn't see it, though he looked in that direction, too.

She said, dolefully, "I thought he might have been saving, but he hadn't. Not a penny."

"No need to worry over that, Mrs. Thorley. Your husband had a week's wages and some bonus due to him. There is the future to consider, but you may leave that to me. And I feel that your religion will be some consolation."

Interested, as he always had been in his employees, Mr. Orford could remember the fuss there had been about Bill, a Methodist, if anything, marrying Effie, a Catholic.

"It would, if only he'd changed," Effie said, shedding some more tears, but edging herself between Mr. Orford and the business drawer. "Most things Bill was reasonable about and he did agree that the children. . . . Except when I was laid up, I never missed a mass or a day of obligation. And though this is not the time to say it—he'd have been a happier man if he'd been reasonable about that and taken instruction. And more reasonable about his family. I mean grieving over that Anna. Not living with him—and I must say he always pulled himself together when he went to work—you'd hardly believe what Anna did to him. I mean her death. Off his food, awake half the night. Out of his mind, nearly. That's how he got himself run over. He knew the train times. He just wasn't thinking."

It was perhaps, Mr. Orford reflected, an easier interview than it would have been had the woman appeared to be more thoroughly grief-stricken. He would very much have liked to look at that policy, but to ask to do so might seem like prying with a view to adjusting what provision he was prepared to make in accordance with what Bill Thorley had left. It was not the amount that interested him; it was the date, but that could be easily ascertained from another source. Thinking these things, Mr. Orford said all the right things, Effie must try not to fret too much, she had her children to think of, she would have to be both father and mother to them in future. Then he asked, "Have you informed his father?"

"No. How could I?"

"I think he should be told. And it would come better from you than from casual gossip. Do you feel capable of writing just a line to him? I will see to its delivery."

"You are so very kind," Effie said, and cried a little more.

While she wrote, sniffing, Mr. Orford cast a calculating eye round the parlour and entertained the odd thought that it was not unlike Rose's own room, on a miniature scale and in, naturally, a cheaper version. Everything that could be draped was draped, and there were yards and yards of the bobbled fringe which he detested. An upright piano stood against one wall, its front quilted red silk behind a fretwork of wood, its candleholders fitted with candles that had never been lighted.

The house, Mr. Orford knew, was bought and paid for; when Bill applied for a mortgage, he himself had sponsored him as a reliable person in a well-paid job. Bought in that way, it had cost two hundred and seventy pounds. Its present market value was perhaps two hundred and ten. The little woman with the toffee-coloured hair would be provided for, whatever the small print, which so few people ever bothered to read, had to say. She could take one lodger or two, and he would guarantee her a pound a week, whatever her circumstances; otherwise, twenty-five shillings should the small print make nonsense of it all.

Mr. Forbes, seeing Mr. Orford's gig halt by his door, was confirmed in his belief that his luck had changed. Another client! He was glad that on Saturdays he did not make his rounds, heralded by children calling, "Mum, here's the death man." On Saturday morning he stayed at home and did what he called his bookwork, all too scanty until now, when he really had something to report.

"My name is Orford," Mr. Orford said, "and I would like a word with you, Mr. Forbes. One of my employees, Bill or William Thorley, met with a fatal accident last evening. I am given to understand that he had insured his life with you."

"He did indeed, sir. What a catastrophe." Mr. Forbes realised that had he been out and about this morning, he would have heard by now; news took no time at all to travel along the railway line. Insulated in what he liked to regard as his office, he was taken by surprise.

"When?"

"A mere two days ago. Thursday."

"Immediately effective?"

"To an extent," Mr. Forbes said. "The first premium was paid in cash, no delay about cheque clearance. Thirty pounds."

Precisely the sum of which Bill, peculating for the second time, had robbed his employer.

"There are, naturally, what we call exculpatory clauses," Mr. Forbes said, only too well aware that this might, after all, turn out to be less of a good transaction than it had seemed at the time. Slap down thirty pounds on a Thursday, leave a claim for three thousand pending on Saturday; who could remain in business on such terms?

"Is suicide excluded? I ask because to some extent his widow and children will be my responsibility. I should like to know where I stand."

"This is our typical form, sir," Mr. Forbes said, handing one over and indicating with his finger the small print about which so few people bothered. "There is nothing secret about it," he said a trifle defensively. "Most firms impose the same restriction."

"Mr. Forbes, your work brings you into touch with many people. Did you notice anything unusual about this unfortunate man?"

"The sum itself is unusual for a man in his position. A

thousand, fifteen hundred perhaps, is generally regarded as adequate. Paying the first year's premium in one go; that, too, is unusual; we accept quarterly or even monthly deposits."

"About the man himself?"

"He seemed to me to be under some kind of strain. He did not look well. Yet he had provided himself with a doctor's certificate of good health. The strained look certainly lifted when I assured him that if he were run over in the road, the policy would be valid. He left by that door, rather like a man who had shed a load. But of course, in a case of suicide. . . ."

"Well, that is not for us to decide. The coroner's jury will do that. It is a fact, however, that the poor man had suffered a bereavement which he took much to heart, so that at times he seemed almost out of his mind. That is, according to his widow."

Mr. Forbes' work did bring him into contact with many people, and he now noticed something extremely unusual about Mr. Orford. He seemed almost to welcome the idea of suicide which would nullify the policy and thus increase his responsibility. Still, peculiar as this attitude was, it pleased Mr. Forbes and led him to hope that he had not on Thursday insured a man who had met with an accident on Friday.

Eager to be about his masters' business, Mr. Forbes took himself by train to Bressford, there to sniff out, by all possible means, any details about the accident.

Anxious not to face his family with what Bill Thorley's visit to the police station *might* imply weighing on his mind, Mr. Orford lingered at Wyck-on-Rad, looking in at the brewery and at the bacon factory. Both had minor problems, of which he made the most, insisting on handling personally a case of a consignment of malting barley which was not up to the standard of the sample—that involved quite a drive. And Mr. MacDonald at Kilburnie was showing himself to be obstreperous; under contract to the factory, he'd claimed the business to be uneconomic and said that there was no power on the earth below or in the heavens above which could compel him to deliver pigs which did not exist.

"That is what he *said*, Mr. Orford. But I know for a fact that he has sent pigs which should have come to us to Eltwell," Mr. Stubbs said earnestly.

"I'll call upon him, too," Mr. Orford said, glad to have something to take his mind off what Bill Thorley had said at the police station.

Mr. MacDonald had no idea that he and Mr. Orford had once stood beside each other in the light of Gregson's suspicious eye.

"Look about you," he said. "There isna a pig on the place except for the old sow and her young—kept for family purposes." It was true that the family's diet of porridge and skim milk was fortified by home-bred pork, fresh—a great treat—or salted down, or smoked into bacon in the wide chimney. The real, marketable, under-contract pigs were safe at Angus' place, from which they would go, under a new and better contract, to Eltwell.

"There was no profit in it," Mr. MacDonald explained. "And no law that a man should labour for nothing."

"I could sue you for breach of contract," Mr. Orford said.

"Aye, so you could. And much good it would be. Even yon lawyers could not get around it; I havena any pigs. As I said, look around you."

It had all taken time, and Mr. Orford was late home. He'd had nothing to eat since breakfast, and the brandy and soda which he had been sipping when Edda came to announce the presence of the police made a small guggling noise in his empty stomach as he went down the beautiful staircase. But he was armed, prepared for the worst thing that Gregson could say.

Gregson said it. Bill Thorley had told all. The letters, the hundred pounds, everything. Mr. Orford listened impassively. No more than he had expected, no worse than he had feared, and nothing that he was not prepared for.

He said, "Dementia takes many forms, of course. In fact poor Thorley, in putting himself under a train, spared me the unenviable task of dismissing him."

"Why," Gregson asked sharply, "do you assume suicide?"

It almost certainly was. In the ordinary way a death on the railway, by either accident or intention, would not have concerned a police officer at inspectorate level, but Gregson was interested in Bill Thorley and by virtue of his office knew something that the general public did not yet know.

"Various reasons," Mr. Orford said. "Certainly in the early part of this year he robbed me a little. Some trifling sum, to help his family—including that unfortunate girl. But he was a good man, and I overlooked the offence and arranged that he should pay back, on easy terms. This week he robbed me again, of thirty pounds—I will not bother you with details. On Thursday he went to Wyck-on-Rad and insured his life for three thousand pounds, paying the first premium in one sum, in ready money. My money. Would any man in his right mind, not planning self-destruction, have done such a thing? Knowing that by the end of the month his defalcation must surely be exposed and his dismissal certain? And then—this may sound trivial to you, Inspector, but to me it was profoundly significant, a sure sign of derangement—as an excuse to run across the line, he took *ham*, saying it was for the family supper."

"Is that so significant?"

"To me, yes. His wife is a devout Catholic. The two little girls are being reared in the same faith. The day was Friday. Surely no sane man after years of marriage. . . . He was distraught, poor fellow."

Gregson had Bill's statement in his hand, and now he

stared at it, remembering the man's earnest manner, the clarity of his story. Remembering, too, his reference to himself as Judas. Judas because of the stealing? Because he knew what this confession implied?

"You look upon this," Gregson said, "as the product of a distraught mind?"

"Largely, not entirely. Letters, Inspector! I should doubt very much that the girl could read or write. That is, of course an assumption, but based on reason. When Bill Thorley first came into my employ, *he* was barely literate. Indeed, it was at my suggestion that he joined evening classes—with the view of becoming a manager one day. The girl with the same background would be unlikely to have received more education than the boy. That is, of course, conjecture. What is *not* is the fact that I am not the man to pay a hundred pounds for a few letters—unless they had great historic value—written by Shakespeare, for instance."

"Did you give the girl anything at all?"

Mr. Orford managed a gesture of repudiation.

"I sent her, through Bill Thorley, her fare back to London. Mere self-defence. While she was at home and dependent, the temptation to pilfer again might well have overcome him. Of the dead let no ill be spoken. But he was extraordinarily attached to her. One offence can be condoned; I was not prepared to be so lenient again."

Flexible as always, Gregson shifted ground.

"Your son, Mr. Orford, was twice seen in company with the dead girl."

"Yes, on the usual wet Easter Monday. Any young man, indeed any decent man—I am no longer young myself, but I could have done the same, and so could you—would offer a girl in the rain a lift in a gig, a warming drink in some nearby hostelry. Would that damn us if several weeks later the girl was found dead in a ditch?"

"According to this," Gregson said, tapping his paper,

"the letters were said to be compromising. Promises of marriage. . . ." And yet Bill Thorley himself, on the verge of
self-destruction, had said he had never seen them, had only
taken Anna's word.·

Mr. Orford, out of his great, his almost overwhelming
weariness, permitted himself a small sigh.

"But as I said, he was much attached. . . . The inquest,
what Dr. Clarke in his evidence revealed. . . . Poor man, so
devoted, so deluded, he felt compelled to convince himself,
to convince others that Anna had only fallen from virtue
under promise of marriage. Excusable. In a way. *He was in-
tent to clear Anna's name.* His last act, one might say."

There was half a minute's silence during which the
sound of voices and footsteps—the movement of people towards the dining room could be heard. The background
noise of family life. Hitherto Gregson had thought of Mr.
Orford as a father only in relationship with Charlie. He
allowed his imagination an inch of sentimentality—the
boy's mother, his sisters. Then the policeman in him resumed control. Anna Thorley had been killed. And there
was the bank bag. The most meticulous and stringent enquiries had failed to discover another of its kind issued anywhere to anyone during the relevant time. And was not this
man's immensely rational explanation of everything in itself suspect? Clever? And that Mr. Orford was clever there
was no doubt; it took a very clever boy to rise from the Pike
to the place which Mr. Orford now held.

Gregson said, "Mr. Orford, I think it would be to everybody's advantage if your son came home and answered for
himself. May I ask you to recall him?"

"You may ask—you may indeed order. Anxious as I am to
comply with a wish, to obey an order, the truth is I have not
the slightest idea of my son's whereabouts. Look at this."
Bending over to open the bottom drawer of his desk, Mr.
Orford felt the pain strike, but in a new way. Not the sudden gripping pang, but a remote, ominous ache, not unlike

the start of a toothache. (Once, in the old days, he'd had a tooth that gave him agony, not abated by the chewed clove, the hot bag of salt. In the end his mother had said, "Ed, there's only one thing for it. Be brave!" She had pried out the rotten tooth with a pair of scissors, the abscess below it had broken and drained, and he'd slept, free of pain. Now, after all those years, he felt the similar, not immediately urgent, but equally unevadable kind of pain in his chest, not in his jaw.)

Ignoring it, he handed over several papers, held together by a pin. Proof of Charlie's indecision. The P and O liner on which he had embarked, well before Anna Thorley was dredged up out of the weeds and the mud, put in at Marseilles; there it took on passengers, bound for the East, who had travelled overland in order to avoid the misery of the Bay of Biscay. Against the ship's arrival date there, carefully labelled "Approx," somebody—Charlie—had pencilled "c/o P and O office." His first address in a foreign land.

There was another page, handwritten in well-licked indelible pencil, informing anyone who could read, about the movements of trains, from Marseilles along the coast to Genoa and thus to Italy. Against the purple-smudged words "Rome," "Venice" the ordinary pencil had made a question mark.

There was a third sheet, printed, giving information about French ships, roughly the equivalent of the P and O liners: the *Lamartine*, for like every nation temporarily defeated, the French were harking back to earlier, more glorious days, and the *Aida*, named for the opera so closely connected with the opening of the Suez Canal. The *Lamartine* put in at Venice and at Levkas, in Greece. The *Aida* went straight to Egypt. There were little pencilled crosses and question marks.

"As you see," Mr. Orford said, fighting back the pain, "my son was, to the last moment, indecisive. He may well have decided at the crucial moment against Greece, against

Egypt, and be now in Rome, Venice, Naples. His trouble was—and frankly I do regard it as a disability—too wide a choice and too little compulsion. No need to decide or to plan."

Gregson then slapped down the last card in this peculiar game—not a good one; in fact, in view about what Marsh had discovered about extradition, a very poor one indeed, almost a fake. He said, "The police in other countries are sometimes willing to be helpful."

The deadly words went on ringing through Mr. Orford's head after he was alone.

Wherever he was, Charlie would be conspicuous, English, handsome, free-spending. Police in other countries, France, Italy, Greece, or Egypt, would be helpful, would track Charlie down, and send him home to face questions for which he was unprepared, against which he could not be warned. His very innocence would be a drawback. He didn't even know that the hateful girl was dead—that news in itself would shock him past any consideration for his own safety. He knew nothing about the sale of the letters. Oh, yes, he'd say, I wrote to her. I loved her. I wanted to marry her.

They'd believe that.

Then he'd say that she jilted him, went off to London to marry somebody else.

Who would believe that—with Charlie so eligible, handsome, and rich?

Nobody! And the mere fact that he was rich would count against him. So obvious a pattern, rich young man, seducing with gig rides, with letters, with promises of marriage, a poor honest girl. And then when infatuation had faded and the time came when the promise should be, must be, kept—murder!

The pain, so different from the other, which was short and sharp and incapacitating for a moment, grumbled on. Mr. Orford ignored it. He slipped into his place at the merry table and said, "No, my dear, no need to recall anything. I'll join you here." Here was chicken, tasteless as flannel. He apologised for being late: "A bit of tedious business. And more to do afterwards I am sorry to say."

He made genial remarks. He looked round and thought: They are all happy. Even Edda. She'd hesitated over the engagement, but once she had decided. . . . And one thing about Simon Talbot: For all his solemn demeanour, he had a sense of humour which matched Edda's; she'd just said something which made him laugh. Louise and Algie Hepworth were obviously made for each other. The Babcock boy was not what he would have chosen for Maude, but he seemed a nice enough boy and Maude was glowing, not the younger sister left out as she had been lately. It was indeed Maude who said, "Mamma, if you would play, we could dance."

The girls were rolling up the rugs in the hall, the young men shifting the piano nearer the drawing-room door as he went back to the library and settled down to write. The music came to him, just a noise; he couldn't tell a waltz from a polka. . . . He was aware of a break in the noise and then a new beginning, slightly louder, less smooth. He heard laughter, too. But he wrote steadily.

Presently he opened the door. Rose was laughing, flushed, pinning her hair into place.

"Really," she said, "Algie is naughty! He insisted that I should dance, too. Some new, very strenuous dance."

Just as Louise was her favourite daughter, Algie Hepworth was her potentially favourite son-in-law. He never treated her as though she were old.

Women can always rejuvenate themselves, Mr. Orford thought, remembering how his mother had rejuvenated herself when moved from the Pike to those old panelled rooms over the shop, how his mother-in-law had rejuvenated herself when she moved to the house in the Avenues.

"I want," he said, "two witnesses to my signature."

"Of course," Simon Talbot said.

"Would I do?" young Babcock asked, ready to ingratiate himself.

"He *can* write," Algie Hepworth said. "He used to do about a thousand lines a week—his own and mine."

"I think that after all this we need some refreshment," Rose said.

"It is merely a formality," Mr. Orford said, writing his own name firmly at the bottom of the sheet of paper of which the upper half was covered by blotting paper. Edwin Orford.

Chelsworth.

Antony St. Barbe Bevan Babcock.

"Thank you," Mr. Orford said. "And now let us see what we have to refresh us."

The party had moved itself, because of the piano, into the drawing room, after all. The evening was mild, and nobody noticed the lack of fire in the grate under the indecent mantel. Rose looked about her with complacency just tinged with disapproval; she still considered the room too bare. Edwin would not even allow her to drape the piano with a beautiful Indian shawl she had bought for that purpose.

The young men went at last. The engaged couples were allowed a chaste kiss. Tony Babcock, who had spent a year since leaving school on making the grand tour of the Continent, indulged in the foreign habit of kissing hands with a bow. By the strict rules of etiquette one should only kiss the hands of married ladies; he knew that but thought that perhaps these less travelled people did not, and it offered him a chance to kiss Maude. He thanked Mrs. Orford for a most enjoyable evening and Rose said almost automatically, "We shall hope for many more." But even as she said it, she could see complications ahead. Edwin was too well mannered to make the boy feel unwelcome once he was across the threshold, but he was almost certain to have something

to say through the intervening doorway while she brushed
her hair. She was slightly relieved when at the foot of the
stairs, he kissed her as well as the girls, and said, "Good
night, my dear. I still have a little tidying up to do."

"May I help, Papa?" Edda asked.

"No. It's a mere nothing. You go and get your beauty
sleep."

"You must be tired, too," she said. She, alone of the company, had been conscious of something strained, a trifle
forced behind his genial manner. A little too genial? No, he
was always a good host. And it might simply be her imagination. She was the only one to whom he had confided the
sad news. She was the only one who took sufficient interest
in the businesses to realise what the loss of a man like Bill
Thorley would mean to him.

In their little satin slippers, with their silk skirts rustling,
they went up the beautiful staircase. He called a final good
night and turned back to the library, where he folded what
he had written, chose a suitable envelope, addressed and
stamped it. Then he set himself to wait until Edda was in
bed. Otherwise, she would almost certainly offer to accom-
pany him.

His thoughts were varied, but there were no self-
reproachful ones. He had simply done—as was his habit—
what seemed to be best for everybody. Over the accident he
had been unlucky, he who had always been so fortunate
once Old Born Drunk was dead.

He thought of Dr. Sapey advising moderation in all
things, sensible advice which applied equally to angina
and to indigestion. *If* the pills in the blue phial relieved the
pain, angina was indicated, and in that case his whole way
of life must be changed, for though angina in itself was seldom a killer, it could be associated with a serious heart condition.

This evening he had been anything but moderate in his
drinking. One brandy and soda in his dressing room, anoth-

er before facing the ordeal of the dining table, a third while writing his letter. Two during the refreshment period in the drawing room. Most men would now be feeling the effects, but perhaps Old Born Drunk's son was immune. All the brandy had done for him was to keep the pain sufficiently at bay as to enable him to appear normal. After all, before the discovery of chloroform men underwent the most savage operations with no other anaesthetic than alcohol.

The pain was encroaching now; it filled his whole rib cage. He took another drink, to dull it a bit, and to make sure that he was well on the excess side of moderation.

"In the meantime," Dr. Sapey had said, "try to avoid any undue physical exertion or worry." A stupid sentence, linking what was possible with what was not. A man who was his own master and rich could spare his body, but what guard was there against worry? *The police in other countries are sometimes willing to be helpful.* The vision of Charlie, out of his very innocence, condemning himself.

Holding his letter, he went into the hall, climbed six steps, no more, for he did not wish to provoke this thing prematurely. He mastered his impeded breathing long enough to call, "Rose, I am just going to stroll to the postbox. Something"—he gave a quick gasp—"for the first collection."

Rose, just coming to the end of her dedicated ritual, said, "All right." Perhaps Edda was already asleep. No sound from her.

Mr. Orford opened the front door quietly and stepped out into the drive. The moon rode high; the half-denuded trees cast shadows. Carrying his letter, and his pain, increasing now, despite the last palliative draught, he moved carefully through the stripes of light and dark. It was essential, he knew, that the letter should be consigned to the exclusive care of Her Majesty's Mailservice, where it would be safe, delivered to the person whose name it bore.

He reached the cattle-grid and crossed it. The lodges

were in darkness. Here was the gaping, trustworthy mouth which had received his false letter to that wretched girl. As he pushed this letter in, he thought: Nobody can prosecute a dead man. He thought that he had been, in a way, lucky to the end. Even the witnesses. Chelsworth, a magistrate, and young Babcock the son of one, one who might have been inimical, would assure that no fuss would be made. It would all be hushed away.

Returning, he took a running jump at the cattle-grid and fell amongst the soft, fallen leaves. He crawled a little way and was violently sick—far more than the scanty meal and the drinks warranted. Disgusting, humiliating. He crawled away from it. Only his mind seemed to be unaffected by this collapse of heart and of lung and of stomach. He could still think; though as he thought of Rose, happily established in *her* right place, Sunnybank, the thought was interrupted by a woeful noise. Some animal in a trap; a neglected baby. . . . It was with surprise that he realised that he was whimpering from pain. He'd always tried not to cry when his father beat him, partly because it upset his mother. Now he was whimpering because this was a hitherto-inconceivable pain, inflicted not from without, but from within. A killing pain. But welcome. A death as well managed as his life had been. Seemed to be. . . .

Hidden from him by the curve of the drive, windows darkened, until only one, the lamp he had left burning in the library, remained to shine until morning. A little breeze sprang up, and a few of the last leaves fell.